The
Collective

The
Collective

A Novel

ALISON GAYLIN

wm

WILLIAM MORROW

An Imprint of HarperCollins*Publishers*

THE COLLECTIVE. Copyright © 2021 by Alison Gaylin. All rights reserved. Printed in the United States of America. No part of this book may be used or reproduced in any manner whatsoever without written permission except in the case of brief quotations embodied in critical articles and reviews. For information, address HarperCollins Publishers, 195 Broadway, New York, NY 10007.

HarperCollins books may be purchased for educational, business, or sales promotional use. For information, please email the Special Markets Department at SPsales@harpercollins.com.

FIRST EDITION

Designed by Diahann Sturge

Library of Congress Cataloging-in-Publication Data has been applied for.

ISBN 978-0-06-308315-8

21 22 23 24 25   LSC   10 9 8 7 6 5 4 3

For Beverly LeBov Sloane. Love you, Mom!

Hate is a bottomless cup; I will pour and pour.

—*Medea* (Euripides)

The
Collective

ONE

The ceremony starts in twenty minutes. I'm climbing out of the subway tunnel, a thousand unwanted smells in my hair. I'm not used to being around this many people— the stink of them, the heat, the noise. The noise especially. I just shared a subway car with a group of high school girls, and their laughter still swirls in my ears. I probably should have driven, but it's been hard for me to drive long distances since Emily's death. My thoughts start spinning along with the wheels, memories of road trips, of carpools and radio sing-alongs and petty arguments, and before I know it, I'm aiming straight for the divider.

The venue is just three blocks away. I walk slowly, slower than everyone around me, trying to catch my breath, to still my thoughts, to think of nothing but the sidewalk and the cold night air and where I need to be.

From half a block away, I recognize the Brayburn Club. I know it from the photo I found online. It's located in a

Gramercy Park brownstone with leaded windows and wide, majestic steps. It's a week past New Year's, but the Brayburn Club is still decorated for the holiday season, a lush wreath filling the front door, icicle lights dripping from the window-sills like fresh beads of sweat.

I pass a group of young women smoking last-minute cigarettes—friends of his, maybe?—and I think back to the time I caught Emily smoking weed with her friend Fiona. She must have been fourteen, always a little old for her years and bored of our small Hudson Valley town. I got so angry with her. Grounded her for two months. Her dad thought it exces-sive. *We smoked pot when we were that age*, Matt said, miss-ing the point. Yes, we smoked pot when we were fourteen, but Emily wasn't us. She was better than us.

I won't do it again, Mom. I promise. Her voice in my head is as clear and real as the shrieking laughter of the girls on the train. I want to lose myself in it and never come back.

It isn't until I'm at the top of the stairs, after I've handed the boy at the door my invitation and I'm in line for the coat check, that Emily's voice quiets and I remember where I am and why I'm here.

"Anything else, ma'am?" says the coat check girl. She has a freshly scrubbed look and shiny dark hair and she's wear-ing the Brayburn College colors—crimson jacket, gold blouse. "Anything else?" She says it like she's prompting me from a script.

"No. Nothing else. Thank you."

The girl's nose scrunches up. She looks at me funny, and I wonder if she can sense what I've been up to. Who I am.

THE EVENING'S MAIN event is the first alumni dinner of the year. It will be held in the formal dining room—a four-course meal, capped off by a speech by a noted software developer from the class of '98. But I won't be staying for any of that.

They're holding the ceremony first, in the club's library— a sprawling room, with wall-sized bookshelves and grand arched ceilings painted with exotic birds and flowers. It smells of leather bindings and polished floors, and there's a Christmas tree in the corner, decorated entirely in Brayburn colors. I imagine most people are calmed by this place—a respite from the stench and bellow of the city. I relax my shoulders and try my best to act as though I feel the same.

The seats are all filled by the time I'm in the room. A boy in a tuxedo offers me a glass of champagne from a tray. I take it for the sake of having something to hold, and slip in next to a group at the back, waiting.

There's a man watching me. That used to happen all the time, and I used to find it flattering, but I don't like it now. I've lost twenty-eight pounds since Emily's death. I've stopped coloring my hair and wearing makeup and I had the bolt-ons removed, and so I am literally no longer the woman I once was. There is no reason to watch me. No flattering reason, anyway.

The man is around my age, with a thinning buzz cut, his

jacket and tie cheap for the room. He smiles, and I turn away from him, the stem of the champagne glass tight between my fingers.

"Why are you here?" he says, and I think, *Does he recognize me?* I'm hoping my thoughts don't show on my face.

"Excuse me?"

His smile is surprisingly warm. Disarming. "Are you a relative?"

"No."

"Brayburn alum?"

"Yes." The easier lie. "How about you?"

He says nothing. Just nods, as though he doesn't believe me. Then he turns back around. Strange. But then everything is strange here. Like a dream, or maybe an acid trip, the colors too soft, the whispers too loud. I'm feeling a little nauseous. There are other people looking at me—two silver-haired women in the back row. Is my hair okay? Do I have something stuck to my shoe? I almost ask them that, but I stop myself just in time.

There is a podium at the front of the room, and a man pads up to it. He has thin lips, wispy hair, narrow shoulders, everything about him meager and unobtrusive. His name is Richard Waverly, and he's the dean of the School of Humanities. He introduces himself as such, but I already know those things. I take a big swallow of champagne and then another and then the glass is done when I hadn't even intended a sip. The room shimmers and blurs. The silver-haired women whisper like snakes.

Waverly says, "The recipient of the Martha L. Koch Humanitarian Award this year is a young man who exemplifies public service," and that's when I finally catch sight of him, standing in the rear corner of the room, his golden curls slicked down, his parents sentries on either side of him. I'd recognize them anywhere. The father is square-jawed and straight-backed, the mother blond and beaming. He's quite a bit taller now, the son. Apparently, he had some growing to do, but the parents haven't changed a bit. The mother especially, in her seasonal wrap dress, big diamond at her throat. *Her death didn't change you.*

I say it out loud. "Her death didn't change you." The hissing women whip their heads around in unison. I can feel the heat of their glares. I aim my eyes at my empty glass and take a deep breath, but then Waverly says the boy's name. A punch to my throat. "Harris Blanchard."

He strides up to the podium, taller Harris with his slicked-down curls, with his expensive suit and shiny shoes, and I hear Emily's voice again. *His name is Harris, Mom. He's really nice.* I remember her Instagram bio, Emily's motto from an Instagram account I'd only learned of after her death, her words on the lips of a defense lawyer as expensive as the gray suit Harris Blanchard is wearing to accept his Martha L. Koch award. My daughter's Instagram bio. The defense lawyer's sneer. *"No fucks left to give." What does that mean to you, Mrs. Gardener?*

Harris Blanchard pulls a piece of paper out of his pocket

and unfolds it. My gaze pings on his mother, just as she mouths, *I love you, sweetie,* and I have no fucks left to give. The word bubbles up in my throat and escapes as a shriek. *"Murderer!"*

I start toward Harris Blanchard. I don't get far.

I'm NOT ALWAYS this way. That is to say, nine-tenths of the time I'm calm and cool and going about my business. I do website design out of my home, and when I meet with clients—usually at the one coffee shop in town, since my house is halfway up a mountain and hard to get to—I put on a dress or a nice pant-suit and heels and behave in a professional manner. I work hard. I don't miss deadlines or pull diva fits when someone wants a change to the design, even an ill-advised one. From time to time, I catch up with old friends over lunch. I make jokes, even.

But Emily is always on my mind, a ragged bundle of memories, cocooned in a constant, gnawing pain. To keep the cocoon tight and the pain at bay, I take pills. In my old life, I had no anxiety that couldn't be cured by my weekly hot yoga class. Obviously, things have changed since then.

The meds I take don't mix well with alcohol, which has never been much of an issue until tonight, when, after arriving at Penn Station two hours early for Harris Blanchard's award ceremony, I stopped at a touristy Italian place, where an organist was playing a Doors medley at an ear-shattering volume.

My ex-husband, Matt, loved the Doors. I suppose he still

does, but it feels weird to talk about him in the present tense, as we've barely spoken in three years. I'd gone into this place solely to get a bite to eat, but by the time the organist had screamed *"Mr. Mojo Risin'"* into the mic for the tenth or twelfth or maybe the hundred and fiftieth time, I'd downed three vodka rocks, and the cocoon had burst open. Emily was with me. I could smell that fruity bubble gum she used to love, her lily of the valley shampoo. I could hear her laughing along with the girls on the subway, and when I looked at the coat check girl at the Brayburn Club, I could see her face. *Get out of here*, I wanted to tell her. *Get away from him.* And then I decided to drink that glass of champagne. . . .

My whole body aches. My throat from screaming, or maybe it's the man in the cheap suit who did it. The way he'd pinned my arms to my back and wrestled me to the floor, my cheek hot against the smooth wood planks, that smell of pine and old books and his sleazy, spicy cologne. It was an overreaction on his part. A show of force, his forearms pressed between my shoulder blades as though I had any chance of getting away, when he had a hundred pounds on me, easy. *I knew it. You didn't fit in at that place any more than I did. And the way you looked at me. That smile . . .* If I'd been sober, if the room hadn't been spinning and shimmering like something out of a bad dream, I'd have figured that douchebag for the rent-a-cop he was.

"Why would you go to the ceremony in the first place?" Reena says. "I don't understand why you'd want to be anywhere near that guy." Reena is one of my two arresting officers, and she is very kind. She knows who I am. She remembers my name from the news five years ago—one of the few people who still do. At the time, she'd been pregnant with her first child, a girl, which made her sympathize with me instead of the rich golden-haired boy with the angelic blue eyes and the premed major. *I couldn't imagine anything worse*, she had told me in the squad car, *than losing a daughter like that*.

Reena and I are in the 13th Precinct house now. I'm being booked, but you wouldn't know it from the way she talks to me, as though I'm an old friend who's hit on hard times. When she asks me why I went to the ceremony, her partner, a stoic young man named Officer Ruiz, raises his eyebrows at her and clicks his tongue once, like a warning shot.

Reena says, "Don't reply." Both of them have the Miranda warning in mind, I know. But I don't care.

"I wanted to see him. I wanted to see if he's changed."

Reena has large, dark, empathetic eyes, and like me she's short, which allows her to gaze into my eyes directly.

I keep talking. "He's taller now. Isn't that interesting? Someone growing that much between the ages of seventeen and twenty-two? You know how tall Emily was when it happened? Four foot eleven. She was a late bloomer. I bet she'd be a lot taller than me now, if he'd given her the chance to grow up."

Reena starts to say something, then stops.

"I know," I say. "I know. Anything I say can and will. Go ahead. Hold it against me. I don't give a crap."

My head has cleared considerably. Enough to know that

I've been charged with disturbing the peace, a violation, and drunk and disorderly conduct, a violation. When Reena initially told me this, I almost corrected her to add "violating an order of protection," but stopped myself just in time. That order expired a year ago. Until tonight, I've done an excellent job of leaving the Blanchards alone.

Reena has removed something from my purse. She replaces it, quick and matter-of-fact, but I'm still able to get a glimpse. A fork from the Italian place. The memory comes to me in stabs, sharp and fleeting. Sliding it into my purse, my palms slippery on the handle. *Kill him. Kill them all* . . . I had thought it was a knife.

Reena hands me a voucher. "You'll get all your possessions back once you're released. You can make up to three phone calls. I'm going to take you to the holding cell now. My hunch is, you'll get a DAT, so you won't have to go through central booking. With any luck, you should be out of here and on your way home within a few hours. You'll get your stuff back then; just give Officer Johnson the voucher. She's the desk sergeant."

She says all of this with a calm assurance, and in that sliver of time I feel protected, as though there's a secret order in this world of which I am a member, and Reena is as well, and that secret, special sisterhood transcends her uniform and my handcuffs and binds us tighter than anything, even the air that keeps us alive.

We are mothers of girls.

I MAKE TWO phone calls. The first is to a client—an artist from Woodstock whose website I'm designing—telling her I probably won't be able to make our eight thirty meeting tomorrow morning. The second is to Luke. Both go straight to voicemail.

The holding cell is empty and quiet. It's located in the building's basement, away from the bustle of the precinct house, but with a sad, restless energy of its own. There is no natural light here. The floor is rough concrete, and the bars are gray under the fluorescent lights. The air is thick with the smell of sweat and with something else I can't name.

There is a metal bench against the wall, a metal toilet in the center of the room. I sit on the concrete floor and close my eyes and try to escape the ghosts, the voices. *Why do you do these things, Camille? Why do you insist on opening wounds?*

My heart is starting to pound. I put my head between my knees and take deep, deep breaths and imagine I'm on the beach, atop a mountain, my feet soaking in a stream. I picture myself at home, at my laptop, out of trouble. None of it works. My pulse is speeding up. I can feel it in my neck, expanding and contracting, the room swelling around me, my breath short and ineffectual. Panic attack. Great. I think of my pills at home in my medicine cabinet. More than 120 miles away. *Don't scream.* My old therapist's voice in my head again. *Don't scream, Camille; find your calming place.*

"Bitch, don't you think that's what I'm trying to do?" I say it out loud. My voice pitches up and quavers, and I actually start to laugh. Thank God I'm alone in the holding cell, or they'd cart me off. Maybe I should be carted off; maybe that would be an act of kindness. . . .

I put my hands to my face. I feel the cool of my palms, focus on it, as Joan would have advised if she were here. Joan, my old therapist, with her red-framed glasses, her wild steel-colored hair, jasmine incense burning in the corner of the dimly lit office. The soft leather couch. Joan's dry hands on my shoulders and the sound of wind chimes, like children laughing in another room. *Find your calming place.* I can see her face in my mind, the smooth young skin incongruous with the prematurely gray hair, hazel eyes magnified by thick lenses, the gentle scold in them. *Breathe deep, in and out. Feel the weight and substance of your own body.* She died a year ago, Joan. A late-night fall from the top of a staircase, and she was gone, at thirty-five years old. Like me, she lived alone and secluded. No one heard her cries for help. It was over a week before her body was found, glasses broken, back broken.

I shut my eyes tighter, and Joan's face becomes the face of Lisette Blanchard, Harris's mother, with her chemically smoothed brow and unnaturally bright smile. Her hair highlighted like mine used to be. She was wearing a red velvet dress at the ceremony. A wrap dress. Emily used to call wrap dresses Mom Uniforms, and she wasn't wrong. There's something so safe about them. *Basic*, as Emily would have said, how they flatter every shape in such a demure, dull, predictable way.

Lisette Blanchard has the same eyes as her son—blue and

twinkling and completely untroubled. Before the rent-a-cop wrestled me to the floor of the Brayburn Club library, I caught a glimpse of the two of them: Lisette and Harris Blanchard staring at me with those wide blue eyes, delicate mouths dropped open. Identical masks of pity.

Find your calming place, Joan would say if she were here, if she were alive. *They don't matter. Their pity doesn't matter. Nothing matters but the sound of the chimes.* The sound of wind chimes. The laughter of a child I no longer have.

I'm screaming now, trapped in that dream I'll never wake up from. The nightmare I've been living for the past five years, where the rich boy takes my daughter from me and smiles and thrives and wins awards.

I scream until I have no voice left and my throat is raw and bloody-feeling. I scream until I've screamed every thought out of my head, and I no longer care about the nightmare, or anything.

I curl up on the floor, the concrete cold of it, my forehead smashed into my knees. *You're a mess*, I tell myself. More of an observation than a judgment.

When Emily was seven years old, she caught a bad case of the stomach flu. Matt and I were up all night with her, presumably taking turns, though I couldn't sleep during my supposed downtimes. I was so concerned about Emily getting dehydrated. Between trips to the bathroom, I was trying to feed her tiny sips of ginger ale from a plastic cup with a teaspoon, the way my own mother used to do when I got sick.

Finally the fever broke. She fell asleep with her little head on my shoulder, the spoon to her lips. *Because you're my mommy*, she said as she was drifting off. *Because it's your job to keep me okay.*

It's strange, being this alone, without my phone or my laptop or even the TV to interrupt my thoughts. *City girl in the country*, Matt used to call me. But it isn't technology I crave; it's the way it numbs me.

Matt lives in Colorado now, atop a mountain. He skis and works at a marijuana dispensary, a twentysomething free spirit trapped in a fifty-year-old body. He's been aging backward since I first met him, but Emily's death accelerated the process. *Come with me, Cammy*, Matt begged me three years ago, when our marriage was still hanging by the spindliest of threads. *Come with me and let's start all over.* I said no, and he got angry. Blamed Luke. *The way you sneak out to see him, to be near him. You're attached to him, and it's sick, Camille. You're sick.*

I'm relaxed now, the fight screamed out of me. I stretch my legs and close my eyes for what feels like hours. I drift off, and come back and drift off again, waiting for whatever it is that's going to happen next.

As it turns out, what happens next is Luke.

TWO

When we're outside the police station, Luke tells me I look like shit. He asks if I've eaten or slept since the last time I saw him, and even though the last time I saw him was five and a half months ago, he makes it sound like that's a serious question.

I force out a laugh. "Of course I have."

"I don't believe you."

"Stop it."

"Well, I'm taking you out for pancakes, whether you want them or not."

Luke says it like a tough guy. Well, as tough as any guy can sound when saying *I'm taking you out for pancakes*. I can't help but smile at him. "Whatever you say, Sarge."

I know it'll make him roll his eyes, and it does. Luke Charlebois is a successful character actor with a master's degree from NYU. He's played Falstaff in a Shakespeare in the Park production of *Henry IV, Part 1* and understudied Lennie in

Of Mice and Men on Broadway. He's been singled out in *The New Yorker* for his turn as a dying high school football coach in an Indie Spirit–nominated film, and he's won three Obie Awards and received an Emmy nomination for Best Supporting Actor in a Limited Run Series. But it's his current TV role, as tough-as-nails Sergeant Edwin "Sarge" Barkley on the network crime show *Protect and Serve*, that's put Luke on the map. When he came to pick me up at the police station, no fewer than half a dozen cops asked him for his autograph.

"That line can and will be held against you," says Luke, who is far too highbrow to be anything other than embarrassed by his cop-show fame, and far too sensitive to badger me for answers regarding my drunk and disorderly arrest. He knows me well enough to guess the reasons, and for him, I suppose, that's enough.

I put a hand on each of his big shoulders and gaze up into his broad, dimpled face in the purple glow of the Manhattan night. It is the kindest face I've ever known. "I'm sorry."

"For what?"

"Well . . . for one thing, dragging you out of your home at . . . what time is it, anyway?"

"I'm a New Yorker. We never sleep."

"I think the saying is about the city. Not the people who live there."

He kisses me on the forehead, and I'm aware of someone watching us. A fan of his, probably. They're everywhere. "You know I love you," he says, and I don't care who's watching.

"Luke?"

"Yeah?"

"Can I?"

He holds out his arms. I rest my face against his chest. Press my ear to his thick sweater and wind my arms around him, pulling his body close enough so I can hear the heartbeat. We stay like that for a long time, my head pressed against him, Luke tolerating my embrace in the gentlest of ways until finally I get it together enough to pull away. "Thank you."

Maybe I am sick. Maybe something inside me got broken when Emily died, and it will always be there, rattling around, hurting me. I accept that. I'd rather be hurting forever over Emily than living the way Matt does, as though she never happened.

Luke brushes a lock of hair out of my eyes. "When are you going to stop all this stuff?"

"With the Blanchards?"

He nods.

"Maybe when they die." I'm joking, I think.

He sighs, condensation spilling out of his mouth. "That anger, Cam. That's what I mean."

"Look, I can't help the way I—"

"And it isn't doing a thing to them. You get that, don't you? They're going on with their night, drinking champagne, toasting their award-winner. They don't think they've done anything wrong, and they never will. They see themselves as the victims. They see *him* as the victim."

"How do you know that?"

He stares at me for what feels like a full minute.

I pull my coat closer. It's cold out, but not with the energizing bite of a typical winter night. It's more insidious, the chill seeping under the collar of my coat, through the weave of my tights, sliding down the back of my neck until my whole body is shivering and it feels more feverish than weather-related, not energizing at all. "I didn't want to show you this," Luke says.

He's scrolling through his glowing phone, and then he's handing it to me. I gape at the screen: The Blanchards grin back at me, hands grasping each other's shoulders. Harris holding his golden award. A perfect little family.

Luke follows Lisette and Harris on Instagram (the father, Tom, doesn't have an account). I know this. In fact, I was the one who asked him to do it, more than a year ago, figuring I'd get blocked if I tried. But the photo still gets to me. How could it not? Imagine looking at a posed picture of your child's murderer. Imagine him basking in the warmth of his parents' embrace. Imagine he's staring straight at the camera, smiling up through his eyes, healthier and happier than you'll ever be. . . .

"Read the caption," Luke says.

I read, my fingernails digging into my palms.

Kudos to our Harris, recipient of the Martha L. Koch award!!! It seems like just yesterday you were a little boy, chasing Buster around the yard and dreaming of playing for the Yankees. Now you're all grown up and surpassing OUR dreams. We couldn't be prouder of the brilliant, thoughtful young man you've become!!!! #blessed

I skim the comments—hearts and happy faces and praying hands sprinkled throughout them like confetti.

"Did you see the last comment?" Luke says.

I do now. It's from Lisette. I look up at him.

"You see what I'm saying? Do you understand?"

"There's a video?"

"There's always a video."

I glance back down at the screen, read the rest of the comment:

To those of you who wrote us after seeing the video: Thank you, dear friends, for all your support. But this is a deeply disturbed woman. Please DON'T HATE HER. We DON'T. We forgive her, and you should too.

"'We forgive her,'" I whisper.

"Do you understand, Cam?"

I don't know what to say. I don't understand anything in the world. Nothing makes sense. Nothing is fair. I haven't understood anything since he killed her.

"Excuse me?"

It's an older woman in a camel hair coat, and she seems to have appeared out of nowhere. She places a light hand on my shoulder, and my first thought is that she's a *Protect and Serve* fan, wanting Luke's autograph. "I won't take up too much of your time." She says it to me, though. Not Luke. "I know you've had a rough night."

Condensation rushes from my nose. I glance at Luke, who is shaking his head. Then back at the woman. There's something about her I know, but I can't figure out what that thing is. "You're a reporter," I try. "I've seen you on TV."

Luke hails a cab, steps back as it screeches to the curb. "We were just leaving," he says.

"I'm not a reporter." The woman clasps my wrist and stands very close to me, as though we're not strangers at all but confidantes, in on the same secret. Her eyes are blue, and startlingly bright. *I do know you. Where do I know you from?* She takes my gloveless hand and presses something into it. A business card.

"It's a group," the woman says. "For people like us."

"People like us?"

"I know who you are." She is still holding my hand and grasps it tighter, her skin cool and dry. "I know how you feel."

She leaves. As I slip into the cab, she hurries to the end of the street, her silver hair catching the glow of the streetlight. In a flash, I understand who she is and why she looked familiar to me. She's one of the two women from the Brayburn Club— the ones whispering, like snakes.

I settle into the back seat and open my hand and stare at the business card: black, with one word written at the center in elegant white letters. No address. No phone number, email, or website. Just that one strange word: *Niobe*.

"WHAT DID THAT reporter give you?" says Luke once we are in the cab, speeding downtown through the empty streets toward an all-night diner on Greenwich that he knows of.

"She's not a reporter."

"Really?"

I don't tell him where I've seen her before. I'm not sure why. I've only spent seconds with this woman, but I feel strange about those seconds, as though they're something to be guarded. "She said she wasn't."

I almost don't want to hand him the card, but I see he's noticed it and so I do.

He looks at me. "What is this?"

It's a group. For people like us. "I have no idea."

"Niobe," he says. "From Greek mythology."

"I . . . guess? I'm not much of a Greek mythology fan."

He nods slowly. "Weird." He hands the card back to me, his gaze fixed on the cab's TV screen, footage of colorfully dressed dancers in some Broadway show, spinning, then leaping, the grins never leaving their glitter-painted faces.

I watch Luke watching them. I've had a few actor friends in my life. They all seem to be obsessed with Greek mythology. "So," I ask finally. "Who's Niobe?"

"The wife of a king." He says it quietly, his gaze still locked on the screen. "She lost her children."

The diner is called the Acropolis and it's nearly empty, which isn't surprising. It's four in the morning, after all, and OPEN 24 HOURS sign or not, it feels more like a daytime place, the lemon scent in the air a little too thick, the lighting too bright and cheery for the after-club crowd. There are potted plants everywhere.

We take a booth next to the window. "I Can See Clearly Now" is playing over the speaker system—a song I've heard at least four times in the past few days. I'm starting to feel mocked by it. A tired-looking waitress drops menus in front of us and walks away. I smile at Luke, my throat dry and ragged. "So, how's the show going?"

"Fine, I guess," he says. "I've been getting weird emails from this fan."

"What kind?"

"You know what slash fiction is?"

I let out a laugh.

"So you do."

"I'd think it would be flattering to have erotica written about you."

"My character. Not me. Let's not get carried away here."

"Even more flattering. A testimony to your acting ability."

He sighs, shakes his head. "All I can tell you is, I can't do scenes with Lieutenant Mitchell without picturing him in leather chaps."

I stifle another laugh. "I hope that, at least, they're accurate procedurally."

"You think I'm going to show this stuff to Jim Grady?" Jim Grady is the show's on-set consultant—a retired NYPD detective who probably thinks slash fiction has something to do with vandalizing tires.

"Good point," I say. "But still—"

"Can I just ask you one thing, Cam?"

My smile fades.

"Why were you at the Brayburn Club? How did you even know about the awards ceremony?"

"That's two things."

He just looks at me.

I take a swallow of my water. "If you must know," I say, "I got an invitation."

"What?"

"I'm serious. I was emailed an invitation to the ceremony. I don't know why. I've gotten other things from Brayburn, though, over the last several months. I think one of the times when I was on their site, I got put on their mailing list."

Luke purses his lips. Gives me flat eyes, like a disapproving parent.

"I look at their website, Luke. Sue me."

The waitress is back. I don't know how long she's been standing there, but I think it's just been for a few seconds. Luke orders a cup of tea, a short stack, a side of bacon. "She'll have the same," he says. He knows enough not to ask me first. Back home, I subsist on stacks of canned soup and frozen meals I buy based more on price than on content. I don't care what I eat, as long as it fills me up and gives me enough energy to move through the day.

Before she leaves the table, the waitress takes a closer look at Luke, then me. "Aren't you . . ." She breathes out the words.

Unlike the older woman on the street, I don't assume she's going to ask Luke for his autograph. The waitress is very young, with dyed orange hair, bars in her ears, elaborate tattoos snaking up both arms. The wrong demographic for *Protect and Serve*; the right one for a semi-viral video. "You're—"

"I'm not anybody."

But her gaze stays locked on my face, recognition dawning in her eyes. I'm newly aware of the sweat stains on my dress, the moldy scent of the holding cell in my clothes and hair, the blotches on my skin from crying. "I'm a hungry customer." I try a smile. "That's who I am."

She gives me a weak smile back, her pale cheeks flushing red. She leaves quickly with our order.

I look at Luke. "I don't like being more famous than you." Out of the corner of my eye I can see her raising her phone to take a picture.

Luke spots her too. "Oh shit," he says. "We should leave."

But I'm already up and heading toward this girl.

"Camille," Luke says. "Camille, wait."

Within seconds I'm inches away from the waitress, glaring into the lens of her phone. "You want a close-up?"

"Uh . . . I . . ."

I swipe the phone out of her hand. Her mouth drops open,

and she looks like Lisette, then Harris, then a combination of the two. I clutch the phone so tightly, my hand hurts. I want to smash it to the floor, but I don't. I don't. I can't. *You can't do things like that.* I stare at the screen—at my own face in the picture she's taken, gaunt and unfamiliar. She's about to text it to someone. *It's her,* the waitress has typed, along with a goggle-eyed emoji and a half-dozen exclamation points. *The crazy bitch from the Brayburn Club!!!!!!*

I delete the text. Hand her back the phone. My voice is calm and quiet and feels as though it's coming from somewhere else. "You know crazy when you see it, huh? You can diagnose these things?"

Her mouth is still open, her eyes aimed at the floor like a chastised kid.

"Look at me."

She does. Her eyes are hard and defiant—at least they seem that way to me.

There's part of me that understands. This girl is eighteen years old. Nineteen tops, meaning that she was around thirteen years old when Emily was killed, and likely didn't follow the news. In other words, like most of the teenagers snapping and GIFing and spreading the video around, she has no idea of the backstory. But that doesn't make me any less angry.

I can feel Luke behind me, his weight shifting. "I'm a human being," I tell the waitress quietly. "I am not your entertainment."

There may be a change in those eyes, a softening. But I'm

not sure. It's probably my imagination. Luke hands me my purse and phone, which is still powered off. I may never turn it on again.

I head out the door with him close behind me. For the length of the cab ride back to his apartment, we barely say a word.

LUKE'S APARTMENT IS in a Brooklyn Heights brownstone—a lovely place, but small and with thin walls. He bought it a couple of years after graduating NYU and, despite his success, has never thought of upsizing. ("I like it here," he says. "It's home.") So while it goes unsaid that I'll be crashing on Luke's couch tonight, it also goes unsaid that I need to be very quiet about it. His girlfriend, Nora, who spends most nights here, is an attorney with a morning commute. She needs her sleep. I get that. What I'm not quite prepared for is that he's already made up the couch for me, sheets tucked neatly over the cushions, two fluffy pillows resting on a pale blue comforter. My throat clenches up and my vision blurs a little. When I thank him, it comes out the thinnest of whispers. "You're so good to me."

Luke waves it off. "I'm out of pancake mix, but I do have eggs and toast," he whispers. "I can make it for you now. Or do you want to sleep first? Have breakfast in the morning, which is, of course, in about five minutes . . ." He turns to look at me, but I'm already on the couch. "I guess you want to sleep," he says.

I grab his wrist. Pull him next to me. I don't want to cry.

Luke puts his arm around me. "You want to listen?" He says it very softly.

I want it more than anything. A tear rolls down my cheek. Then another. He lies back on the couch, his head against the pillows. He pulls me to him.

"But . . . Nora . . ."

"She doesn't mind," he says. "She understands."

I wipe the tears from my face, but more follow. He's doing this because he feels as though he owes me. I know that. I'm taking advantage of him, of the fact of his being alive. It's not right. But I'm not a good enough person to pull away.

"It's okay," Luke whispers. "It's okay, Cam."

Will I ever be whole again? Will I ever be normal? I rest my head on his chest, and as he strokes my hair, I find it. The heartbeat. My daughter's heartbeat.

I fall asleep listening to it, forgetting my troubles, marveling at its strength.

THREE

It was my decision to donate Emily's organs. It made Matt feel squeamish, I think, but I didn't care. He owed it to me. It had been him, after all, who let Emily go to the fraternity party. As she lay in the hospital, slowly slipping out of even the artificial life the ventilator could provide, we agreed to donate her lenses, liver, kidneys, and heart.

I was told they all went to patients who needed them. But Luke, the heart recipient, was the only one to write me a letter. I wrote him back, and then we spoke on the phone. A friendship was born. Or, as Matt used to call it, an addiction.

Matt's description may have been accurate, I don't know. I do remember Luke's and my first meeting—at the Applebee's in Woodbury Commons, an enormous outlet complex off the New York Thruway, with a parking lot bigger than the entire town I live in. Luke chose the place, claiming it was a halfway point, though I knew from the map he had to travel a lot farther. I tried to tell him we could meet in the city, but he wouldn't hear of it. "It's the least I could . . ." he started. Then he stopped—embarrassed, I suppose, by his own indebtedness.

At any rate, we drank a couple of beers and talked about things I no longer remember. The weather, maybe? The news? What I do recall is the feel of the conversation—like a job interview you know you've aced, and you can't wait to get past the formalities and go to work.

I could have watched him move and speak for hours, if only to marvel at the livingness of him, my daughter's living, beating heart.

While we were waiting for his Uber to arrive, he asked if I wanted to listen to it and of course I said yes. The disparity in our heights made it easy, as though it had been planned. All I had to do was move closer and my ear was to his chest. When I put my arms around him, it was so satisfying, the final piece fitting into the jigsaw puzzle.

Maybe it was an addiction. Maybe it is.

When I wake up in the morning, my head is still resting on Luke's chest and I realize I've been dreaming about my Emily. In the dream, we've been climbing a mountain. The air is thin and our breath is heavy, but we're smiling, covered in sweat, both of our hearts beating so hard, it's all we can hear. *Almost there, Mom*, Emily says. *Soon we'll be able to jump off together.*

I spring away from Luke, my face flushing. "What time is it?"

"Huh?"

The sun's pressing through the windows, and the door to

Luke's bedroom is open, Nora having left for work. I yank my phone from the nearby charger, power it up, and look at the screen. Eight a.m. My screen is striped with texts, three of them from women I used to know, mothers of Emily's closest friends. Their names are Lisa, Denise, and Sylvie, and when I read their texts, it's hard not to picture the three of them clustered around a cauldron.

Camille!! Are you okay?

> Saw what happened at the Brayburn club. If
> you need someone to talk to, I'm here. . . .

Honey, you need help. Please seek it. I'm begging you, as a
caring friend.

The final text is from Glynne Barrett, the Woodstock artist. It's the only one I don't delete: Does 2 p.m. work for you?

I text back quickly: Yes!

"I need to get home."

Luke says something about giving me a ride to Penn, but I tell him the subway's faster—I'll probably make it there before he's able to get his car out of the garage. I kiss him on the cheek. "Thank you," I tell him. Even though he hates it when I thank him for anything. "And please thank Nora for me. It can't be easy, sleeping alone while you're out there on the couch . . ." I decide not to finish the thought. "Anyway. I wish you guys would come up and visit me sometime. I have a big house. Lots of room. I'd like to return the favor."

"Thanks, Cam. We just might do that."

Once we've said our goodbyes and my hand is on the doorknob, Luke touches my shoulder. I turn around and look into his eyes and know exactly what's on his mind. Luke is so easy to read. I often wonder if it's because of his acting training—that Stanislavskian tearing down of walls over years and years and years—or if it's simply me, the connection we share. "I'll be okay," I tell him.

"Can you promise me something?"

"Depends."

"The next time you plan on doing something like you did last night, can you call me first?"

Interesting choice of words. I never *planned* on doing what I did last night. I'm not *that* crazy, and I tell him so.

He says nothing.

"Come on, Luke. You know me." I start out the door, but he blocks my way.

"There's this one director on *Protect and Serve*. He meets the leads privately once a week, shows us our worst takes."

"He sounds like an asshole."

"Most people think so. But I find it helpful."

"Like a 'scared straight' thing? Only it's bad acting instead of drugs?"

"Yes. Exactly."

"Why are you telling me this?"

"I'm not going to show you the video. But . . . I took a look at it last night, after you fell asleep. And I think you need to watch it. On your own. When you get home."

"To scare myself straight."

"Yeah. Kind of."

He's serious. I can't believe this.

"I had some drinks to calm my nerves. They didn't mix well with my antianxiety meds, which . . . I guess is kind of ironic, really. When it comes to calming a person down, two rights can make one hell of a wrong."

"Camille."

"That wasn't me at the Brayburn Club, Luke. It was a bad chemical reaction."

He sighs heavily. Says it again. "Camille." It makes me hate my own name, that tone of his. It annoys me nearly as much as the concern-trolling of Lisa, Denise, and Sylvie, who, by the way, I haven't spoken to in probably a year.

Luke isn't like them. He has a good heart, in every sense. He just doesn't know me quite as well as he believes he does. I give him a forced smile, a hug goodbye. "Your concerns are duly noted, Sarge."

I say it because I know it will piss him off.

WHEN I GET back to the Rhinecliff station, there's a ticket on my car. I parked in the short-term lot rather than the overnight one and thus overstayed my welcome; I hadn't expected, after all, to spend the night in jail. But the car hasn't been towed, and I choose to take that as a positive.

It's twenty degrees colder up here than it was in the city—a bracing cold that bites at my cheeks and makes my eyes water. And as I drive over the Kingston-Rhinecliff Bridge, over the frozen tundra of the Hudson River, the crumbling piles of ice blending into the dull sky, I think about how I used to love the winter when Emily was alive. I was in a poetry workshop back then, and I wrote some terrible haikus about the "kindest season," how it buried the dead leaves and blown-down branches of fall beneath a blanket of white and put everything to sleep. Winter was, I believed, a chance to hide all the year's mistakes, to freeze them dry. It was a chance at rebirth.

What a load of crap that was.

My phone dings. An incoming text, but I don't even glance at it. After an arrest and a parking ticket, the last thing I need is to get pulled over for texting and driving. It dings again and then, when I'm over the bridge and heading up Route 209, it rings into the Bluetooth and I answer it.

"Oh, hello, Camille." It's Glynne Barrett, and she sounds strange—as though she's surprised to hear from me, even though she's the one who called. "I just texted you."

I glance at the clock on my dashboard. It's 1:25. "Hi, Glynne. See you at the coffee place? I just have to run by my house to pick up my laptop, so I may be, like, five minutes late—"

"Listen. I . . . uh . . ."

"Yes?"

"I don't think I'll be in need of your services."

My fingers tighten on the wheel. "Oh."

"I . . . I rechecked my finances and it's not in the budget. Sorry."

"But we didn't even go over pricing. I work on a sliding scale." I don't like the tone of my voice, the desperation in it, but I can't help it. I know why she's pulling out. I know it has nothing to do with money, and I know she won't be the last to do this to me. "We can figure something out. I really think you'll be pleased with the designs I've come up with. . . ."

"I'm truly sorry."

"Glynne."

"Yes?"

"You've seen the video."

"Yes."

"I can explain."

"Camille. You truly are a dear, but . . . I think you need a rest right now."

"You have no idea what I need. You don't even know me!" I shout it into the windshield. Thankfully, she's already hung up.

I stare out at the gray road, the sky already starting to darken, that bleak, mummified winter sky. Here's the thing: I don't need Glynne Barrett's money. Matt and I paid off the mortgage on the house a long time ago. Plus, we got a big settlement in our wrongful death suit against Pi Sigma Phi—a move that made Harris Blanchard's lawyers categorize us as moneygrubbing opportunists but that left both of us more than comfortable, even after the divorce. The way I spend, which is hardly at all, it'll take me decades before I make a dent in it.

No, I don't need money. I need the job. I need to spend a certain amount of my day focused on things like fonts and resolutions and links, or else my mind will go to that dark, cold place it goes whenever it has nothing else to do. I'll relive that night five years ago, relive it over and over again but with different outcomes. Impossible outcomes. I'll break things. I'll drink. I'll hurt people who don't deserve to be hurt, when the one person who does deserve it continues to thrive. To sparkle. To win awards. I need this job to survive.

I hit redial on my phone, expecting Glynne Barrett's voicemail. She picks up, though. "Camille," she says.

"I'll do it for free."

"What?"

"You said it wasn't in the budget. I'll redo your website for free."

"Oh, come on." Glynne sighs out the words. "That's silly."

I clutch the wheel. "Yeah. It probably is."

She says nothing for a while. I see my exit ahead, and I take it as she breathes into my Bluetooth. "Okay," she says finally.

"Great. Great. You won't regret it." Duh. At the very least, this is a two-thousand-dollar job. I'm doing it for free. Obviously, she won't regret it. "So . . . see you at two?"

"How about you just email me your ideas?"

My cheeks are hot. The parking ticket smirks at me from the dashboard. "Of course," I tell her. "Of course, Glynne."

IT'S NEARLY AS cold in my house as it is outside. I kept the heat on when I left for the city; I didn't want the pipes to freeze. But it's a very old house—built in 1800 or so—and terribly drafty. I'd seen romance in the place when we first moved up here from Manhattan in the spring of 2002, a wooden house still standing when enormous steel towers had so recently gone down. Matt and I had come up here for a weekend with our three-year-old daughter and a vague idea of moving away from the shell-shocked city—no place for a child, we had said—and we'd both fallen in love with the house at first sight. Since it was spring, we didn't think about how treacherous the bluestone walkway could be in the winter if it wasn't shoveled and salted, how rarely a peaceful mountain road like this one got plowed, or how expensive it was to heat a big, old wooden Colonial. We just saw budding rosebushes clinging to the side of a sunny yellow house and swooned like lovestruck teenagers. *I can plant ranunculus and hyacinth over there*, I had said. *An English garden that can grow alongside Emily.*

The draftiness was fine when Matt and I slept close together under piles of quilts, or when Emily was little and we'd play Apples to Apples in front of the wood-burning stove, sipping cups of hot cocoa, quilts thrown over our laps. Now that

I'm living here alone, though, it's just an old wreck with sucky insulation. On a typical winter day, I take two or three hot showers and I still can't get the chill out of my bones.

That said, I have no intention of leaving. Leaving this house would mean starting over somewhere else, which is a thing I can't imagine.

I throw some logs into the stove, take a shower that steams up the bathroom mirror, and change into sweats, replaying the conversation with Glynne in my mind, then the one with Luke, that maddening concern in his eyes. *Does the whole world think I'm crazy?*

My office is on the second floor, my desk situated across the room from a large window. I sit down in front of my closed laptop and stare out the window before powering up—the steady wind ruffling the skeletal trees, the sky already darkening. Interesting. Matt and I fell in love with the house in spring, spent so many hot summers entertaining friends in the small backyard where I tended my evolving English garden. On crisp fall days, we hiked to the top of this mountain—Mount Shady, it's called, same as the town—and gazed out over acres of fiery leaves. But the past five years have been nothing but winter after winter after winter, one dead-cold January bleeding into the next, the other seasons lasting no longer than a clearing of the throat. The roses in front of the house don't even bloom anymore. Or if they do, I don't notice.

I power up my laptop, open the folder of designs I worked

up for GlynneBarrettCreations.com—one simple and classic, gray lettering on a white background; the other a little brighter, the red letters bringing out the colors in the painting she chose for the title page. Glynne is a skilled artist, and popular in our neck of the woods—a landscape specialist, very Hudson River School. She had been a fresh talent when we first moved up here—a break from all the nature photography and album cover art that filled most of the galleries. We bought one of her paintings, of a barn at sunset. It was the first new decorative thing we purchased for this house, and it still hangs in the den. I like to sit across from it, watch the changing light play on the painted sky. Some quiet days, I've gotten lost in it for hours.

Glynne doesn't know any of that, but I had been hoping I'd be able to work something out with her—another painting, maybe in exchange for web optimization or two years of free updates. No such luck now, I suppose. I let out a long sigh. What would it be like to delete the past twenty-four hours from my life?

I don't want to go online, but I have to. Luke was right— well, partially. I do need to watch the Brayburn video. Not so I can learn something about myself, as he suggested, but so that I know what I'm up against and how long it's likely to last.

I have a Twitter account—zero followers, an egg for an ava- tar, a series of numbers for a name. I created it seven years ago in an effort to stalk my rebellious thirteen-year-old daughter, and I've used it only a handful of times. I tired of it quickly after discovering that Emily only used the platform to tweet heart-eye emojis at members of One Direction. But I do remember my password: 417Dumpling. Emily's birthday, combined with my nickname for her when she was a baby.

I log in to Twitter now and search for "Brayburn Club" and the video pops right up, along with related searches (#Psycho Mom, #KochMeltdown #MeltdownMom #MarthaMeltdown. #KochBlock. At least that last one is kind of clever).

Bitches be crazy, one of the first tweets reads. I click on the video link. It makes me freeze inside, but I watch it twice more, then three, four times. It's like watching a stranger, a bad actor in a bad play I can't take my eyes off of.

I scroll through the rest of the #PsychoMom tweets. Turns out someone's made a GIF of me screaming *"Murderer!"* Over and over again on my laptop screen, the twisted face, the wild eyes. The first comments I read are from clueless teens:

What's wrong with this lady lol?

Go home, Aunt Cheryl. You're drunk.

But then I get to the people who do remember:

How sad for #HarrisBlanchard.

I'm cringing all over. I can't even with what she's doing to this LEGALLY EXONERATED kid.

If he were my son, I'd sock her in the face.

When you can't tell the difference between legit rape and your own bad parenting.

Women like this make it harder for real victims of assault.

And then this one, accompanied by a "before" picture of me at the trial, coifed and curvy in an ill-advised pencil skirt: OMFG. THIS is Camille Gardener??!!!

There are the sympathetic tweets, of course, plenty of them, from bleeding hearts with hashtags like #Justice4Emily and #BelievetheWomen. In a way, these are even more upsetting, the users treating me as part of a public agenda, hoping I can *get some inner peace* and *move past the outrage* so the patriarchy won't win.

One of them has tweeted out a personal message: Camille, please. This isn't what Emily would want.

The presumptuousness of Twitter. The fucking nerve. But then again, look at me. Look at what I did. If ever someone demanded this type of attention . . .

I scroll up to one of the links, watch the video again. The scream from the back of the room, Harris Blanchard on the stage, ducking down fast, as though he's been shot. My face, just before the rent-a-cop takes me down. The eyes. The teeth. "What is wrong with you?" I whisper at the lunatic on the screen. "Who are you?"

VIDEO LINKS ARE one thing, but GIFs last forever. That "The lies, the lies!" one with the Real Housewife, for instance. Nobody remembers what that was about, do they? But it doesn't matter. It's the incongruously formal dress, the way she flails her hands around, the flash of anger in her eyes. Most of all, it's her face. I'd know that face anywhere, and I haven't watched any of the *Real Housewives* shows in years.

After I've made my way through most of my Twitter hashtags, I go to the downstairs bathroom, gaze into the mirror, and see her gazing back at me. #PsychoMom. #KochBlock. I wince, and PsychoMom does too.

In the cupboard next to the sink are some of Emily's things—a plastic tub full of brightly colored nail polish; another, packed with wild lipstick shades: glittery green, gothic black. And yet another full of hair dye. I've kept all these things because I still can't bring myself to throw them out— these souvenirs of my daughter's over-the-top preteen tastes, slumber parties, and school dances, the white marble sink tinged electric blue from boxed hair dye. . . .

I grab a box of dye in the most conservative color I can find, which happens to be called Raven's Wing. Not great for my skin tone, but it beats trying to look for something more complimentary and getting spotted in CVS by people who used to know me. All I want is to look different from the woman in the video, and Raven's Wing can do that job.

I open the box, grab Matt's old hair clipper and the scissors I used to cut Emily's hair with when she was a little girl. Within the hour, my waist-length dirty-blond, gray-streaked hair is shiny black and barely reaches my chin. I examine my face in the mirror, the way the cut accentuates the sharpness of my jaw, the dark circles under my eyes, and my eye color, which the black dye seems to have brought out—a vivid, shattered green. I didn't think a new hairstyle could make me look angrier, but that is what I seem to have accomplished. If I saw me walking down the street, I'd cross to the other side. Not a bad thing, really. And I do look different.

I run the blow-dryer over my hair, then go to the kitchen and heat up a can of soup, which I eat in silence, then grab a few slices of bread and eat those too. I'm hungrier than I thought. I wash it all down with a bottle of seltzer, then a glass of wine. By the time I head back upstairs to my office, the sun is setting.

Twitter is still up on my laptop screen. When I left the room, I'd been exploring the #MarthaMeltdown hashtag, and I see there are several more entries if I choose to refresh. I choose not to.

I'M EMAILING MY designs to Glynne when I notice another email, this one from Facebook. *Invitation to Join a Group*, it's titled. I open it up, recalling the silver-haired woman outside the police station. The card she'd given me: *Niobe*.

It's a group, she had said. *For people like us.*

Unlike Luke, I've never heard of the Niobe myth. Outside of my art classes, I was never much of a student—more interested in socializing. I did have a Greek mythology class sophomore year of college, but it was at nine a.m., so I was either dozing in my seat or back in my dorm room, nursing an Everclear hangover. I took the class pass/fail and barely passed. I learned nothing.

So I google Niobe now, and read her sad story, how she bragged about her dozen children so much, she enraged the Titan Leto, who sent her kids Apollo and Artemis down from Mount Olympus to kill all twelve of them.

It's the price you pay for being dumb enough to feel secure in your life.

After her children were taken from her, Niobe was so destroyed by grief that she turned to stone and became part of a mountain herself, the face of Mount Sipylus, known in Turkish as Ağlayan Kaya ("the Weeping Rock"). Niobe's tears turned to waterfalls that have never stopped rushing.

People like us.

I log in to Facebook, which is a kinder, gentler place than Twitter. At least, it is for me because I have very few friends and haven't posted on it in five years. If anybody's posted my viral video, they haven't tagged me. But even if they have, that's not why I'm here. I click on my messages. I've gotten a few—"inspirational" chain letters from people who honestly believe they're "paying it forward" by clogging up people's inboxes, plus some "are you okays" from Mount Shady acquaintances. I don't open any of them. But I do click on one—the same invitation to join the private group Niobe. I accept.

The banner at the top of the group's page is black, the word printed across it in simple white letters. Just the black box and the word. And a slogan at the side of the page. There are 132 members in this private group, which frightens me. It's bigger than I thought. But maybe there's safety in numbers.

At the right of the page is this description: Don't let your pain turn you to stone.

I scroll through the page and start to read the posts. Tales of heartache and sleeplessness and agonizing grief, all from women. All from mothers. A retired high school teacher in Washington, D.C., awakened at three a.m. by a phone call— her only daughter, dead from a fentanyl overdose, administered by a rich druggie boyfriend who subsequently checked into rehab and spent no time behind bars. A nurse from Texas, her unarmed teenage son shot in the back by a man who successfully claimed in court that the boy "was behaving suspiciously" by walking through his neighborhood. A stay-at-home mom from Connecticut, her kindergartner the victim of a hit-and-run driver, never caught . . . Women from Miami and Los Angeles and rural Wyoming and the Boston suburbs, all of them robbed of their children by the actions of others— drunk drivers, incompetent doctors, and, yes, murderers with intent—all of whom, like Harris Blanchard, never got what they deserved. Women trying to accept their losses when their losses are unforgivable, unimaginable, unacceptable . . .

And here's what I notice: None of these stories are told in the context of time. The deaths could have happened yesterday or last month or twenty years ago; no one specifies how much time has elapsed since the death of their child because they all understand that time doesn't matter. The hurt's the same. The wound never heals. The details never fade.

My son was wearing his varsity jacket. He was carrying his gym bag. He cut through that neighborhood coming home from a game. He had a calculus final the next morning. He texted me, asking if there was any ice cream left.

I keep reading as night falls outside my window and the room goes dark and cold. And as I read, I think again about that silver-haired woman—how she and her friend had watched me at the Brayburn event, the hiss of their whispers (had they said, *That's her*?). I think about how she'd somehow known to find me outside the police station, at the exact moment I left with Luke, before we'd gotten into our cab. I think about how strange that was, yet somehow comforting, too, not so much the actions of a stalker as those of a guardian angel.

Tell your story, the angel tells me, over and over, in the depths of my imagination—that hiss of a whisper. A snake, wrapped around nourishing fruit. *Tell your story. You'll feel better. I guarantee that you will.*

I haven't told my story. Not since five years ago, when I took the witness stand in my ill-advised pencil skirt, the defense lawyer smirking at me, my daughter's angel-faced, wide-eyed murderer mouthing *It's okay* at his weeping mother. I've never told the story without being judged for it, and so I've promised myself that I'll never tell it again.

Again, that tempting whisper. This page is no courtroom. These people do not judge. They are people like me.

People like us.

I create a post:

Camille Gardener
January 10 at 1:41 a.m.
I'm ready to tell my story now.

My finger is on the touch pad, my gaze pinned to the screen, to the tiny pointing hand hovering above the post button.

Do it, the angel whispers.

I hold my breath. My finger moves.

FOUR

NIOBE

MEMBERS: 132 MEMBERS

Description: Don't let your pain turn you to stone.

Camille Gardener

January 9 at 11:42 p.m.

Hi. My name is Camille, and I live in upstate NY. Thanks for inviting me to join this group.

Seen by 110 people

30 ♥, 20 👍 10 comments

Daria Ann (admin): Welcome, Camille! Do you want to share your story? Niobe is a safe, judgment-free space full of like-minded mothers. Many of us (me included) have given up traditional therapy since sharing here.

Camille Gardener: Why are there no men?

Melissa Reese: Too much mansplaining!

20 👍, 10 😃

Daria Ann (admin): Lol, Melissa. We did have some dads in the group when we started, Camille, but we found it made it more difficult for some of us to share.

Tara Jacobson: In other words, like Melissa said lol.

Violet Langford: It isn't their fault. It's just the way we've all been conditioned. Every parents-of-victims group I've belonged to has been mostly women, yet there's always been a man in charge. They talk, we listen. It's the way of the world, but it's also part of our pain and anger. On top of everything else, we don't ever get to feel heard. Men don't understand that, bless their hearts.

7 😞, 3 ❤️

Daria Ann (admin): It's not that way of *our* world, though. We listen to each other.

Tara Jacobson: Amen.

Camille Gardener: Well, thank you again. But I don't think I want to tell my story. Is that okay?

Daria Ann (admin): Everything is okay here, Camille.

Camille Gardener

January 10 at 1:41 a.m.

I'm ready to tell my story now.

Seen by 79 people

45 ♥, 30 👍

Daria Ann (admin): We're listening.

Camille Gardener: My daughter was killed at a fraternity party. It happened in January, on a Friday night. She was fifteen years old. I wasn't around when she asked if she could go to the party. She had been invited by a boy—a freshman at Brayburn she had met a few weeks earlier. Her dad said yes. I wouldn't have. For years I've tried to think about my ex-husband's line of reasoning: This boy wasn't the first older friend my daughter had made. She was an only child, and wise beyond her years. She had several close friends who were seniors, and a college freshman didn't seem that different. Brayburn is small and not that far away from us, and it's not a notorious party school. She promised she would be home by her eleven p.m. curfew. My ex-husband, I'm sure, had any number of reasons. I still wouldn't have let her go.

Anyway, at the time, I worked for a Hudson Valley tourist magazine, and we were closing an issue that Friday, and so I didn't get home until close to eleven. It was one of those nights that was too cold for snow, a clear night with a sky full of stars

and a full moon. I looked in the closet and saw that her winter
coat was missing, and I remember saying to her dad, "At least
she brought her coat." We both knew how she hated wearing
a coat, no matter how cold it was. She found it constricting.
She found everything constricting—her school, her town, her
parents. It was nothing unusual. She was just at that age. My
husband said, "I'm sure she'll be home soon. She's a good kid."
But then midnight came, and there was still no sign of her.
She didn't answer our texts. That was when her dad told me
it was a college fraternity party she'd gone to, and that she'd
gone with a boy who had picked her up at our house. Her dad
didn't have a cell phone number for the boy, just a name. The
boy she had met a few weeks before at a friend's house. I can
recall my daughter saying that this college freshman was "very
nice," and that I would like him if I met him. The good news
was, my husband remembered the name of the fraternity. We
looked up the number and called its landline, over and over and
over, hoping to find him and our daughter. No one answered
for a long time. Then finally someone did. It was a very drunk-
sounding boy. He said he couldn't find either one of them, and
that he was pretty sure there were no underage girls at this
party, which from the sound of things was still in full swing.

We called the police. They told us "don't worry" and to "sit tight."
But of course we worried. Before I tell more of this story, there's
something you all need to understand. Our daughter may have
been sophisticated for a fifteen-year-old, but in our town, all that

meant was that she wore a lot of black and colored her hair and listened to music with swear words in it. She didn't drink or do drugs. She'd never had a boyfriend or even been on a date. She worked hard in her classes and played the piano in the school jazz band. She liked to bake cookies. She was a virgin.

I was furious at my husband for letting her go to that frat party. I yelled and screamed at him, and he yelled back, telling me at least he had been around, that I was never around, always working. At dawn we got into my car and we drove to the campus. We saw some kids coming home from parties, and we asked them if they had seen our girl. Finally we found the frat house. Her winter coat was in the bushes outside the front door. She was found later that day, in the woods behind the school, barely alive. She clung to life in the hospital for three days—enough time to give us a shred of hope. Before she lost consciousness, she said, "He gave me too much to drink. He took me to the woods. He raped me." She said it to me directly. She said it clearly, as weak as she was, because she needed me to know the truth. And then she said, "I'm sorry, Mom." For going to the party, I guess. For believing a monster was "very nice." I don't know for what exactly, because those were her last words. I'm sorry. She apologized. Her murderer never did. He claimed they had consensual sex at the frat and that afterwards, she refused his offer of a ride home and drunkenly "ran off" with a "stranger" he "never got a look at."

Daria Ann (admin): That's heartbreaking, Camille.

Camille Gardener: There was no stranger. My daughter said his name. She told me her killer's name, and it was the same boy my husband had allowed her to go to the party with.

Daria Ann (admin): Could you ever forgive him?

Camille Gardener: If you mean my ex-husband, yes. If you mean the boy who raped her and left her to freeze to death? No. Never. Not even after he's dead himself.

70 ☹

FIVE

Emily is buried in Mount Shady Cemetery—a tiny graveyard situated, oddly, next to the town playground. Matt
and I had thought about cremating her body, but I couldn't
bear the thought of losing any more of her than I already had,
and so we bought a simple gravestone, the plot just twenty feet
away from the swing set she used to love when she was little.
I haven't been here in months because, to be honest, I don't
feel her presence at the grave site. Not the way I do when I'm
listening to Luke's chest.

But I am here now, nearly twelve hours after telling my
story. A few of the women in the Niobe group suggested I do it.
They seemed pretty adamant that it would help me "heal" and
"get on the road to moving on," and so I told them I would. I
don't think it will, but I respect them enough to keep my word.

I parked the car up the road, and I'm walking down the
icy, pitted sidewalk in snow boots, the hood of my puffy
coat pulled over my newly black hair. I bought flowers at the

supermarket—pink roses that will surely die fast in this arctic weather—but after last night, and all the memories that came with it, I feel the need to leave something for her, something fresh and new and perfect.

It's about one in the afternoon, but the sky is such a peaked gray that it feels more like early morning. There are hardly any cars driving up and down the streets, and the air is so cold, it sears my eyes. It's impossible not to feel déjà vu. It was a record cold winter five years ago, and in the weeks following Emily's death, I spent most of my waking hours outside, standing in the yard, or more often struggling up the mountain to the spot Emily and I used to picnic in when she was little—a big smooth rock next to a stream we named Unicorn River. Unicorn River was a sheet of ice at that point, and I'd sit on that rock and stare down at it until my feet felt dead and my lips turned blue. *Reverse projecting*, my therapist, Joan, called it. *You're trying to feel the way she did at the end.*

Joan understood. Not because she was a therapist with a medical degree (from Brayburn of all places), but because she'd lost somebody too—her little brother, when she was a teenager—and it turned her hair steel gray forty years too early. Joan was the only one who knew how I felt. A young woman with an older woman's name and hair and hardship, a psychiatrist who specialized in patients coping with the untimely death of a loved one and knew the feeling intimately. *You have to stare it down*, Joan would say. *You turn away from grief and it will sneak up on you, grab you, smack you to the ground.*

Our friends, on the other hand, kept trying to put me to bed. *Get some sleep. You need your strength.* People always tell the grieving to get some rest, take it easy, go to sleep. They ply us with chamomile tea and sleeping pills and bake us soporific casseroles. They shove us into bedrooms and cover us with heavy blankets and beg us to sleep, to stay out of the way, to remain unconscious so they won't have to endure the discomfort of having to talk to us.

I found it all so disingenuous back then, but it didn't really matter, as it turned out. A day after they posted bail, Harris Blanchard and his parents gave an interview to *Rolling Stone*, and that interview changed things. It was picked up everywhere, posted and tweeted and screenshotted and even discussed by the ladies on *The View*. And, since it was 2015 and fits of outrage weren't quite as frequent or as disposable as they are now, it did not pass through the news cycle quickly. The story lingered like a bad storm. Reactions to it were ugly, even among the people who actually knew Matt and me. The awkward visits and casseroles and entreaties to sleep gave way to icy stares in the grocery store, my coworkers at the magazine literally whispering behind my back like third graders. *She must've known what her daughter was up to. What kind of mother would let a girl run wild like that? Have you taken a good look at Camille, though? Seems genetic to me.* Finally the editor in chief suggested I take a leave of absence. I didn't fight it.

The gist of the article, in case you haven't guessed: Rape

charges aren't always true. Sometimes the man or boy accused is the real victim.

Harris and his parents told quite a vivid story—something straight out of a Lifetime movie, where a self-destructive teenage townie seduces a loving couple's innocent son and runs off to meet her tragic end, leaving the poor college boy alone, confused, falsely accused. *Mother May I Binge Drink with Danger?*

The girl Harris Blanchard and his parents described in the article was a stranger—an invented character, not even remotely close to the person my daughter was. But the reporter couldn't have been more sympathetic to the Blanchards. We probably should have returned his calls for comment, but we were grieving and could barely talk to anyone, and by the time we realized what was happening, it was too late. Harris and his parents had written the narrative. And their legal team took over. They found Emily's secret Instagram accounts and filled in the story with lurid colors. And pictures. Someone in their ranks leaked the pictures to the press.

At the trial, two surprise witnesses came forward—both claiming they had seen Emily talking to "a stranger" long after Harris alleged they'd had consensual sex. One of them, the fraternity's president, said he saw her walking with this stranger into the woods. *A tall dark guy with a beard,* he said. *I couldn't see him very clearly.* I was the prosecution's only witness. They had tried to call a young girl who said Harris had forced himself on her when they were both in high school, but the judge wouldn't allow it. Though only Harris Blanchard's DNA was found in the rape test, the defense easily pointed out that this stranger could have worn a condom.

In the end, all we had was what Emily had told me in the hospital—what's known as a "dying declaration" in a court of law. *Of course you believe her,* one of the defense lawyers had said to me, her voice laced with false sympathy. *She was your daughter. You loved her.*

I believe her because I knew her, I replied. *None of you knew her. You're just making her up as you go along.* It didn't matter. Nothing I said mattered. The judge threw out the second-degree manslaughter charge, the jury quickly acquitted Harris Blanchard of rape, and his parents embraced him in front of snapping cameras, weeping tears of joy.

I felt as though the truth had been stolen from me. I made a secret vow never to speak of it again to anyone—to keep the facts close, so they couldn't be warped and damaged any more than they'd already been. So last night was a gift: an opportunity to tell a group of people what really happened to Emily that night and be believed. The thing is, though, I don't feel the relief I expected to feel. If anything, I hate Harris Blanchard more than ever.

I'm in the graveyard now. I can see the playground from where I'm standing, the pink roses cradled in my arms like a baby. Her grave is just a few rows up from where I am, and as I move toward it, I speak to Emily in my mind. I subscribe to her high school newsletter, and so I tell her about the new gym they're building, about the marching band winning a state championship, and how Miss Habler, the home ec teacher who seemed ancient to Emily when she was a freshman, is at long last retiring. It's all small talk, of course—things she'd probably roll her eyes over if she were alive. *And I'm supposed to care about this, Mom, because . . . why?* But it's all just a warm-up, leading to Niobe.

Emily, I found some new friends. They've lost their children, too, just like I have.

I imagine her response: *Come on, Mom. You told them you can't forgive Harris and all they did was throw a bunch of sad faces at you. They're just as judgy as the rest.*

"Yeah, well, at least they believed your story."

It isn't a story. It's real. It's what happened to me. Harris killed me. You have a right to be angry about that, Mom. Nobody should try to force you to forgive him.

Of course, it's me responding, not Emily. She isn't here, and she never will be. I'm alone in a graveyard on a freezing day, talking to myself. I wouldn't exactly call that healing or moving on.

I find Emily's headstone. It's pink marble and reads, *Emily Cheyenne Gardener 1999–2015 Beloved daughter,* with this inscription underneath: *"If there ever comes a day when we can't be together, keep me in your heart. I'll stay there forever."*

The quote is from *Winnie-the-Pooh,* Emily's favorite book when she was a little girl. Matt chose it, as well as the pale pink marble, and if you don't look at the dates, it would be easy to think she died at eight rather than fifteen. Matt liked to think of her that way, young and uncomplicated. When the pictures from her secret Instagram accounts came out, he refused to look at them. I got it, of course. But I couldn't look away. To me, they were more evidence of naivety than worldliness. She was a little girl playing with a camera, much the way she used to play dress-up alone in her room, never imagining that, after her death, those pictures would kill her for a second time. *She just wanted to be liked.* I tried explaining that to Matt, to Luke, to one of the reporters, whose name I can no longer remember. All of them got that same pitying look in their eyes. Nobody understood.

I bend down to set my flowers on the grave, and my breath catches. There's a bouquet here already—a dozen white roses. They're fresh and alive, and with the weather the way it is, they couldn't have been placed on Emily's grave much earlier. Who could they be from?

There's a tingling at the back of my neck—that primordial sense that someone is watching me—but I'm not afraid. I feel protected.

At the center of the bouquet rests a business card, glossy black against the ivory blooms. I remove it and turn it over, my breath coming out fast, a burst of condensation in the still air. There are two words on the card—the same font as the one the silver-haired woman gave me in the city, thin white letters against the black.

Ağlayan Kaya

The Weeping Rock. The unbreakable thing Niobe turned into, once her grief became too much.

"CAMILLE?"

I'm leaving Cumberland Farms, a to-go cup grasped in my hand, when I hear my name. My first impulse is to ignore it. I can't even remember the last time I was happy to run into someone I know up here. She says my name again, and I recognize her voice—Denise, the second witch in the texting trio. Her daughter, Chloe, was in Emily's class and had made her cry in the seventh grade by posting pictures on Instagram of a sleepover she hadn't been invited to. By the beginning of high school, Emily had taken to calling Chloe and her friends "basic bitches," and to be honest, I've always felt the same about their mothers.

I keep my eyes aimed at my shoes, but Denise is relentless. "Camille? Camille Gardener?" She's facing me, the two of us the only people on the sidewalk, and so I have no choice but to acknowledge her. "Hi, Denise." My voice comes out a rasp. I'm no good at this anymore. There was a time when I was the outgoing one in my family—an extrovert with golden highlights and fake boobs who wore makeup and went to PTA meetings and smiled a lot and did 99 percent of the social planning, but I can safely say I'm no longer that person. Since Matt left, I've sometimes gone for days without speaking and, like any unused muscle, my personality has atrophied. I can't fake a smile to save my own life, especially with a basic bitch like Denise. I try to move around her, but she puts a hand on my arm.

"Jesus, here we go." I actually say that out loud.

Denise keeps her hand on my arm. "You changed your hair."

"Yes."

"It's different."

"That's what I was aiming for."

Denise takes a step closer. She peers into my eyes as though she's trying to force her way in. "Did you get my text?"

"No . . . I mean, yes." I clear my throat. "Yes, I did get your text."

"And?"

"Thank you."

"Camille," she says. "I meant what I said."

"And . . . what is that, exactly?"

"Look, I know we haven't been as close in the past few years. But that doesn't mean I haven't been thinking about you. I know you're hurting. I saw the video. What can I do to help you move on?"

I stare at her. The pink cashmere gloves. The pink nose. The shiny blond hair and the spotless white wool coat, like a giant white rabbit. What am I supposed to do? Thank her for thinking about me? I try that, just to lose her.

I have so many problems with Denise and her ilk, but here is my biggest one: All of us will experience loss in our lives.

We will cry until we have no tears left and then we will hurt even more. Even for the luckiest of us, life is mostly pain, with moments of happiness thrown in just to keep us vertical. But the Denises of the world don't understand that. They think pain and loss is for other people. They say things like "Everything happens for a reason," and they *believe* it because it comforts them, the idea that people like me must have deserved what they got. "I don't really want to move on," I tell her. "But thanks."

"Camille, please. Call me, okay? We can talk."

The paper coffee cup is warm in my hand. I jam the other into my coat pocket, where the business card is waiting. *Ağlayan Kaya.* The face of a powerful, immovable mountain. "I will," I tell Denise.

She smiles like someone who's gotten what she wants. "Thank you."

We both know I'll never call her, and that's fine with us both.

THERE ARE FIVE websites I designed that I continue to manage, and ever since Glynne texted me yesterday, I've been checking my phone more often than I should, fully expecting at least one of them to fire me. Having watched the video myself, I wouldn't blame them if they did, but so far, so good. When I get home, I've even gotten a few updates from one client—an elderly Vassar professor who self-publishes science-fiction books on the side. I spend most of the afternoon scanning and positioning the three new covers he's sent me—the most memorable featuring a pink planet, ringed and glowing. *The Lost Souls of Chymera*, the book is called, and when I take a break to lie down and rest my eyes, I have a half-dream I'm there, on the beach of Chymera, my feet warmed by soft pink sand, watching Emily splash in rosy waves. *Don't go out too far*, I tell her. *Stay close to Mommy. . . .*

When I wake up, it's already dark outside and my face is wet with tears, like it always is when I wake up from a dream and feel reality setting in. It's a few seconds before I register the chirp of my phone, a few more before I get that it's not the alarm; it's actually ringing. My phone so rarely rings.

I grab it from the nightstand and check the screen. *Matt.* I can't remember the last time we've spoken. Six months ago? A year? But of course he's calling now. That damn video. Against better judgment, I answer it.

"Hi, Cammy. Long time, huh?" He says it like he's trying not to break things.

I rub sleep from my eyes. I remember now. The last time I spoke to Matt was February of 2019. I was feeling especially lonely and called him, ostensibly to wish him a happy birthday, though I was a month too late. I'd forgotten about the time difference and so it was seven a.m. Colorado time when I called. A very young and sleepy-sounding woman answered. *A friend from the dispensary*, Matt said. But after enduring an incredibly awkward conversation with them both, I checked out his Facebook page and learned he was engaged to a girl named Star, born the same year Matt and I had gotten married.

It didn't upset me as much as you might think. It was in character for my reverse-aging ex-husband, who had been wise and serious beyond his years when I met him—a computer coder before anyone even knew what that was, a PhD from Stanford, and not yet twenty-four. Now he's skiing and selling weed and engaged (maybe married?) to a woman half his age. The last time I looked at his Facebook page, he and Star were on their way to Coachella, and I realized that I really don't know Matt, not anymore. Maybe that isn't so bad. Both of us have been through the same awful thing, and it's changed us. Why should I be upset that we changed in different ways? "Hi, Matt."

"Listen, Cammy . . ."

"I know."

"I got a call from Lisette Blanchard."

I wasn't expecting that. Her name feels like broken glass in my ear. I open my mouth. Close it again. I have no idea what I'm supposed to say.

"I guess she didn't know I moved," Matt says. "Anyway, she said she was calling because she was worried about you. She wanted me to watch the video of you at the Brayburn Club. She sent me a link, and I watched it while she was on the line. She wanted me to talk to you and see if you're okay."

My voice comes back. "For fuck's sake."

"Cammy . . ."

"I don't want to talk about this, Matt, all right? I know I shouldn't have done it. I shouldn't have gone to that stupid award ceremony in the first place, but I did. It happened. And frankly, if you're going to be worried, I'd be more worried about someone who can't see that her son is a fucking sociopath than about someone who had a little too much to drink and called him out on it, but *maybe that's just me.*" I say it loud enough to hurt. My hands are trembling, my cheeks burning hot. I take a deep breath, listening to the silence on Matt's end of the line. "Matt?"

More silence. Matt's always been like this. Quiet during arguments, disappearing into himself. Avoiding conflict at all costs. I would mention this, but what's the point? I've said it probably a dozen times, in front of two different couples counselors, and all it got him to do was leave me.

"So, how's Colorado?" I ask him finally. "How's Star? You guys married yet?"

Matt says, "I told her to fuck off."

"What?"

"Not Star. Lisette. I told Lisette Blanchard to fuck off and never call me again."

My eyes widen. "*What?*"

"Star and I aren't going to get married, Cammy. She doesn't believe in contracts, and tbh, we're trying to downsize, so we don't need all those gifts."

"Can we get back to Lisette Blanchard?"

He exhales into the phone. "Sure."

"You really told her that?"

"Yes."

"I'm . . . I'm kind of amazed."

"You shouldn't be." His tone is quiet. Measured. "Lisette Blanchard has no right. She knows she doesn't. She knows everything her son took from us, because she isn't an idiot. But she survives on delusions, and the more people believe those delusions, the stronger she gets. I'm not interested in helping her feel better. She can fuck right off."

I swallow hard. "Thank you."

"Please don't thank me," he says. "She was my daughter too."

Darkness presses against the window. I shift on the bed, the springs whining. From far away, I hear the screech of tires—someone making a sudden turn all the way down the mountain, in town probably. It makes me aware of how isolated this house is, and how alone I am in it. "Matt?"

"Yeah?"

"What do you survive on?"

He laughs a little. "Indica," he says. "Edibles. I can't stand smoke."

"You know what I mean, Matt. How do you make it through each day without wanting to . . . well, do what I did on the video. Or worse?"

He inhales sharply, then lets it out. "You remember Gerard Krakowski?"

"I don't think so."

"I didn't, either, but he was in the news ten years ago. Wingnut vigilante in Texas. He killed a black kid. The kid was an honors student and a varsity baseball player, but Krakowski and his lawyers claimed he thought the kid's varsity jacket was gang colors and he was behaving suspiciously. If the neighborhood had security cameras back then, we'd have seen he wasn't doing anything suspicious, unless you count walking through that asshole's neighborhood."

"Right."

"The kid was unarmed. Krakowski shot him in the back. Killed him instantly, but he got acquitted. Never spent a day in jail."

"Terrible."

"I know," he says. "But . . . I guess you didn't see the news a couple of days ago. . . ."

"I hardly ever read the news."

"Me neither, but this popped up on my home page. Krakowski was cleaning his gun, and it went off and killed him. He shot himself, Cammy. If that isn't karma . . ."

"You believe in karma?"

"Maybe."

"You think that someday Lisette Blanchard will lose her son just like we lost our daughter."

"Payton Ruley's mom had to wait ten years for it, but it happened."

I exhale hard, a strange feeling coming over me. It's jealousy. I'm jealous of Matt. "You honestly have that kind of faith."

"You asked me what gets me through each day." He says it very quietly. "I just told you."

It isn't until I hang up with him and I'm downstairs in the

kitchen, pouring myself a glass of wine, that I think about that name. *Payton Ruley.*

On the kitchen table, my laptop is still open to the Vassar professor's website. I close that screen and click onto Facebook and head straight for the Niobe group.

I scroll down past three or four new posts, then my own from last night, down further and further until I find the one I'm looking for—one of the much earlier posts I'd read when I first found the group. *My son was wearing his varsity jacket. He was carrying his gym bag. He cut through that neighborhood coming home from a game. . . .*

The date on it is June 3—more than six months ago. I stare at the poster's name for what feels like a full minute: Rachel Ruley.

"Karma," I whisper. I google Gerard Krakowski, read up on the details of his death. Then I start to compose a private message.

> **Camille Gardener:** Hi, Rachel, I am a fellow member of the Niobe Group and recognized your son's name in the news. I know we're not official Facebook friends and I imagine you're getting barraged by private messages from reporters, but I hope this finds its way to you anyway. I really wanted to reach out and say that, as un-PC as this may sound, I'm glad Krakowski is dead. Personally, I hate it when people tell me I should forgive my daughter's murderer, that forgiving him and

his parents will stop the flow of hate in my veins and give me some closure. There is no closure for me. I will never stop hating him. And I hope I'm not presumptuous in thinking we might feel the same. We were robbed of our children. How can we be asked to stop hating those responsible???

That said, it gave me a lot of satisfaction to see the man who murdered your son get exactly what he deserves. EXACTLY. Before I joined the group, I had stopped telling people what I really want for my daughter's murderer, because it seemed like whenever I did, people would respond with, "Two wrongs don't make a right." What they don't seem to understand is that his death wouldn't be a wrong. It would be karma, if you believe in that crap. I don't. I prefer to call it justice.

I'd love to talk with you more about this if you're so inclined. If not, I understand. Just know that I'm on your side.

I read over the message twice—once for grammar and ty-pos, once for "Do I have any right to say these things to a stranger?" And then, without thinking too long about it, I hold my breath and tap send. It feels like pulling a trigger, and after I do, I stare at the screen, my heart pounding when the little check appears in the chat window: *Rachel Ruley has read the message.*

Then come the pulsing ellipses at the bottom of the window. I watch and wait. . . .

The ellipses stop. Start again. Stop.

"What are you typing?" I whisper. But no words appear. The ellipses stop.

It's six thirty, so I put a frozen meal in the microwave. I eat it slowly and in silence, thinking about Rachel Ruley, how it must have felt to read the news stories. Her son's murderer, dead by his own murderous hand.

Once I'm done eating and I've washed the dishes, I open my laptop again, head back to Facebook, and open the message. There is still no reply from Rachel Ruley. She has nothing to say to me, and that's fine.

I go back to my design files—the Vassar professor's website, the specs I recently sent to Glynne. After I finish all the updates, I upload them and go to my website email and send them to my client. Once I'm done, though, I notice that my website has received two new emails: one from Glynne titled These look great!

They'd better. They're free. When I open it up, though, she says she has "just a few thoughts" and suggests meeting for coffee tomorrow morning to discuss them. I debate asking her if she's paying for the coffee at least, but instead I just type, *Sure*, adding an exclamation point to show how truly accommodating I am.

The second email is from what looks like a meaningless series of numbers. *Spam*, I think. But then I notice the subject line: Justice.

Coincidental spam? I open it anyway. How can I not?

The message contains one word, and then a link to a site: a random-looking series of numbers followed not by *.com* or *.net* but by *.onion*.

I try clicking on it, but nothing happens. I copy it onto my search bar, but all I get is the blank screen and the note about being unable to access the site. I'm feeling a little panicky, as though I've been treading water for hours, and this strange numbered site is an island—a mysterious, looming thing that could save my life if I just find my way there. I pick up my phone, go to my recent calls, and click on Matt's number. It rings just once, and then he answers. "You again." He says it gently.

"Hey, listen. I have a computer question for you."

"Shoot."

"Can you tell me what *dot onion* means after a website?"

"Well . . . yeah. But why are you asking?"

I stare at the one word on my screen and the lie comes to me fast. "A client. She . . . um. She wants to show me a website as an example, but the link doesn't seem to work."

"Yeah? Well, tbh, I wouldn't bother with that client."

I sigh. Second time he's used the expression *tbh* in two separate phone calls. I suppose that when you hang out with a twenty-five-year-old all day long, text-speak finds its way into your lexicon. "Why not?"

"Websites that end in *onion* are on the dark web. You can't reach the site because you don't have an unencrypted server."

"The dark web? Really?"

"Yep."

"How . . . strange . . ."

"You doing websites for hit men, now?"

I force out a laugh. "I guess I should vet my clients better. Thanks for the info."

"Take care of yourself, Cammy."

"You too." I end the call, my eyes still on the email, on that one, lonely word the sender had typed, before that long, random series of numbers. *Kaya.*

I go to Google and type it in fast: *How to find and download an unencrypted server.*

SIX

It isn't hard at all to find an unencrypted server, and it's not expensive, either. In less than an hour, Tor is on my computer, and I've navigated my way to a site called Ağlayan Kaya, which, at first glance, looks exactly like the business card that had been left on Emily's grave. White letters on a black background. In the upper right corner of the group's page, there's a tiny button marked **chat**, and when I click on it, I'm asked to fill out a form with my first and last name, my email address, and an alias.

Pick a series of four numbers for your alias. All interaction on the Kaya chat is anonymous. If you state your real name, the real name of any of the other members, or of anyone connected to a member, you will be immediately and permanently removed from the chat.

For my four numbers, I choose 0417. Emily's birthday. I check it against the other members' numbers, and then I fill out the form without hesitation. There's no question I'll abide by these rules. I'm grateful for the enforced anonymity—there's freedom in it. And as far as the administrator goes—that unseen person or pile of software I'm providing with my real name and email address—I'm okay with them knowing who I am. It's not as though they've asked for my bank account number or my social. And if trusting this one entity is the price for, as that email said, *justice*, then I'm willing to pay it.

Once I've submitted the form, an instructional page pops up on my screen.

Ağlayan Kaya. Our loss has turned to rage that is permanent, strong, impenetrable. We are the face of the mountain and we will not be moved. We will not forgive. We will not sleep until the unpunished feel the pain they deserve.

Say here what you will. Speak your anger and take others' as your own. Fantasize the worst fates for your children's murderers and we will join you in it. The only words that aren't tolerated here are the ones forced on us by those who aren't part of the mountain—"Moving on," "learning to forgive," "a newfound understanding," etc. These are words we say to make others feel comfortable. We do not appease others by hiding our grief. There is no "moving on" here. We are the face of a mountain. No one can move us. Type "yes" if you agree.

I type yes. A message appears on my screen: 0417, you may enter the chat room, it tells me. I'm filled with a strange energy, a thrill that warms my blood.

MY EYES ARE starting to sting. It's hard to keep them open. I glance down at the lower right corner of my laptop screen. Four a.m. I've been in this chat room for more than six hours, but it feels like just a few minutes. I've made friends here—some thousands of miles away, judging from the way they describe their surroundings, and some closer. I remember the white roses on Emily's grave. *Some very close.*

I'll never know her name, the woman who left the roses. But as I finally log out of the chat room, ready for sleep, I feel as though I know her thoroughly. I know all of them thoroughly. There is strength and power in collective rage, one of the numbers said. It's true. I feel it.

I am no longer alone.

Since Emily's death, I've tried to join other groups. A support group for the newly grieving that met in the social hall of a Poughkeepsie church, an online chat for parents who have lost young children. I once took a memoir-writing class at the Omega Institute in Rhinebeck, where several of us happened to be struggling with the deaths of loved ones and trying to heal by squeezing our memories into words. In all of these groups, we sometimes described wish-fulfillment fantasies, and for my fellow members, those fantasies were almost always the same. *If I could have my child back for one day, this is what I would say to her, this is where I would take her, this is what we would do.* In the memoir class, the instructor even gave it to us as an assignment, and many in the class found it healing. I did not. Having Emily back for one day is not a fantasy of mine. It feels more like a curse, since it ends with losing her all over again.

My fantasies of wish fulfillment do not involve Emily at all. They involve Harris Blanchard, paying for what he's done.

And at last, I've found a group of women who all feel the same.

For the past six hours, these other nameless women and I described the deaths of those who killed our children in as much imaginative detail as we could: the drunk driver, forced into the middle of a highway and run over by an eighteen-wheeler. The druggie boyfriend, injected with bleach. A bully who drove a young girl to suicide, beaten to death by a mob in the school gym. For Harris Blanchard, I chose to have him led out into the middle of the woods in the dead of winter, beaten up within an inch of his life, then tied to a tree and left to freeze.

These women were supportive. They didn't act as though it was unhealthy to have such violent thoughts. And while I know there's no direct connection between this page and what happened to Gerard Krakowski, I almost feel as though this group is powerful enough to have wished it into reality.

The hope that grief counselors and clergy try to make you feel. The phrases well-meaning friends throw at you. *She's out there, watching over you, gazing down at you. She's with you,* *every day, living again in every memory. . . .* It's all a bunch of crap. Emily is not watching me. She doesn't exist. Harris Blanchard took her from me five years ago and she can never come back. Don't tell me that she can, that she *has*, just to quell my very justified anger. It's insulting and infantilizing—a Santa Claus type of lie.

The stories we tell in the Kaya chat, though, are different. They're *possible*. And the more we put them into words that aren't judged or shot down or excused away with *You don't* *really feel like that, honey* . . . the more we agree with those words and elaborate on them and give each other respect for having typed them, the closer our stories get to feeling not just possible, but probable. Achievable.

The sun is starting to rise, and I still haven't slept. I pop a Xanax. Set the alarm on my phone for nine a.m. so I don't miss my meeting with penny-pinching Glynne. As I fall asleep, I feel strange. I realize that it's because for the first time in months, I'm smiling.

"YOU LOOK GOOD," Glynne says. "I like your hair."

She's lying. We're in Mount Shady's one and only place to go out for coffee—a combination restaurant/overpriced antique boutique called Analog, owned by two clearly homesick Brooklynites—and I've caught a glimpse of myself in the cracked $790 mirror directly behind our table. I look pale and drawn, even in the forgiving yellow light of this place, and my chopped-off black hair only accentuates it. As Glynne stirs extra milk into her London Fog, I take a sip of my coffee. It's bitter. "Thanks." I force a smile. "I wanted a change."

Glynne gives me a pitying look. "Good for you." She removes the soft leather messenger bag from the back of her seat and undoes the clasp. Her nails are a shiny conch-shell pink, her skin glowing with the remnants of a vacation tan. I've always thought Glynne Barrett effortlessly attractive, but looking at her now, I can see that she does, in fact, put in a considerable amount of effort. The purposefully windblown hair, the peach lipstick that clashes artfully with the purple-and-red Tibetan scarf, the eyes, too vivid a blue to be natural. She reminds me of my old self—the amount of work it took: the manicures and the spray tans and the designer dresses and shoes—just to look "presentable" for a job at a country lifestyle magazine that was mostly coupons, when most of my coworkers usually showed up in sweats. *You can take the girl out of the fashion rag . . .* Matt used to say. I'd counter that an art director had to look creative and pulled together whether she worked in a glass tower in New York City or an office park in Kingston. But really, I think I was just vain.

Glynne thumbs through a stack of papers in her bag. She removes three color printouts of the designs I've sent her, all riddled with Sharpie scrawl. She lays them side by side on the table between us. "So, here's what I was thinking," she says, then proceeds to explain each scrawled note. "Just a few tiny tweaks," she adds at one point. But there are dozens of them.

At another point she explains, "What I'm trying to do here is match your designs to my vision."

Which would be fine, really, if she were paying for this. If I hadn't had to beg her to suck up her discomfort at being around me enough to benefit from my hard work, cost-free. If she wasn't one of so many people—hundreds more online—to judge me, to look down on me or run from me or laugh at me, to wrestle me to the ground and put me behind bars, simply because I had a normal, human reaction to the garbage who raped my fifteen-year-old daughter and left her to freeze in the woods and then got off because . . . why? Because his parents hired a team of celebrity lawyers.

Am I that hard to understand? Or is it just that they don't want to understand me, people like Glynne Barrett, who curate their wardrobes and fuss over websites and run from anything raw and unplanned, as though my type of pain were catching?

I hate him too, one of the numbers said to me on Kaya last night. Another said, He killed your daughter. He doesn't deserve to live. I said similar things to other numbers, all of us running toward one another's pain, our rage combining until it felt strong enough to take shape, to kill.

"Camille?" Glynne says. "Are you with me?" There's an odd look in her eyes—a mixture of amusement and concern.

"Yes. Why?"

"You seem like you drifted a little. Am I giving you too many notes?"

I nearly tell her about Kaya—not because I think she'd

understand, but because I'd like her to know that there are many others out there who do. But I can't. I know that. The woman in charge of the chat, the administrator of the site, I assume, goes by the screen name 0001. She contributes very little, but last night she did admonish one member (1219, which happens to be my birthday) who said she wanted to tell her husband about us. To be a member of this group is to take an oath of secrecy, 0001 warned. If you tell a soul, Kaya will dissolve. It will lose its magic. Telling one non-member ruins everything for us all.

It will lose its magic. As though we are witches, casting spells on our enemies.

Glynne says, "Camille?"

"No, sorry. I'm fine with your notes." I say it because I feel like I need to keep up appearances. But what I really want to do is cackle.

"Okay. Well, listen. Thank you."

"No problem."

"And I . . ."

"Yeah?"

She clears her throat. "Full disclosure." She tucks a shiny lock of hair behind her ear, revealing a glittering earring—some sort of Creamsicle-colored stone that brings out her lipstick. "I wasn't going to tell you this, but I've known Dean Waverly for years."

In my mind, I grab hold of the earring and rip.

"He commissioned me to paint a piece for the Brayburn

Faculty Club. This was . . . Well, it was probably a year or so before what happened to your daughter."

"Oh."

"When we first spoke about the website, I honestly didn't know that Emily Gardener was . . ."

"It's a common last name."

"Yes, well . . . I just wanted to tell you." She puts a hand on my shoulder. I want to shake it away. "He really did feel awful about what happened. Rick has never approved of fraternity culture."

I swallow hard, a million words running through my head. "Good for him." It's the nicest set of words I'm able to string together.

She gives me a warm smile, as though we've made some kind of real connection. We haven't. I know Waverly is "against fraternity culture." After Emily's death, Harris Blanchard's fraternity lost its charter, and the school put such strict rules into effect regarding underage drinking at frat parties that rush became a nonevent, and enrollment in the Greek system slowed to a trickle. I know all that. I don't care. I don't blame fraternity culture for Emily's death. I don't blame parties or alcohol or the detrimental influence of social media and online porn on Today's Youth. I blame her murderer. Period.

Glynne winds her hand around my back—an invitation for a hug. I don't accept it. People do and say and think whatever they can, just so they can believe they're good. It isn't my job to back them up. "Thank you," I tell her, "for the notes."

As I take her printouts and head out of the café, I'm counting the minutes until I can go to Ağlayan Kaya again.

IT'S A TWO-MINUTE drive to my house, another ten to load more wood into the stove, brew a pot of coffee, turn on my computer, and enter the dark web. As I take all these steps, my breathing is steady, deep, and focused, much the way it was when I used to run every day, each breath propelling me forward along with the music in my headphones, drawing me closer to my destination.

Until, at last, I'm there.

Once I've clicked on the Kaya chat, I type without thinking or censoring or reading anything anyone else has written. It feels like jumping out of a window, all the while knowing there's a safety net below.

0417: I want him dead. For real. I don't care how.

Ellipses percolate beneath my comment. I stare at them, waiting for words to appear. And it isn't long before they do.

2201: I think you were too kind last night, simply beating him up before he gets tied to the tree. I think he could use a knife through the eyeball.

1225: Or try a cut to the carotid, in front of a mirror. Make it shallow so he can see it happen. Then chop off his head.

0104: He raped your daughter, right? Chopping off his dick seems more appropriate.

The comments keep coming, the suggestions grislier and grislier. But while I appreciate the support, the lack of judgment, the complete absence of the words *forgive* and *move on*, I know, on some level, that it's still nothing more than a group fantasy. At this very moment, Harris Blanchard is happily brunching with his parents in New York City or enjoying the company of his fellow seniors or hiking or skiing and posting pictures on Instagram, his grinning face behind a pair of enormous goggles as he enjoys these final weeks of winter break. My daughter—the lack of her—is the last thing on his mind.

I want him dead. For real.

This morning I woke up after just two hours of sleep and showered and dressed for my meeting with Glynne an hour and a half early. I used the extra time to drive across the river to the Brayburn campus. It was the first time I'd been there since the trial, but after talking all night on Kaya about what Harris Blanchard did to my daughter, I wanted to make sure I wasn't remembering things wrong.

I wasn't. The woods where Emily's body was found are a six-minute drive from the frat house—a fifteen-minute walk at the very least. That means he went out of his way to take her there, far away from the party, where no one could hear her scream.

The campus was close to empty for break. But there were still some students wandering around, and I could have sworn

I saw him from a distance, laughing it up with a group of friends, just around twenty feet away from where he'd left an unconscious Emily five years ago.

If it wasn't him, it was someone just like him, because the world is full of young men just like him—unremarkable in every regard, except for the ridiculous privilege with which they were born.

How I longed to lean into the accelerator and head straight for him. Even when I realized it wasn't Harris Blanchard, I still had to stop myself from doing it. And really, would the world be that much worse of a place if I hadn't stopped myself?

4566 asks if I'm still in the chat. I respond that I am. And then I type out everything that's on my mind.

0417: I don't just want him killed off. I want his soul destroyed, his memory ripped to shreds, just like he and his family and their lawyers did to my daughter. After he's dead, I want the whole world to see him for what he truly was. I want his parents to have to live for the rest of their lives knowing what a mistake it was to bring him into the world.

I take a breath and read my words as the rest of the chat room reads them. "That's it," I whisper. "That's what I want."

And then, like an answer, a box appears on the lower right corner of my screen. A private message from 0001. The administrator of Kaya. Did I say something wrong? I thought there was no judgment here.

0001: Did you mean it?

Instantly the message vanishes, a feature of this site I was unaware of—disappearing private messages—0001's words existing only in my memory. *Did you mean it?*

I type a question mark on the screen and hit send. It disappears too, but 0001 replies with a screenshot:

0417: I want him dead. For real. I don't care how.

My own words glare at me, then vanish.
Another screenshot appears. The words I typed moments ago:

0417: I don't just want him killed off. I want his soul destroyed, his memory ripped to shreds, just like he and his family and their lawyers did to my daughter. After he's dead, I want the whole world to see him for what he truly was. I want his parents to have to live for the rest of their lives knowing what a mistake it was to bring him into the world.

I type a reply and send it.

0417: Yes. I meant it.

It disappears, ellipses stepping in.

0001 is typing . . .

0001: What if I told you that we could make that happen?

"What?" I say it out loud, as though I expect her to hear me. "Are you serious?"

I gape at the blank space where 0001's words were, and a chill runs up my back as it dawns on me—what this oasis on the dark web, this place to vent our most destructive thoughts, could potentially be. I remember my last conversation with Matt—how he had said, *You doing websites for hit men, now?* Matt, always smarter than he sounds.

Hit men. I feel as though I'm in free fall, both my chair and the floor pulled out from under me, nothing to hang on to, not anymore. Is that what Kaya is? A murder-for-hire site that specializes in grieving mothers, luring us in with kind words and secrecy and flowers for our dead children, allowing us the irresistible luxury of voicing our rage without judgment, before hitting us with the sales pitch . . .

0417: I am not interested.

After the sentence disappears, 0001 sends me a question mark. And so I type more.

0417: I'm not going to hire you to "make it happen." If I wanted to do something like that, I'd have done it already. What I meant, what I WANT, is the same thing the other women on the chat want: justice for my child. I'm not some Texas cheerleader mom emptying out her Christmas savings so she can pay a big, bad man to snuff out her kid's rival. I want my daughter's murderer to get what he deserves and I want the power to "make it happen" myself. It's something we all want more than anything and will never have. Shame on you for trying to exploit our pain for money.

Several seconds elapse, the private messages box still and quiet. *I guess that's it, then.* I push my chair back. Stand up, my head swimming a little.

Another message appears. After I read it, I sit back down again.

0001: When I said "we could make that happen," I meant all of us. Including you.

0417: ?

0001: I'm a grieving mother too. We all are. We are a collective.

My mouth feels dry. My head light. I'm not sure what to say, and so I stay focused on the blank box, the italics on the bottom:

0001 is typing . . .

And then, finally, the next message appears:

0001: Each one of us is a working part in a great machine. The machine that we are produces justice. We've been doing this for more than three years, and we have been successful. But in order for us to achieve continued success, each part of this great machine must 1) commit fully to our cause, and 2) tell no one about it.

My jaw drops, my eyes salty from not blinking. A collective of wronged mothers. Each one contributing to the murders of our tormentors . . . This can't be real. I don't think it's real.

0417: Is this some type of game?

The question disappears, and I instantly regret typing it. I want to find out more, but instead I've shut her down. The screen is still. No ellipses. I try again.

0417: I want to be part of the collective.

0001 starts typing again. I let out a sigh of relief.

0001: Can we trust you?

0417: Yes.

0001: Do you swear on your daughter's memory that you will never betray us?

The sentence disappears. My jaw tightens. I've never sworn on Emily's memory before. Emily's memory is all I have. I wait for more ellipses, but the screen stays still.

There's an antique grandfather clock in the hallway outside my bedroom. Matt and I bought it eighteen years ago at an estate sale in Accord—our first purchase for this house—and while I continue to wind it regularly, it's been a long time since I acknowledged its existence beyond an occasional cursory dusting. But now, suspended in that moment between a question asked and a question answered, its ticking echoes, as though each second were outlined in black. It continues until I can't take it anymore—the awful loneliness of an inactive screen.

0417: Yes. I swear.

The reply appears nearly as fast as mine fades.

0001: Message me the first and last name of your daughter's killer. I will then give you an assignment. Do not question what you are asked to do—just do it. Like every assignment, it is part of a whole. Upon successful completion, you will be in the collective. Is that clear?

0417: Yes.

0001: If I do not hear the name from you within twenty-four hours, the invitation will be revoked. You will never be offered another. If you repeat any of this conversation to anyone, there will be severe consequences. Do you understand?

0417: Yes.

I gaze at the blank box on my screen. If the collective is some type of game—and I can't help but believe it is—I'm not sure what "severe consequences" means. It must be like the warning signs posted in front of roller coasters, or the disclaimers they used to run before slasher movies. *May cause seizures. Do not watch this if you suffer from hypertension or anxiety.*

In order to buy into any thrill ride, you must feel as though you're risking something big to be there. And it's worked. I've bought in. Wherever this assignment is going to take me, it's already proven more effective than any traditional therapy I've ever had—even Joan. *Even Joan.* I scoot back in my chair and hug my knees to my chest, my heart pounding against them, cheeks flushing, eyes shut. *Alive.* That's what I feel, for the first time in so long.

The good thing about living alone is, you can say things out loud without worrying about how crazy they sound. "All strapped in." I say it loudly, proudly. "Let's get this ride started."

I type out Harris Blanchard's name. Send it to 0001. And wait.

SEVEN

It's been more than twenty-four hours since I sent Harris Blanchard's name to 0001. Outside of showering, I've spent every waking moment on the Kaya chat, reading stories and commenting, commenting, commenting . . . joining in this Greek chorus of grieving women, inventing fitting deaths for the thoughtless drivers and pill-addicted doctors and senseless, shameless, worthless murderers who have stolen our children without paying for it, putting all my thoughts and energy and strength into this thread, to the point where it feels as though we truly are one all-powerful entity, *a great machine*, as 0001 had put it, capable of killing with the combined force of our words.

But I still have not received an assignment.

I'm thinking now that during my exchange with 0001, I flunked some sort of test and now I'm stuck on level one, never to learn the intricacies of the collective. That's fine, I guess, as long as I'm not kicked out of the chat. If that were to happen—

and I know how this sounds—I'm not sure I'd be able to survive on my own.

I haven't been out of the house during this time. I haven't watched the news or checked my email, and I've barely slept or eaten. It's hard for me to believe these other women have accomplished much more than I—and I'm a newcomer. How long have the regulars been on the Kaya chat, starving in front of computer screens, their husbands and boyfriends and living children powerless to stop it? Has it been weeks for some of these women? Months? *What's happening to Mom? Why is she disappearing on us?*

The son of the mayor of 5590's small town was driving Daddy's Ford Explorer when he ran down 5590's eight-year-old son, killing him. I'm describing what might happen if the mayor's son were to be pushed out of a speeding vehicle onto a highway packed with long-haul trucks when I hear the galloping thump of a bass and reflexively delete the comment; I'm so unused to noises.

After a second or two, I recognize the bassline as the opening of Heart's "Barracuda." It's coming from my phone, the ringtone I've chosen for Luke. (Heart. Get it?) I always pick up for Luke, and so I do now. "Hey there," I say, putting him on speaker so I can keep typing.

"Are you okay?" he says.

My eyes stay on the screen, on 5590 telling 2948, The mayor's son never did any time. He was never even arrested. In my town, justice and the Law are two different things.

"In my town too," I whisper.

2948: In my town too.

"Huh?" says Luke.

"Of course I'm okay. Why wouldn't I be okay?"

"You were going to call me when you got home. Remember?"

I have no recollection of ever having said this. "Oh. I'm sorry."

"No worries. I'm just glad you're . . . you know. Alive."

5590 says that the Law shields people like the mayor's son from justice, and 2948 replies that if she were justice, she'd rip him limb from limb. As quietly as I can, I type, We ARE justice.

"You are alive," Luke says. "Right?"

"I've . . . I've been caught up in a work project."

"Oh. Sure." He sounds odd and detached, as though he doesn't believe me. It makes me feel the way I did in high school, when I was stoned with friends and forced, for whatever reason, to talk to my mom on the phone. I have an urge to hang up on Luke, to tell him I'm not feeling well or that I have an appointment scheduled or that there's a call on the other line. It's so strange, this divide between us. It's never been there before.

Just give me a few days, Luke. A few days with my new friends, and then I'll be back to my old self. I promise.

But what's this?

4566: We are MORE than justice. As long as each of us does her part, we are A DEATH MACHINE.

0001: A reminder that this is a public forum.

4566: I wasn't going to be specific. I swear. Sorry. I've had a few glasses of wine.

0001: Log off, please. Get some rest. You can come back when you're sober.

Whoa . . . I open up a private message window and try to type in 4566, but the numbers don't register on the screen. I try a few more numbers from the chat, but they don't either. The only number I can private message is 0001.

Luke says, "Are you typing?"

Please go away. "I'm just . . . Yes. It's . . . it's that work project I was telling you about."

"I should let you go. We can talk later."

"I'm sorry, Luke." And I am. I truly am, but . . . When I asked 0001 if this was a game, she never answered me one way or the other. "I'll be done with this soon."

"No worries. Wait, though. I've been meaning to ask you . . ."

"Yes?"

"Did you ever find out what Niobe was about?"

I squeeze my eyes shut, then open them on the screen.

0001: 0417, check your private messages.

Luke says, "Niobe. Greek mythology, remember? The woman gave you that card?"

My heart is pounding, my hand hovering over the touch pad. I need to get him off the phone, but Luke knows me so well. I've come to believe that when my daughter's heart was implanted in his chest, her intuition somehow came with it. And so I can't lie to him. He'll know it.

"It's just a stupid Facebook page. One of those groups for grieving parents, where they try and help you find 'closure.'"

Luke sighs.

"Exactly."

"That's too bad."

"It's really not a big deal."

"I was hoping you could find some . . . I don't know. Some company."

My gaze is pinned to the screen, the private messages box. I force out a chuckle. "Because misery loves it?"

"No, Cam," he says quietly. "Because you deserve to feel better."

"Luke."

"Yeah?"

"I love you. You know that, right?"

"Yes."

"I'm doing okay. I'd tell you if I weren't."

"Good," he says. In the background, I can hear Nora calling his name. And then: "Is that Camille? Did you tell her?"

"Tell me what?"

"Nothing. I'll tell you next time we talk."

"Okay." Normally, I'd press him a lot more, but I don't even sound curious, which is not like me at all.

"Cam?"

"Yeah?"

"I love you too."

I let out a long sigh. "Let's talk soon."

After I end the call, I click on my private messages again and open it—a one-line message that sticks in my head long after it vanishes, filling me with a strange new sensation, part thrill, part dread, as though I'm at the start of a roller coaster that might possibly collapse.

0001: Look in your mailbox.

I hurry downstairs and out my front door without a coat on, searching up and down my road for a sign of a car, a puff of dust. I don't think I heard one drive by, and I usually do from my office, which faces the road. But sure enough, when I open the mailbox, there's something in there. *Who came to my house? How did they know to come here?* I slip the package out very slowly. Hold it between the tips of my thumb and index finger, as though it's covered in poison.

It's an unmarked manila envelope. Something short and bulky is inside. "What is going on?" I say it as though someone is watching and can answer, and part of me believes that someone is, someone can.

I have an urge to throw the package into the bushes and run back into my house. But the urge to open it is much, much stronger.

I tear the envelope apart. There's a flip phone inside—the kind you get prepaid at a convenience store, complete with a car charger, and when I press the button, it shows that I have one text, from an unfamiliar number.

REPLY "YES" TO RECEIVE YOUR ASSIGNMENT.

I reply yes and receive a lengthy text immediately. It consists of seven steps, the last of which is to place the phone and charger in a plastic bag, drive to a public dump in Red Hook, and dispose of it in the non-recycling bin.

I scroll back up to the top of the text and read step one: Believe in each step. Commit to each step. Question nothing. My face flushes. My blood hums.

Check that one off. I'm ready.

THE REST OF the steps are simple but are described in great specificity. For one of them, there's an actual script.

Twenty minutes ago I finished step two, which was to go to the ATM of my choice and withdraw $140 in cash from my checking account. Easy peasy, as Denise would probably say. But it gets more interesting from here.

Step three involves buying some items at the Walmart at the Hudson Valley Mall, and so I'm in here now—this cavernous blue-tinged store I hardly ever go to since 1) I hate parking at the mall and 2) Walmart makes me nervous. As per the assignment, I'm supposed to use some of the cash I just got to buy a baseball cap (No team names. No bright colors. Nothing identifiable) and two sets of gloves (one wool, neutral color, no pattern; one latex), a pocket notebook, and a pen. I've found the cap already—a plain black one that matches my hair. I've also grabbed a pair of matching black gloves, a no-brainer, as are the notebook and pen. For the latex gloves, I'm supposed to go to the pharmacy (you'll find them in First Aid; they come in packs of twenty, but you will take just two pair (one backup in case the first rips) and dispose of the rest of the pack in the garbage can outside the store). And sure enough, there they are, bottom shelf. Latex surgical gloves. Pack of twenty.

I'm heading for the checkout line when I catch sight of two laughing young women in the makeup department, their faces and voices achingly familiar. I duck into the next aisle before they spot me, and stand here amid the ladies' razors, watching these lovely creatures. "He'll love you in this color," says the taller one, whose name, I remember now, is Gia. "Are you kidding me?" says the shorter one. "It makes me look like his mom!"

The shorter one is Fiona, the girl I caught Emily smoking

weed with when they were fourteen. She goes to Brown now, a chemistry major. I learned that from the high school's newsletter—the issue that came out on what would have been Emily's graduation. Fiona wears a bright red puffy coat and Gia is in yellow—two joyful twenty-year-old women in primary colors—and watching them is to see what could have been, what should have been if there were no such thing as Harris Blanchard.

Gia must feel me watching her because she glances over in my direction, but I turn away in time and all she sees is some woman in baggy clothes, a head of hacked-off black hair. "What do you think of the pink?" Fiona says, her voice as high and plaintive as when she was fourteen. *Don't be mad at Emily, Ms. Gardener. It was my idea, I swear.* My eyes fog up. I turn and walk the full length of the aisle and head for the checkout counter, the gloves and hat clasped in my hands, the flip phone straining against my back pocket.

Get out of here fast—that's the goal. Those words run through my mind as I hand my cash to the bored-looking teenage clerk and collect my change, the laughter of Emily's friends somewhere far behind me, a world away. *Forget those girls, forget the past. Live in the assignment. Move on to the next step.*

STEP FOUR IS to take Route 9 to Staples and use their computer equipment to print out a mail label. Drive .4 miles west, the assignment reads. You will see it on the right. Impressive how correct these instructions are. Staples is exactly that far from the Walmart, and I wonder if 0001 made them up, or if she has regional teams running through dress rehearsals to make sure the game's instructions are as easy to follow as possible.

Once I'm inside, I make the mail label as specified, the address a PO box in Burlington, Vermont, and pay in cash for the use of the computer and printer.

So far, so good, I think, once I'm back in my car. And then I flip open the phone, return to the assignment text, and read step five. It's the one with the script.

SCOTT BROS. HUNTING and Fishing is located fifty-two miles north of Staples, in a tiny strip mall on the outskirts of Albany. As with the rest of the assignment, the directions here are so perfect, I have no need to plug the address into my GPS.

Once I'm in the parking lot, I take a long look at Scott Bros., which is located between a nail salon and a check-cashing place and seems very out of place in a strip mall—all that camo and killing equipment in a brightly lit space that probably used to be a Dressbarn. In a few minutes, I'm going to walk into Scott Bros. and buy a certain brand of hunting knife. There is no mention in this assignment of how or when or on whom the knife will be used. But what I'm supposed to believe is that, at some point in the not-too-distant future, it will play a role in the murder of one of the guilty.

I know that's what 0001 would like us to believe, that this collective is real, that it's been effectively meting out justice for years, none of its members getting caught, all of them (all of us?) working together to form, as 4566 drunkenly put it, *A DEATH MACHINE*.

Part of me wants to believe it. A *lot* of me wants to believe that Gerard Krakowski's accidental shooting death was not some dark coincidence but the work of the collective, and that these steps I'm taking today will result in tangible justice for someone else. But the more I think about it, the more certain I am that this is nothing more than an elaborate role-play exercise, a type of behavioral group therapy for the mortally wronged.

It just doesn't make sense as a real thing. If we truly are contributing to the murders of unpunished child killers, and if this has been going on for more than three years, as 0001 says, wouldn't someone have messed up by now and wrecked the whole operation? We're grieving mothers, all of us. Wild cards. How could this "great machine" continue to run smoothly when all of its parts are faulty and damaged?

The fascinating thing, though, is that it doesn't matter to me. I'm willing to commit to this role-play, to believe in it when I haven't believed in anything at all for the past five years. I'm willing to work my hardest to get every one of these steps to-the-letter right because of the way this all makes me feel—as though my rage has a purpose. As though I have the power to kill, and I'm no longer alone.

And so I do what the assignment asks. I pull out the notebook and the pen and write *Buck 119* on one of the pages, then I rip it out and shove it into my coat pocket and go over the script one more time.

I'm ready.

"So, a knife, huh?" says the man behind the counter—a fifty-ish wannabe tough guy with a bushy salt-and-pepper beard, a tattoo of a fanged snake on his biceps, and a thick chain around his neck that reminds me of a choke collar for a rottweiler.

"Yep."

"Mm-kay." Outside of the accessories, he's not terribly threatening-looking. His build is bulky but soft, his voice nasal and high-pitched, almost boyish. But clearly, he wants to look like he belongs in this place, with its sleek handguns and rifles, its ammo belts and pocketed vests and knives with gleaming blades, displayed under the glass counter like engagement rings. It's freezing outside but sweltering in here, and I imagine it's so this guy can comfortably wear the tight camouflage T-shirt he's got on, along with the matching cargo pants—head-to-toe hunter drag, save for a somewhat incongruous nametag. "Your name is Ashley?" I ask him, going off script. I can't help it.

His face reddens. "My mom was a *Gone with the Wind* fan." He clears his throat, and his voice comes back, deeper. "What are you hunting?"

"Deer." I'm back on script. "Actually, it's for my brother. A birthday present."

"Nice!"

I put on a practiced grin. "I'm a good sister."

"Okay, if you're talking deer, you'll want a pretty big blade for gutting and skinning. Personally, I like the Silver Stag Cascade—"

"I'm looking for the Buck 119."

Ashley's eyebrows go up. "Lady knows her knives. We've sold four of those this week." He beams at me, holding my gaze a lot longer than I'd like. I've dressed in neutral colors—a baggy beige sweater under my puffy coat. Faded jeans. I've combed my hair and put on just enough makeup to cover the dark circles under my eyes. In short, I've dressed like I always do—so as not to be remembered. But not being remembered is easier said than done when you're probably the only female a man has spoken to in weeks, maybe months. "Not many women are into hunting." He says it like he's been reading my thoughts.

"I'm not." I avert my gaze. "I don't know anything about knives, actually. We were talking about my brother's birthday, and he not so casually mentioned the name. See?" I pull the piece of notebook paper out of my coat pocket and show it to him, clueless as can be. "I even had to write it down, so . . ."

The smile dissolves. "Oh. Okay."

He opens the glass cabinet. Removes a large knife with a black handle and a curved silver blade that makes my knees weaken. "This is the Buck 119," he says. "Nothing fancy, but a good, solid, versatile knife. Your brother's got impressive taste."

"I'll take it."

"You want it gift wrapped?"

"What?"

"Kidding. We don't do gift wrapping. I'll need to see some ID, though."

I look at him.

"Well . . . you gotta be eighteen to purchase a hunting knife, young lady."

I force out a laugh. "Oh . . . Ashley."

He winks. "Got ya again." He leans so far over the counter that I have to take a few steps back. "You . . . uh . . . live in this area?"

"Nope."

"You here for a little while? I get off soon and I could show you around—"

"My husband was born here. So I'm familiar with it."

"Ah." He sighs. Back to business. "Okeydoke. Tax included, the knife costs $96.32."

I give Ashley cash, as instructed by 0001. "Here you go." I smile politely.

Ashley doesn't. He opens the cash register, counts out my change on the counter, and slides it to me. "Not for nothing, but you should wear a wedding ring." He says it in a huffy tone, as though I deliberately misled him.

"Tomorrow's another day, Ashley."

He glares at me, and I wince. I shouldn't have said that—

it wasn't in the script. But come on. Who does this guy think he is, scolding me over jewelry choices? Or assuming that buying a murder weapon is the same thing as swiping right on a dating app?

Ashley starts to pack the knife into its box. I want to tell him that frankly I don't give a damn about his stupidly hurt feelings, but instead I hold back. "Thank you. You've been very helpful."

He doesn't look up at me, but his expression softens. "My pleasure, ma'am," he says. Then: "I really do need to see your driver's license."

I swallow hard. The instructions said this would happen. The instructions said not to worry.

He gives me a sleazy smile. "Protocol."

I pull my wallet out of my pocket and hand Ashley my license.

The picture's an old one, taken when Emily was still alive and I was healthy and busty and freshly highlighted. He takes a longer look at it than I'd like. "Camille," he says. "That's a pretty name."

"Thank you."

His gaze shifts from the license to my gaunt face, the amateur dye job, and I can sense him taking it all in, the before-and-after shots. There's a flicker of something in his eyes—understanding? Pity? Recognition? *Please don't let it be recognition.* Whatever it is, Ashley doesn't verbalize it.

He goes back to packing the knife, and when he's done, he presents me with the slim box, pressing it into my waiting hands like a gift-wrapped bauble. "Hope your brother bags himself a big juicy buck," he says.

I'VE DRIVEN EIGHTY-ONE miles to get to step six, which is to be completed at the post office in Ellenville. There's no script for this step, but there is a costume—the black baseball cap, black wool gloves with the latex ones underneath. Like the rest of this town, the post office is small and unassuming—a one-story building made of stone, with blue painted shutters—and I feel strange and out-of-place here, in my serial killer's costume, carrying a boxed hunting knife along with the mailing label I made at Staples.

As I approach the entrance, I spot two surveillance cameras glaring down at me. I reach for the door. It flies open and I jump back, gasping, the box gripped to my chest—an overreaction if there ever was one.

"Whoa, sorry!" says a voice. A man's voice. I don't know what he looks like because my head is down, my gaze glued to the sidewalk. I don't want him to see my face.

"No worries."

I can feel him gaping at me, and my skin prickles.

Believe. Commit. Question nothing.

The post office is small inside, with dark wood paneling and a huge mural on one wall. With the last of my cash, I purchase a padded envelope and, as specified in step six, $14.90 in postage from the sweet-faced elderly woman at the counter. I manage a smile at her as I check the room. It's too warm and library-quiet, but empty, which is the important thing. I hope it stays that way.

I make for a far corner, where I remove my wool gloves, slip the box into the padded envelope and seal it, affixing the label I made at Staples: that PO box in Burlington, Vermont.

As I complete this step, I peer at the mural above me—a group of Founding Father types standing outside an old-fashioned wooden building, some holding muskets, others raising their arms triumphantly. One of them plays with his dog. All of them seem to be watching me with X-ray eyes, the nuclear heat of them boring into the contents of the package and my latex-gloved hands as I smooth the label. The door opens behind me, a whoosh of cold air rushing in. I grab the wool gloves and put them on before turning around. A young woman approaches the window, a stack of packages in her arms. There's no telling whether she noticed me in my latex gloves. But I suppose, it doesn't matter, does it? It's just a game, after all.

Isn't it?

In part two of this step, I will dispose of the baseball cap and both sets of gloves at a rest stop twenty miles south of here. And then, at last, it will be time for step seven. I want it all to be over, but also I don't. There's a rush in this off-kilter feeling, the thrill of secrecy and potential danger blended with something I haven't felt in years—a sense of purpose, I think.

As I drop my package in the appropriate slot and head for the door, I could swear that sweet-faced elderly woman is watching me, too, and smiling. *Do you know?* I want to ask her. *Do you understand? Are you one of us?*

EIGHT

0001: The package has been received. You have officially completed your first assignment. Welcome to the collective. Your loyalty has been proven. But not permanently. It will be expected of you, always.

0417: Thank you. I appreciate the opportunity.

0001: You will be receiving another assignment within the next twelve hours. It may or may not involve interacting in person with another member. If so, are you willing?

0417: Yes.

0001: This is the next level of your involvement. I caution you not to exchange too much personal information. Speak to each other only enough to effectively complete the given assignment. This is necessary, for both your safety and the safety of the collective. Do you understand?

0417: Yes.

0001: It is in motion, then.

0417: Can I ask one question?

0001: Yes.

0417: What is going to happen with the knife I sent to Vermont?

0001 has left the private chat.

IT'S BEEN SIX days since I sent the package to Vermont, and four days since 0001 messaged me, making my membership in the collective official. I still don't know what happened with the knife—probably nothing. But I don't care. Ever since I completed that first assignment, I've been sleeping better than I have in years. My appetite has improved. I'm able to drive long distances without my mind going to dark places, and I worry less in general.

I've been enjoying my design work, too. In just a few hours, I finished all of Glynne's suggested tweaks to her site, and she loved the results so much that she insisted on paying me generously. I even managed a lunch with Denise, who mentioned the glow in my cheeks and asked if maybe I'm dating again. Quite a transformation in such a short time, and I know the reason: I no longer feel powerless. As 0001 said during my most recent conversation with her, *There's a reason why the poor and disenfranchised find direction in the military. There's safety in numbers, yes. But more important, there is power.*

So even though I may not be contributing to the real-life murders of the unjustly unpunished, these strange assignments make me *feel* as though I am. And that, I now understand, is what gives them meaning.

Three days ago I bought two old-fashioned Lux kitchen timers, one white, one pale blue, at a busy indoor flea market in Tannersville and placed them in the mailbox of an abandoned pre-kindergarten in Lenox, Massachusetts. Two days ago I purchased a flip phone from a convenience store in Nyack, called a Florida phone number with it, read a series of letters, numbers, and symbols into the voicemail, then disposed of the phone at a public dump in Ramapo.

And then, last night, I finally came in contact with another member of the collective. She was a pale young woman with damp hair and big, frightened eyes, and I met her at two in the morning in the parking lot of a dilapidated mall in Bridgeport, Connecticut. My task was to drive her, in my own car, to the New Birmingham rest stop on the New York Thruway—a drive that took close to two hours. But I was too worried about following 0001's rules to ask for the woman's name or even her Kaya screen name, and so we spent most of the ride without speaking, the only sounds in my car the rasp of her breathing, her chattering teeth. I wanted to ask what she was doing with wet hair on such a bitter cold night, but she seemed so fragile to me, the way her small hands gripped the seat, her left knee bouncing furiously. Rules aside, asking her anything felt invasive and wrong.

Just before she got out of my car, she placed a hand on my shoulder. "Sister," she said. She left before I could respond, hurrying through the rest stop's nearly empty parking lot to another waiting car, its headlights blinding me before it disappeared into the night.

I'm thinking about her face now, the terror in it, and then her voice, the steely resolve in that final moment when she called me sister. Her wet hair, the smell of her sweat. How real it all seemed—as though she wasn't just pretending, as though she'd evened a score by committing some awful act she'd never thought herself capable of and, having crossed that line, was now stronger than she'd ever imagined possible.

I thought, watching the other car speed away, *Maybe this is more than role-play.* But remembering it now, with the distance that comes from a good night's sleep, I see it for what it was. The girl was very young to have had and lost a child—a

child herself, really—and the young are the best at pretending. Those comic book conventions where they dress up as
characters and fully commit to the roles, the online games
where they waste entire days in a cartoon landscape, spending
play money and living out alternate identities, even falling
in love . . . You have to have one foot in childhood to commit
to pretending that intensely, and they do. These kids do.

Anyway, all this speculation is really just something to keep
my brain occupied as I work on my one ongoing assignment—
sitting in a parked car outside the train station in Croton-
on-Hudson from eight p.m. on, recording the times when a
short, impeccably dressed man with a shaved head arrives
from the city, gets into a silver Porsche, and roars out of the
parking lot. Truth told, it's the dullest assignment I've had yet.
The man has been arriving at the same time every night, always parks in the same space, and speaks to no one on his way
there, a true creature of habit. It might help to know who he is
and why I'm watching him, but I've been given nothing other
than a single picture. **Names are dangerous**, 0001 says. But
then again, so is boredom. Knowing the man's name and what
he's done might revive my interest in this assignment. Would
it be so bad to break this one rule, if doing so makes me more
devoted to the game?

The Porsche has M.D. plates, so that narrows things down.
I click on my phone's web browser and scroll through doctors
with practices in Croton-on-Hudson and NYC—a very long
list, shortened only slightly after I rule out females. I'm about

to give up when I remember that *Catfish* TV show Emily used to watch, how the host was able to drop a photo directly into the Google Images search bar on his laptop and identify the subject. I look up "how to search an image on iPhone" and the process is quite similar. . . .

It works. Dr. Porsche's real name is Edward Duval, and the photo is clipped out of a three-year-old group shot, taken at a conference put on by the New York Society of Plastic Surgeons. A plastic surgeon. Of course that's what he is.

The alarm on my phone goes off: 8:44 p.m. That's four minutes before the time Dr. Duval has arrived for the past three days—8:48 sharp. And sure enough, as I watch the cluster of people leaving the station at 8:48, there he is—predictable as clockwork and alone as ever as he hurries down the stairs, straight for his usual space, so lean and purposeful, that bounce in his step, a man with somewhere important to be.

Maybe 0001 was right. Maybe names are dangerous. Because as Dr. Edward Duval, plastic surgeon, slides in behind the wheel of his shiny Porsche, I have such a powerful desire to start up my car and follow him that I need to restrain myself. One of the murderers mentioned in the Kaya chat was a plastic surgeon—a man who botched someone's forty-year-old daughter's breast reconstruction, succeeding in what cancer had failed to do. Insurance did pay the daughter's husband an undisclosed sum, but the plastic surgeon did not admit error or guilt and kept his license in good name. "Is that you, Dr. Duval?" I say it out loud in my empty car, only vaguely aware

that I've turned the ignition, that I'm pressing ahead and tailing him out of the parking lot, making a left shortly after he
does. *I'll just follow him a little way. He won't notice.*

The chrome bumper gleams in the streetlamps, the car it's
attached to a sight to behold, the cost of it at least a year of tu-
ition at Brayburn, maybe more. While we're at it, that suit he's
wearing is probably two months of the mortgage Matt and I
were paying, and I can only imagine what his house looks like,
or the details of his most recent vacation. But there's one thing
I know for sure: Whether or not he's truly the same plastic
surgeon who killed that woman's daughter, Dr. Edward Duval
is rich enough to have gotten away with it.

With the back of his carefully shaven head in my sights, I
feel the same rage that I did a week ago on the Brayburn campus, when I saw the boy who wasn't Harris Blanchard but may
as well have been. *I could kill him,* I think. *I could kill him,
and no one would see and the world would be a better place
for it.* . . . Just a little push on the gas, enough to send him flying
across the overpass, that shiny silver Porsche sailing through
the air, and it would no longer be role-play. It would be real.

If I were to do that. If I were to live out this fantasy and lean
into the accelerator and smash into that Porsche with every
ounce of anger inside me, if I were to crush the life out of him
in this expensive sarcophagus he bought for himself, would I
ever feel bad about it? I don't think I would.

Shit. I'm following too closely. When he makes a right, I'm
less than a car length behind him, and for a few seconds we're

both exposed in the brightness of a streetlight. I can see into the Porsche, his eyes in the rearview, aimed at me.

I ease my foot off the accelerator. He guns his. Zips through a yellow light and then through another. I stop at the red, breathing hard. *Stupid, stupid, stupid.* He saw me. I know he saw me. I tell myself that this is just a game. A role-play involving driving long distances, tracking the movements of strangers, buying knives . . . Elaborate, yes. But our grief is elaborate, messy, chaotic. It takes a lot to ease minds as damaged as ours. Ask any professional. Ask Joan, who once told me, *We're all going to die someday. Maybe you can at least find some comfort in that.*

No. You can't ask Joan. Nobody can ask Joan. Not anymore.

I pull over to the side of the road. It's a quiet street, but I put my hazards on anyway, just in case. I click on the dome light, and in the ledger notebook I've bought especially for this assignment, I write down the date and the time of Dr. Duval's arrival in the train station, just as I've done the previous three nights. My pulse races. I'm worried my sweaty hands are dampening the page, that when I eventually rip it out and send it to the PO box provided by 0001, the ink will be smeared and she'll figure out that tonight I did something so wrong, it made me sweat.

I'll have to keep my distance tomorrow night, that's all. Tuck my hair under a scarf or a cap, maybe rent a different car. *Don't diverge from the rules. Don't ever, never again.*

I turn off my hazards, make a U-turn, press home on my

GPS, and do exactly what it tells me, step by step by step. It isn't until I'm back on the thruway that my breathing slows down and I'm relaxed enough to turn on the radio.

I press scan and stop at the first NPR I get—the end of some local program, where they're talking about the best Indian restaurants in Westchester County. I listen without thinking, the smooth tone of the announcer's voice like a long, warm bath, the melodious sound of the dishes a type of meditation. *Saag. Curry. Vindaloo.*

By the time the show is over, I'm relaxed again. *It's fine. It'll be fine.* Dr. Duval has probably forgotten about me already— and even if he hasn't, there are only two more nights to this assignment. I'm smart enough to record his arrival time for two nights without being seen.

The regular news starts up—the numbing grate of politics, some climate conference somewhere, designed to make us feel as though we still have control over something. I'm about to click off the radio when another newsreader takes over—a local one, a man, less polished-sounding than the first. Something about his voice makes me want to listen to what he's saying, and when I do . . .

There are moments in my life—just a few of them—when the present and the future seem to bleed into each other and I see everything from the strangest perspective, understanding before I even know what's happening that from here on in, nothing will be the same. Matt proposing to me was one—or rather, that moment just before he proposed, when he opened his mouth to speak and time stood suspended. Another was picking up the phone to learn that I was pregnant, my knees buckling before the IVF nurse said a word. The last time I felt it was in those few seconds before the police officer told me that Emily's body had been found. I've always assumed it would never happen again, but I feel it now, as the announcer discusses an ongoing story, about a man in Colonie, New York, who died of an apparent suicide at three a.m. this morning, a homemade bomb strapped to his body. *The collective is not role-play. The collective is real.* I know it deep within me, even before the announcer identifies the suicide victim, and I bite my lip so hard, it bleeds. "The victim, fifty-five-year-old Ashley Shawger," he says, "was the manager of Scott Bros. Hunting and Fishing in Troy, New York."

NINE

I pull off the thruway at the first rest stop I reach. Once I've parked, I take out my phone and look up every article I can about Ashley Shawger's suicide. *Don't jump to conclusions,* I try to tell myself. *Coincidences happen.* And the first one I find is somewhat calming. According to one of his neighbors, Shawger was an "eccentric" and a hoarder—a dumpster diver with a garage full of found objects, many of which could have been pulled together to make a bomb. *"I was shocked to hear Ashley blew himself up," said the neighbor. "But when I thought about it, there were warning signs."*

Another article, this one in the *Colonie Herald*, quotes a coworker as saying that Shawger "hadn't been the same" since the death of his mother, whom he'd been caring for, alone, for years: *"Ashley looked like a tough guy. But beneath the tattoos and the spiked bracelets, he was very sensitive."*

There's a link beneath the piece that reads ASHLEY SHAW-GER'S ACT OF HEROISM, and when I click on it, I'm directed to a *Spotlight* article from March 5, 2008. It's topped by a picture of Shawger—jeans and a ZZ Top T-shirt, thinner, less gray in the beard. And the headline is LOCAL MAN SAVES DROWNING GIRL. I read some of it, which details how Shawger jumped into the freezing Hudson River to save five-year-old Portia Conrad, who had fallen from a lookout point at a nearby park. *"You don't meet that many purely good people in this world," Portia's mom, Carol, said of her daughter's rescuer, who at press time was in the hospital, recuperating from injuries incurred in the incident. "As far as I'm concerned, Ashley Shawger is one of them."*

Maybe it really was suicide, I keep telling myself as I google Portia Conrad's name and find her listed on the 2019 fall quarter honor roll at Colonie Central High. *Maybe he wanted to be with his mother. Maybe he was lonely and depressed and too sensitive for this shitty world. . . .*

I go to Google Images next, where I find photos of Shawger with his wheelchair-bound mother, with his dog, with a group of friends on a hunting trip, posed around the carcass of a deer. I even find a photo of him eating ice cream cones with Carol and Portia Conrad, a reunion that took place two years after the rescue. The picture that draws my attention, though, was posted within the last hour by an unnamed witness with a phone—snapped through a charred window of the remains of Ashley's home, one of his tattooed arms visible in the lower left corner of the frame with a yellow circle around it, a red circle around something else, closer to the center. *What's left of the bomb,* the call-out reads.

I tap the screen for a closer look—a scorched mass of wires and fuses, a metal ring that looks like a giant handcuff, and something else, a small object that jumps out at me, a startling pale blue. *No, no, no . . .* I know what it is. I know it before I tap the picture to make it bigger, before I stretch it out with my fingers until the image fills the screen. Even with half its face blown off, I can identify it: an old-fashioned Lux kitchen timer, exactly like the blue one I bought at the flea market in Tannersville, three days after my awkward, too-memorable encounter with Ashley Shawger.

TEN

AĞLAYAN KAYA

PRIVATE MESSAGES

January 19, 4:00 a.m.

Participants: 0417, 0001

0417: You never said that the collective targets innocent people.

0001: The collective targets no one who doesn't deserve to be targeted.

0417: Ashley Shawger didn't deserve it. He saved a child's life.

0001: How do you know he was targeted by anyone other than himself?

0417: The timer. I saw it in a picture. One of the articles said two Lux timers were used to make the bomb. And I saw one of the two I bought.

0001: Read this.

https://msn.com/en-news.ny//bombsuicidevictimwasahoarder/ar-byybk

0417: I've read everything about him. I know he was a hoarder. You expect me to believe those kitchen timers were his?

0001: I expect you to believe that it's possible they were. I expect you to take comfort in that and move on.

0417: You sound like my old therapist.

0417: Are you still there?

0417: Hello?

0001: Harris Blanchard just won a humanitarian award at school. Do you feel the good deeds he racked up to win that award outweigh what he did to your daughter?

0417 is typing . . .

0001: How do you think the mother of Richard Ashley Shawger's victim feels when she hears about what a "lifesaver" he was?

0417 is typing . . .

0001: You don't think someone else would have saved that girl if he hadn't been there?

0417: What do you mean, his victim?

0001: You buy into this narrative that Shawger was a hero. That he saved that girl out of the goodness in his perfect, self-sacrificing heart. You believe everything you read in the press. Is that right?

0417 is typing . . .

0001: If we only knew each other from press reports, we wouldn't know each other at all. How is it, 0417, that I have to TELL you that? YOU of all people, who have been so terribly misrepresented and maligned.

0417: Did you know who Ashley Shawger was before you sent me to his store? Did he kill someone's child? Was this all planned?

0001 has left the private chat.

I KEEP THE private chat window open, even though it's a blank box and I'm alone in it, the conversation lingering in my mind like a scene out of a fever dream I haven't completely woken up from.

"I thought the collective was a game," I whisper.

But did I? Or did I just believe that it was possibly a game? So I could take comfort in that and . . . On the main chat page, a member called 6267 is venting her rage over the loss of her teenage son, shot dead by a woman who claimed self-defense and got away with it. My son was learning disabled, she's just typed. He knocked on her door to ask directions, and she killed him. Ours is a "stand your ground" state and she said he was trying to break in. He wasn't. He was lost. He never hurt anyone. Her attorney called my dead son "dangerous" in the courtroom, in front of me. In front of his grandmother.

2223 is the first to respond. I know her story. Her teenage daughter was one of many girls lured into "working" for a fifty-year-old billionaire who had promised her a modeling career. Her first "photo shoot," 2223 had told us, was in his Mercedes, on a desolate road in Rockaway Beach, twenty miles away from the New York City studio where the fourteen-year-old thought she was going. She was drugged throughout it. There was no crew or photographer.

2223 has never mentioned the billionaire's name, but I know it. We all do. He was big in the news five or six years ago, accused of running a child sex ring but convicted on much lesser charges—attempting to solicit a minor, as I recall—by a friendly DA. He served a few months in a Club Fed, then went back to his Long Island mansion and his hedge fund business, telling the world that he'd "simply befriended the wrong people" and he just wanted to "lead a quiet life."

Meanwhile, 2223's daughter got addicted to drugs, lost thirty pounds, pulled out most of her hair, and jumped out of a twenty-story window.

In a just world, 2223 tells 6267, you could put that murderer's own gun in her mouth and pull the trigger. In front of her lawyer. Call them both dangerous, because they are.

More numbers join in, agreeing and commiserating, and I'm struck by how many of us there are here, on this one page in the depths of the dark web. It must be one of the most common things in the world—losing your child to a murderer who continues to thrive.

Before I fully realize it, I'm typing too. I read my comment after I've posted it and it feels as though it was written not by me but by *us*, this thing I'm a part of. I want to beat her to death for killing your son, I've just typed. I want to break every bone in her body.

I don't remember typing it.

I'm thinking now about what 0001 told me several days ago, about there being safety and power in numbers, how the poor and disenfranchised can find strength as a large group. She mentioned the military, but doesn't this concept also apply to cults? Are we being brainwashed? Am *I*?

This is real. It's not group therapy or role-play, and I should care about that. I *do* care about that. 0001 has all but admitted that the group killed Ashley Shawger, and they've probably killed many, many more. And yet, here I am. I haven't left the group, I haven't told the police, and I know I won't. I can't. Why? What is wrong with me?

I think back to my private chat with 0001—how she'd gone silent at the mention of my therapist, then switched lanes, insisting Shawger's death was somehow justified. *How do you think the mother of Richard Ashley Shawger's victim feels when she hears about what a "lifesaver" he was?* The specificity of that sentence. The mother. The singular victim. Shawger's full name.

She wants me to look it up.

"Richard Ashley Shawger." I say the name out loud as I type it into my search engine, along with "kill" and "victim."

The search takes me all the way back to 1990. To news reports of a nineteen-year-old named Nathan Langford, shot dead by a hunter.

An accident. That's the way most of the archived news stories I find describe the death of Nathan Langford of Havenkill, New York, who was killed by twenty-five-year-old Richard A. Shawger, of Cairo, New York, in the upstate town of Roxbury. The two young men had been acquaintances, Nathan a former classmate of Richard's cousin. They'd gone into the woods to camp out and hunt deer with half a dozen other young men, and Shawger had accidentally shot Langford, mistaking him for a deer. It was all very tragic, according to all of those quoted.

An awful miscalculation but all too possible within those dense woods. Richard Shawger was young. He was contrite. No justice could be found in sentencing him to any jail time.

One lengthy article in the *Buffalo News* included the judge's brief speech from Shawger's sentencing, in which he'd described the shooting as *"a tragedy, nearly as painful for Richard Shawger and his family as it is for the Langfords."*

"Why should yet another young life be ruined?" the judge said after letting Shawger off with a ten-thousand-dollar fine and a year of community service. *"This young man has suffered enough for his mistake. He's clearly traumatized by it."*

Involuntary manslaughter. No jail time. Not a single day.

For someone so traumatized by a hunting accident in his youth, Ashley Shawger had certainly made an odd career choice—not to mention the hunting trips he continued to take, right up until his alleged suicide. That photograph I saw of him and his friends posed around the deer carcass, rifles resting against their sides like drunken prom dates, beer cans raised high . . . According to the caption, it was taken just this past August.

I had a bad tequila night when I was twenty and I still can't stomach a margarita. Ashley Shawger killed one of his friends while hunting at roughly the same age, yet look at him. Living it up with a dead deer, or as he might have called it, *a big juicy buck.*

How do you think the mother of Richard Ashley Shawger's victim feels . . .

I look for more articles about the sentencing until, finally, in the one from the Roxbury paper, I find a picture of the Langford family. In the photo, they're leaving the courthouse, the mother held upright by two men, one her age, the other much younger and taller and wearing an army dress uniform. I read the caption: *Lionel Langford, who read a statement at the sentencing, was accompanied by his wife, Violet, and their older son, Corporal Thomas Langford, twenty-four.* The mother's eyes are closed. She looks as frail as a crushed leaf.

In Lionel Langford's statement, he reportedly said that as a good Christian, he had no other choice but to forgive Shawger for killing his son. *My wife and I asked God for guidance,* he told reporters after the sentencing. *He showed us the right path.*

I look at that mother. Her closed eyes. Her drawn cheeks. According to the article, she said nothing at the sentencing. She had no statement for the press. She let her husband do the talking, but was he really speaking for her?

In the same article, there's a picture of a group of young men posing in camo, rifles at their sides. It reminds me of the recent photo of Shawger and his buddies, only minus the deer, and there are no beer cans in sight. Half of them look too young to drink legally. From the caption, I learn that Nathan Langford is the one on the far right—a thin boy in a baggy flannel shirt who looks like a gawkier version of his older brother. Next to him stands Shawger, with a thick, dark beard and shaggy Kurt Cobain hair. Shawger is smiling. Nathan

Langford is not. Shawger's got his bulky arm wrapped around Nathan's neck, fake-strangling him. *Good one.* My eyes find the photo caption: *Courtesy of Violet Langford.*

She did make a statement of her own after all.

I think about googling Violet Langford's name, because there's something familiar about it. I can't tell, though, whether I really do know it from somewhere, or if it's simply one of those names that sounds like I should.

My eyes are so salty, though, the lids heavy. My vision starts to blur, my body telling me that it's going to sleep, whether I want it to or not. I move away from the computer and collapse onto my bed, the fever dream taking over. I'm floating through the night sky, a sea of stars that's all milky swirls, like camouflage. And Nathan Langford is out there, beyond my reach. Nathan's in his flannel hunting shirt and he's showing Emily his forehead, whispering something I can't get close enough to hear. . . .

When I open my eyes again, the sun is bright outside my bedroom window and it feels as though I've slept for days. When I glance at the phone, though, I see that it's just six hours later. Ten a.m. I guess that was all I needed. I head into the shower and let the hot water pour over me, the steam clearing out my lungs, my mind.

Violet Langford. It isn't the sound of the name that's familiar. It's the *look* of it. I've seen it in print.

I get out of the shower and dry off, the name still in my head. Violet Langford. As I wipe the fog off the bathroom mirror and brush my teeth, I try to recall where I've seen it. The font. The size . . . The color. It's blue. Facebook blue. "That's it," I whisper. That's where I've seen her name. Violet Langford is a member of the Niobe group.

I HAVEN'T BEEN on Niobe in ten days. Compared to the heroin of Kaya, it's like the weed I used to smoke in high school. But once I'm on Facebook, I'm able to find the group quickly, and it seems as though no time has passed. So many new posts since I've been here last, women pouring out their grief, drowning in it, trying—and mostly failing—to help each other to shore.

I click on the member list and scroll through it until, sure enough, I find the name. Violet Langford. I was right.

I click through to her personal page. It's public, which is a good thing. I can learn about her.

Violet Langford. She supports the Sierra Club. She works full-time at the Havenkill Library. She likes to garden. She has three cats, and she frequently posts pictures of them. The cats' names are Skip, Elsie, and Coconut, and judging by the number of pictures, Coconut may be her favorite. She posts no pictures of herself, though. Not even in groups.

Violet Langford's husband and older son are both dead—which makes me choke up when I realize it. On the anniversaries of their passings, she posts old, happy, uncomplicated photos—Lionel in his wedding tuxedo, Thomas as a baby. I scroll back until I can find her talking about the circumstances of their deaths—Lionel of a heart attack twenty-five years ago, when he was only in his early fifties. Thomas in an IED explosion in 2005, during his third tour in Afghanistan.

Violet Langford never remarried. She has only around fifty Facebook friends, most of them female and most of them, like her, use photos of their pets as profile shots. Like me, she leads a solitary life, in a house too big for just one person, a house full of memories of the dead.

How does she do it? I wonder, as so many of my "friends" must wonder about me. *How does she go on living like this?* I must focus on what's important, though, and that is just one item of information: Violet Langford lives in Havenkill. And that's only a forty-five-minute drive from my house.

HAVENKILL IS ONE of those picturesque Hudson Valley towns—full of historic plaques and statues of men on horseback and window boxes and white Colonial buildings with lacquered black shutters. Matt and I used to love to spend long weekends at Havenkill bed-and-breakfasts when we lived in the city, daydreaming about moving to the town (which I believe is technically a hamlet). *We can be just like George and Mary Bailey*, we'd say. But they really were just daydreams. The truth is, there's something we both found slightly offputting about Havenkill—a judgy, insular quality behind the Bedford Falls veneer. The big, unapologetic cross in the town square at Christmastime; the hardness in the eyes of some of the smiling store owners—especially when you'd mention you were visiting from the city; the enormous historic mansions at one end of town and the tiny tract houses on the other, never the twain shall meet. It gave both Matt and me a hinky feeling, so that when we decided to move to this area, we steered clear of Havenkill and the neighboring towns on the east side of the river and opted instead for the more rugged terrain of the west.

We might have been over-suspicious, but I do recall one incident, years after we moved to Mount Shady. Matt and I were having dinner in Havenkill when a couple of burly young cops rousted a drunk from outside a neighboring bar in the middle of a rainstorm, one of them using so much force that I thought he might dislocate the guy's arm. It was around the same time as the town made headlines over a high school hit-and-run case, in which the rich people involved behaved just as disturbingly as those cops. I don't recall the details, but I do know that Matt and I spoke then about having made the right decision in putting the river between us. And I still feel that way as I stop at a red light on Havenkill's main drag, allowing a picture-perfect family to pass in their matching Canada Goose coats.

The library is located at the end of a side street, in one of the more modest areas of town. It's a boxy brick building with ionic columns out front that seem a little too important for such an unassuming-looking place, and when I see it, I remember that I've been here before, with nine-year-old Emily, when she was researching a paper about the Hudson Valley and the Revolutionary War. Violet Langford could have easily been there that day, but if she was, we didn't speak to her. Emily didn't like to ask for help, even back then. She preferred to discover things on her own.

I park my car and walk into the building. As mentioned on its website, the Havenkill Library is open seven days a week, but it isn't a large library at all—just two small wings, the adult one to the left, children's to the right, and a small bank of computers at the center, in the area in front of the checkout desk. I start toward the adult area, but then I hear a young voice saying, "Thank you, Mrs. Langford," and I spot her in the children's section, replacing a picture book on one of the higher shelves and then turning. "Of course, Charlie." She smiles at the boy, and I'm surprised at how strong she looks, how healthy. She's wearing a fuzzy red sweater and pressed jeans, and when she dusts her hands off on them and says goodbye to Charlie and his two friends, I'm aware of how much taller she is than I thought. Her posture is perfect.

She goes back to the shelves, and I head over to her, aware of my surroundings, my steps light and unobtrusive. When I speak to her, it's in a voice that's barely above a whisper. Libraries intimidate me. They always have. "Excuse me, Mrs. Langford? Can I speak to you for a few minutes?"

Violet turns. Looks me up and down. She wears her reddish hair in the same short, curly style as she had at the courthouse thirty years ago, and she doesn't seem to have aged much since then. Of course, that's hardly saying anything, frail and spent as she'd looked in the black-and-white photo. Violet Langford in the flesh is quite vibrant, her eyes a striking pale green, like sea glass. Her smile is tentative, but still warm and inviting. She smells faintly of vanilla cookies. I imagine she must be a hit at story hour. "Are you looking for a book?" she says.

"No, ma'am. I wanted to talk to you for a few minutes."

Her smile fades a little. "About what?" she says.

I force the name out of my mouth. "Ashley Shawger."

"I see." The smile disappears. "Are you a reporter?"

"No. I swear."

"Who are you, then?"

I take a step closer. She's easily five inches taller than I am, and her ramrod posture gives her something of a military look. I think of her son Thomas. There is a strong resemblance. "I'm a mother," I tell her. "Like you."

She stares at me, pink circles forming high on her cheekbones. "You look familiar."

"I'm Camille Gardener. We're both in the Niobe group."

She narrows her gaze on me, then lets out a long sigh. "Oh yes." She smiles again and puts a hand on my shoulder, as though I'm an old friend she hasn't seen in years. "I remember you now."

THE LIBRARY COURTYARD is small and probably charming in the spring. But right now it feels like something in mid-hibernation, the fruit trees skeletal, the rosebushes as gray and threatening as balled-up barbed wire. Violet says, though, once we're out here, that it's the perfect place for a private conversation. "It may not be comfortable," she explains, "but it's a small price to pay for no surveillance cameras."

Violet has brought out two hot coffees, and she hands one to me. "To thaw you out a little," she says, and the heat of it through the paper cup and the warm steam in my face couldn't be more welcome. She gestures to one of the stone benches and I sit down, Violet sitting beside me, the cold of the concrete biting through my jeans, the back of my puffy coat. My nose is starting to go numb. "What do you want to know?" she asks.

Between the cold and the subject I want to discuss, there's no point in taking time for formalities. I jump right in. "How did you feel when Ashley Shawger died?"

She opens her mouth, then closes it again. "*Richard* Shawger," she says. "The night he died, I was at an all-night bingo game at a church in Pleasantville. Proceeds went to a children's literacy organization, and I'm proud to say, I won. Just ask anybody who was there. I was *elated*."

"Did it . . . did it take away your pain?"

"Winning at bingo?"

I just look at her.

Violet blows on her coffee, takes a tentative sip. "It's interesting," she says. "After Nathan was killed, our pastor told us we could find comfort in our suffering. He pointed out how, after you've wept really long and hard, you're flooded by this sense of calm and peace. Do you know what I'm talking about?"

"Sort of. I always thought it was exhaustion."

"Well, the pastor told us that it's God. Literally. 'What you're feeling is God.'"

I have no idea what to say. "That's . . . interesting."

"He also said that God only gives you as much as you can take, and that the Lord bestows the most suffering on His favorite children. Lionel loved all that. I thought it was a load of horseshit."

I smile.

"I mean, really. I wept more than I ever have when I found out about Nathan. I cried myself hoarse when Richard copped a plea and when the judge gave him a sentence that would have been better suited to a jaywalker. For that year and easily several times a year following, throughout all the years since it happened, after my husband drank himself into a heart attack, during and after all those tours Thomas insisted on going on in Afghanistan, all of them suicide missions and he knew it . . . After all of that suffering, I would come home from this job and cry and cry until I had no tears left. I've cried more than any person has a right to, and I have felt a hell of a lot of things while doing it. None of them have been remotely close to God. I've walked through fire, Camille."

I take a sip of my coffee and watch her face, those eyes, flashing. I ask, "Do you feel God now that Shawger is dead?"

"Yes."

"He saved a life, you know, about five years ago. A little kid."

She gives me a small, sad smile. "I know. I read about it in the paper. And if all I knew of him was what I read in the paper, or what that judge said about him, I'd think he was quite the little hero."

"What don't I know?"

"A lot."

"Tell me."

She exhales, condensation floating from her lips. "Nathan was different," she says. "Sensitive. Artistic." She gives me a look.

"He was gay?"

"Maybe. We didn't talk about those things back then. Not in our town. In our church . . ."

"Okay . . ."

"Anyway, even though they were a good deal older than Nathan, Richard Shawger and his friends used to tease him mercilessly. They did since he was a boy. I was shocked when Richard invited him on that hunting trip. I tried to convince him not to go, but Nathan was old enough to make his own decisions, and for whatever reason, he wanted to be their friend. I think he was thrilled to have been included."

I stare at her.

"I think it was a setup."

My eyes widen more. "They said it was an accident."

"I'm not saying Richard Shawger shot Nathan on purpose. He may have just been trying to scare him," Violet says. "But just as I know that he did not invite my son on that trip in the spirit of friendship, I don't believe for *an instant* that he *confused him for a deer.*"

I close my eyes, remembering it in frames. Harris Blanchard

outside the courthouse. His friends and parents embracing him as the photographers snapped away. Lisette taking the microphone. *As the mother of an only boy, I feel so very grateful to the jury for seeing the truth.*

Violet says, "A few years ago, I bought a gun. I'm not going to tell you how often I drove by that awful store where he worked. I didn't care if I was caught. But I couldn't . . . I couldn't bring myself to . . . I'm too weak. I couldn't do it alone."

"I know exactly how you feel."

"I know you do, Camille. I saw your video."

I move closer to her, the words rushing out of me. "I used to think, maybe someday, when he's older, he will understand what he did. If I shout loud enough, he'll hear me. He'll really hear me and he'll see how much he's hurt me, how he's destroyed my life, my family. . . ."

Violet sets her coffee down on the bench, places a warm hand over mine. "I used to feel that way, too, my dear. But it's a pipe dream. Your child's murderer. Mine. They're all the same. They believe what their defense lawyers say about them. They need to be punished to feel guilt, and then they're never punished, so they never do. We suffer and we weep and they don't care. They never learn. They never understand. Not until . . ."

"Until what?"

"Until their last sentient moments on this earth. Then they get it. All of it."

"How do you know?"

She squeezes my hand tightly and leans in close, her lips to my ear. "You can see it in their eyes, and all over their faces as they're begging and pleading," she whispers. "You can feel it. You can feel it, sister."

IT'S NEARLY FOUR p.m. by the time I get home. The sky is tinged with coral—the start of sunset, but it feels as though several days of sunsets have passed. I've been driving around for hours, a mess of questions in my head, Violet Langford's voice drowning them all out. *They need to be punished to feel guilt, and then they're never punished, so they never do.*

Once I'm in my house, I head upstairs and do something I haven't done in a while. I find Brayburn College's public Instagram account on my laptop, and then I find him. He's in the far right picture in the top row, wearing his navy-blue sports coat and crimson tie, and he's standing in front of that Brayburn Christmas tree, smiling next to his parents and Dean Waverly, the Martha L. Koch Humanitarian Award clutched in his hands. I read the cheery caption, about how award-recipient Harris Blanchard "took a gap year, but is certainly making up for it!"

So that's what they are calling it now—the time before and after he stood trial for the rape of my daughter. *A gap year.*

I grit my teeth. Stand up. I head downstairs to the kitchen and pour myself a glass of wine. Toward the end of our conversation, Violet Langford had taken out her phone and shown me an article online that will be appearing in tomorrow's print edition of the *Colonie Herald*, detailing a suicide note emailed to the newspaper by Ashley Shawger half an hour before the bomb exploded. The newspaper hadn't released its contents until they'd been able to confirm that it had, in fact, come from Shawger's computer, and Violet had peered over my shoulder, reading the words along with me: *I killed a young man thirty years ago. I destroyed a family in the process. In detonating this bomb, I am simply doing to my own body what I did to the Langfords' lives.* Since the explosion had taken place at three a.m., Shawger had died on January 18—the thirtieth anniversary, to the day, of Nathan Langford's death. "Karma," I had whispered.

And she had replied, "Took the damn thing long enough."

I think about Violet's face, her green eyes clear and sparkling, her movements so light, as though she'd been dragging a weight behind her for years and had just cut it loose. She deserves that feeling, that lightness, the ability to move, to live again. *We* deserve it. I raise my glass to karma—which, I'm realizing, is sometimes a group effort.

I take a long swallow, and then I drink again, to the woman who typed out the note on Shawger's laptop and sent it to the paper, to the ones who built the bomb, and to the others, myself included, who purchased its parts. To those who confronted Shawger in his home, who looked into his eyes as they attached the collar and the belt and set the timers and experienced his remorse—thirty years too late—and forced on him, the same way he had forced an early death on a woman's son. *To you who saw it. Who felt it.*

I toast to those who drove the bomb makers to Shawger's home and to those who picked them up and to 0001, who had so efficiently sent me to Shawger's store to purchase what will no doubt be a murder weapon in another incidence of karma, eliminating a potential future witness in the process. Most of all, though, I toast Violet Langford, who has managed to live in this cold, chaotic world long enough to see justice served, at last.

After I've drained my glass, I go back upstairs, back to the dark web and back again to Kaya, where I send a private message to 0001.

> **0417:** I was wrong to doubt the intentions of the collective. I never will again.

It's all I write. The words disappear, but she doesn't respond. I stand up. Walk downstairs. Pour myself another glass of wine. "Please answer." I take a huge gulp, and then another, and before long I find myself pacing the kitchen in increasingly tight circles, finishing the glass but tasting nothing. "Please answer."

I shouldn't drink anymore. The room is starting to shimmer, and the meds/wine combination is making me weave on my feet.

When I look at the clock, I see that it's been fifteen minutes, so I hurry back upstairs. Check the screen.

Still nothing.

This isn't at all like 0001. She always answers private messages immediately. "No. Please. I want in. *Please.*" I start for the stairs. Turn back around. I can't leave the room. I feel shaky, desperate. I turn back to my laptop, my eyes starting to fog. "Please don't do this to me. *I want in.*" My voice cracks.

And then it comes. My answer. A faint beep, letting me know I have a new private message from 0001. "Please." I open it, my hands trembling. . . .

0001: Do you watch *The Bachelor*?

ELEVEN

Weird that 0001 would bring up *The Bachelor.* When Emily was eleven, I caught her watching the dating reality show on her iPad and got so angry with her, I took her device away for a week. An overreaction, I know—particularly since I'd never watched *The Bachelor* myself and was basing everything on preconceptions. But somehow the idea of all these intelligent young women competing pageant-style for the love of some blandly handsome pharmaceutical sales rep who kept talking about his "journey." . . . It seemed to me like the ultimate wrong lesson for a girl her age to be learning. (If she wanted to watch reality TV, I reasoned, why not something like *Survivor* or *The Amazing Race* or even *American Idol*, where winning was based on real *skills*?)

I suppose deep down, I was afraid of her growing up with the priorities I'd had as a young woman in Southern California, when I spent a year and a half saving eight thousand dollars for a boob job because, college education or not, design skills or not, my dream, as taught to me by my own mother, was to be the final destination of a man's journey.

Anyway, as far as I know, Emily stopped watching. And I didn't think of *The Bachelor* again until one time a few years ago, when Luke and I were talking about the Harris Blanchard trial, and he said to me, "You got the villain edit."

When I asked him to explain, he somewhat sheepishly told me that it's a "Bachelor Nation term" for how one's words and expressions can get spliced together to turn even the most reasonable person into the bad guy (or girl, as it were), all for the purpose of creating the most compelling narrative.

I said, "Did you really just use the phrase *Bachelor Nation term*?" And he confessed: Not only were he and Nora cardcarrying citizens of Bachelor Nation who faithfully watched the show and all its incarnations, from *Bachelor Pad* to *Winter Games*, he also had a personal connection. Years before he met Nora, Luke had actually auditioned for *The Bachelorette*. "Ali's season," he told me. "I got a callback, but I didn't make the final cut."

At the time, I said something like "Ali's loss is Nora's gain," and quickly moved on to the next topic to save him any further humiliation. But now that 0001 has told me that the first part of my next assignment is to 1) catch up on this season of *The Bachelor* via streaming platforms and recaps, and 2) announce my newfound love of the show to whomever I can, I'm on the phone with Luke for the third time in six days, reiterating my anger over the current Bachelor's poor choices. "I don't understand why he kicked Alayah off," I'm saying now, the passion in my voice surprising me. "Sure she's a little annoying and over-the-top. But if Pilot Pete were to send home every single person on that show who is annoying and over-the-top—"

"This is weird, Cam."

"What's weird?"

"This. The *Bachelor* talk. I mean, come on. You don't even watch TV."

"What's weird," I tell him, "is that I didn't discover *The Bachelor* earlier." I'm surprised at the conviction in my own voice. But then again, when I commit to something, I do it fully. "I don't know. Maybe starring in a viral video has made me rethink my feelings about shows where people humiliate themselves."

"Really?"

"Also, I love the travel photography."

He laughs a little. "Hey, maybe if you're in the city sometime, you can hang out with Nora and me and watch Pilot Pete make more bad decisions."

"I'd love that." The back of my neck is starting to sweat. I'm not used to keeping things from Luke—not important things, anyway.

It's necessary. I understand that. I can't tell anyone about the collective—for their safety as well as for the safety of the many women involved. But it is disheartening that, for the sake of my "sisters," I have to pull away from the one person in my life who truly feels like family.

Luke says, "I'm glad you finally appreciate quality television."

I'm in Poughkeepsie now, heading into the parking lot of a bar called the Wild Rose. "Oh my God, look at the time," I tell him. "It's almost on."

"In half an hour."

I clear my throat. "I'm going to a viewing party."

He says nothing for at least ten seconds. And then, finally, "Are you kidding me?"

"God's truth. I'm in Poughkeepsie. This bar called the Wild Rose holds viewing parties every Monday night. It's known for them. There are drinking games, and some people even dress up. It's fun."

"This . . . Okay, this is really super weird."

"It's not." After I turn off the engine and switch from my Bluetooth to my earbuds, I catch sight of someone pulling into the parking lot slowly, a few spaces down. Silver Camry. Just like 0001 said in the instructions she private messaged me. The Camry flashes its lights a few times, and I'm able to see its license plate: the same one I'm supposed to be looking for. "Oh good, my friend is here."

"Your friend?"

"New friend. *Bachelor* friend. I met her on a Reddit thread."

"Cam?"

"Yes?"

"This is going to sound patronizing. And I don't mean it to. . . ."

"What, Luke?"

"Are you still on your antianxiety meds?"

I take a breath. Let it out slowly. "Do you remember what you said to me? The morning after I got arrested?"

He says nothing.

"You told me to watch the video of myself."

"Right."

"Well, I did. And I got why you told me to do that."

"Okay, but, Cam, that was harsh of me and—"

"You were right. I need to put all this stuff behind me—the Blanchards. The trial. All of it. And if I'm going to do that, I need activities. New friends who don't associate me with . . . with what I went through. Friends who see me for who I am now."

A woman gets out of the Camry. I roll down my window and look at her. She's several years older than me but in great shape, with short, sensible brown hair and clear-framed glasses. She's wearing ripped jeans and cowboy boots and a shearling coat. I think she looks like an early retiree taking a line-dancing class, and I wonder what she thinks of me. She gives me a tentative wave, and when I wave back, she opens her trunk and heads for the bar. "I need to move on, Luke," I tell him as I grab out of the back seat, a plastic bag with black jeans, a black hoodie, and black boots inside. "And if that means hanging out with some random woman I met online to obsess over the marriage prospects of a Delta pilot, then so be it."

As I pass the Camry, I casually toss the bag into the trunk and slam it shut. Luke hasn't said anything for a while. I never answered his question about going off my meds, and I'm worried he's going to bring it up again.

Finally he speaks. "I'm really proud of you."

I close my eyes. *Good. This is good.* "Thank you," I tell him. "I'm trying."

I say goodbye to Luke and head through the parking lot and into the bar, where country music blasts through the speakers and garlands of fake roses hang from the walls and two hunky young waiters wearing tight white dress shirts and pilot hats work the mostly female crowd. There's only one bartender—a woman in a sparkly evening gown and false eyelashes, her shiny red hair in a tossed-around updo. Clearly, she loves her job. Or *The Bachelor.* Or both. The costume is spot-on; she could easily be a contestant, were she around ten years younger. Maybe, like Luke, she even auditioned in the past. She's in constant motion, juggling two cocktail shakers and laughing with customers, and she's wearing a huge handmade button that reads *FLY ME, PETE!* in swirly red letters. A sign over the bar announces two-for-one cosmos and a disturbing mixture of rum, Cointreau, apple cider, and grenadine called the Final Rose. I've never been in a scene like this before— not as an adult, anyway. It makes me nervous, but I have to say, it's also kind of exhilarating.

I scan the crowd for my new friend with the clear-framed glasses and the Western wear, hoping I'm able to recognize her. For the past week, she and I have been openly and purposefully chatting on a *Bachelor* subreddit called *Pilot Pete*

Belongs with Alayah. But beyond that, I know nothing about her other than her first name. Wendy. Her name is Wendy. I think about what I said to Luke, about meeting new people who know me for who I am rather than what I've lost. A partial truth. I am who I am because of what I've lost. I can't change that, and so I have found new friends who are as burned and shaped and redefined by loss as I am.

"Camille!" Wendy is standing up. She's saved us a table for two near the TV, and she says my name so loudly, it cuts through the music and the whoops and the chattering voices. More than half the bar turns to look at us.

I smile, like someone smiling at an audience. Then I rush at my new friend Wendy and embrace her as though we've known each other for years.

WENDY DRINKS TOO much. It's intentional—part of our script. But she is getting so shit-faced, it concerns me. She and I have a long evening ahead of us.

We're well into the last half hour of the show, and here at the Wild Rose it's gotten increasingly rowdy, all of us fans cheering for our favorite contestants and booing the ones we hate and chugging our drinks whenever anyone on-screen says, "She's here for the wrong reasons," "at the end of the day," or, of course, "journey."

But even in this *Bachelor* bedlam, Wendy stands out. Half an hour ago, I had to break up a fight between her and another woman over whether or not Victoria P. is surgically enhanced (Wendy was Team Yes and apparently felt so strongly about that, she was willing to "take this outside"). And now that Alayah has returned to set the record straight with Pilot Pete about what a scoundrel Victoria P. is, my Reddit friend has gone into overdrive again, standing up at the table and screaming at the screen, "Tell it, bitch! Tell it like it's the last thing you'll ever tell anyone!" as shushes erupt all around her.

"Can you *please* control your friend?" says a woman at the next table. "I can't even hear what's going on."

I look up at Wendy, who has just polished off her fourth Final Rose. I'm midway through my first glass of wine, which I doubt I'll finish. "Hey, take it easy. People are trying to watch."

"Camille, come on." She drains the rest of the glass and slams it on the table, sending shards of ice flying. *"It's Alayah's moment of truth."*

"Quiet down!" shouts someone at another table.

"You quiet down!" Wendy hollers. It sparks a mini-riot, the women in the bar yelling at Wendy as Alayah's fellow contestants yell at her—a strange mirror image, though Wendy gives it back a lot better than Alayah does.

"Get her out of here!"

"Hey, fuck you, it's a free country!"

"Sit down and shut up!"

"Don't you tell me to shut up, bitch! I'm a paying customer!"

She's going to get us kicked out of here. She's supposed to. For reasons unknown to me, that's part of the script too. My guess is, we're building an alibi. But I didn't expect her to be this disruptive. I'm having flashbacks to my own behavior at the Brayburn Club, and I'm half-expecting a bouncer to grab Wendy and wrestle her to the floor.

The show is ending now, *TO BE CONTINUED* . . . at the bottom of the screen. Alayah will live to see another week, but, because of Wendy's antics, no one's been able to hear how. Someone throws a glass of wine at Wendy, and her jaw drops open. I gape at her, the purple stain spreading down the front of her white shirt like a gunshot wound. She whirls around, red-faced. *"What the fuck?"* But then the bartender is at our table in her evening gown, arms crossed over her chest, one of the hunky waiters standing behind her. "Excuse me," she says quietly.

"You're going to pay my dry-cleaning bill, you piece of—"

"Excuse me. I'm going to have to ask you ladies to leave."

Wendy collapses into her chair. "Why?"

"Well, for your own safety, for one thing."

Wendy says, "I think I'm gonna throw up, Camille."

"Oh Jesus," the waiter says.

I turn to Wendy. "You think you can make it outside?"

"Maybe."

I lean over, and she puts her arm around me. "I got her," I tell the bartender. "I'll give her a ride home."

The table next to us starts slow-clapping as I pull Wendy to her feet. She's broad shouldered and strong, with about five inches on me in those cowboy boots. I'm struggling to hold her up.

"I'll help." The bartender puts her hand on Wendy's shoulder, and Wendy flings her other arm around the waist of her glittery gown, the remains of her drink still in her hand, red droplets flying.

As we move past the bar and to the front door, the whole room claps us out.

We have another assignment after this. I've yet to know the details—Wendy supposedly has a burner phone that will receive them as texts, one by one, throughout the evening. According to 0001, the assignment is better accomplished with two people, but from the looks of things, I'm going to have to drive Wendy home, take the burner, and do it alone.

"You gonna be okay?" says the bartender as we reach the front door.

"Sure," I tell her. "She's just . . . She's a big Alayah fan."

"So am I."

"Yeah?"

She nods. "Those other contestants could give Regina George a run for her money. Who the hell are they to call anybody phony?"

"Right? That's what I was telling Wendy on our thread." I clear my throat. "It's a Reddit thread. We met online."

"I know."

I stare at her.

The bartender takes a quick glance behind her, then gives me a wink. "Good luck out there, sister."

She turns and heads for the bar without looking back at us. Her dress shimmers.

After the door shuts behind us, I lead Wendy to her car. "You got the keys?"

She puts her lips to my ear. "They're probably watching us through the windows, so I'm gonna let you haul me into the passenger seat." She presses a set of keys into my palm. Her voice is calm, sober, the slur completely gone. "Once we get out of here, we can switch."

"We can?"

"She was serving me virgins all night," Wendy whispers. "We're everywhere, Camille."

As I DRIVE Wendy's Camry to the Poughkeepsie Galleria, the only sounds are the quiet roar of the engine, the crunch of the wheels on the near-empty road. I keep sneaking looks at her, my partner in crime—the benign smile, the sensible hair, the peaceful gaze, all so removed from the screaming drunk at the Wild Rose. I want to ask her if she's ever studied acting. I want to ask her a lot of things, really. Her age for one. Back at the bar, I'd figured her for mid-fifties, but during this brief drive she's looked a few years older or several years younger depending on the light. I want to ask her what she does for a living, whether she's married, how she stays in shape—anything to break this silence. I want to ask her if she minds keeping quiet as much as I do, but from the looks of her, she doesn't. I imagine she's been in the collective longer than I have, so she's more used to these rules.

I pull into the parking lot, turn off the car, and pop the trunk.

We open our doors silently, walk around to the back of the car, and remove our plastic bags full of clothes before slamming the trunk shut.

Wendy changes in the front seat, I change in the back, yet somehow, it takes us the exact same time to don our black hoodies, black jeans, and black boots. *In synch*, I think. *A well-oiled and silent machine.*

A little too silent, but what can you do?

Wendy takes the wheel, and I get into the passenger seat. But instead of starting the car, she sighs dramatically. "Fuck this."

I turn to her.

"Listen, I know rules are rules, but too much quiet triggers my anxiety. If I have to shut my mouth for this entire friggin' night, I'll have a goddamned heart attack."

I smile at her. I'm not sure I've ever liked someone so much after exchanging so few words with them.

"So, Camille. You up for a gab?"

"I thought you'd never ask."

"I'M GONNA ASK you something," Wendy says, "and I want you to be completely honest with me."

"Shoot."

"Did you ever watch *The Bachelor* before last week?"

"No."

"You're not shitting me. You swear on it. As a sister."

"Yes. I swear."

"Okay. I believe you." She breathes out slowly. "Me neither, by the way. But . . . I think I may have gotten too into character, or whatever. Because I'm kind of obsessed."

I laugh. "What is it about that show?"

"You too?"

"*Yes.* I'm so ashamed."

It's close to midnight, and we're heading north on Route 9, as per the second text on Wendy's flip phone. I have to say, my first impression has proven correct. I really, really like Wendy. Ever since we peeled out of the Poughkeepsie Galleria parking lot, we've been talking nonstop.

And while we have indeed broken a rule, it feels like it's for the better good. I'm not just giving her a ride, after all. We're doing this assignment together. It requires a good deal of trust, and for that to happen, we have to, at a bare minimum, be comfortable in each other's company.

So now we are. We've even exchanged last names. (Interestingly, Wendy and I are both divorced but have retained our married names. Hers, she told me, is Osterberg—"Iggy Pop's real last name, but despite my ex's rangy build and out-of-control stage presence, he's sadly no relation.") I know about her ex-husband, how they still work at the same accounting firm and how, more than once, they've gotten drunk and made out at Christmas parties. I know about her sister-in-law, an actual FBI agent who "makes me feel like Walter White whenever I'm around her." She knows about me and Matt—how close we were until we weren't anymore and how these days I barely know him. She knows how my best friend in the world is Sarge from *Protect and Serve* and how that may or may not be because my daughter's heart beats inside Sarge's chest.

And now we're on to lighter topics. "I think that if *The Bachelor* had been around when I was young," I tell her, "I would have tried out for it."

"Oh, me too. But I would totally be there for the wrong reasons."

"Instagram fame? Casual sex with crew members?"

She shakes her head. "Free booze."

I start to laugh.

So does she. "Instagram fame," she snorts. "I'm sixty-five, for godsakes."

I blink at her. "You *are*?"

"I take that as a compliment."

"You should."

She grins. "Hey, age ain't nothing but a number. Who said that again?"

"R. Kelly."

"Oh, right. Gross. Never mind."

The flip phone dings, and she turns to me. "What's it say?"

I pick the phone up from its resting place under the radio. Flip it open and read the text:

Where are you now?

"She just wants to know where we are." I look for the nearest mile marker and text it.

Another text quickly arrives—a set of directions, beginning with a drive through the town of Red Hook and ending on a small stretch of access road that doesn't even have a name. "Okay," I tell Wendy. "We have to keep our eyes open now."

She nods. I tell her to make a left on Old Post Road and she does, slowing down so we can read the signs. "So," she says, "where do you think this night will take us?"

"No idea."

"Are you nervous?"

"A little."

"Me too. I mean . . . We were given each other's real first names and asked to use them a lot, which can only mean alibis, right?"

"Yep."

"Triple-Oh-One said we'll be fine as long as we follow the instructions, and if we can't trust her . . ." She doesn't finish the sentence.

I glance at the text. We have two miles before the next turn, which is enough time to ask her what I've wanted to, this whole ride. "Wendy?"

"Yeah?"

"Have you ever killed anyone?"

She answers more quickly than I expect her to. "Yes."

"For the collective?"

"Yes."

"How did it feel?"

Wendy watches the road. Her face is uncharacteristically still, and it strikes me how different she looks when she isn't smiling. "Easy," she says. "Surprisingly easy."

WE'RE SUPPOSED TO switch cars with two other women on the unpaved stretch, but once we reach it, it's so dark that I don't see the other car until we're just feet away from it.

"Our partners," says Wendy, and I see them in the glow of our headlights—two figures, all in black, same as we are, hoods pulled over their heads.

I flip open the phone and send the text I've been told to send:

> We are here.

The reply comes fast:

> Is the other car there too?

> Yes.

> Leave the keys in your car. The two sisters will drive it to the park and ride at Exit 19 off the NY Thruway and leave it there, to be picked up once the assignment is complete. In exchange

for this burner, they will hand you a sealed envelope. Inside will
be the rest of your assignment. DO NOT OPEN IT until you are in
the other car and they have left in your car. Understood?

Yes.

Go.

I show Wendy the text thread. We slip our hoods over our
heads and open our doors at the same time. The black-clad "sisters" approach us as we reach the distance between the bum-
pers of our two cars, one slipping me the envelope, one taking
the burner from Wendy. It almost feels biological, the rhythm
of it all—as though we're working parts of the same organism,
our movements as perfect and involuntary as the beating of
a heart. There's comfort in that rhythm, in the way we move
in unison, in not seeing either of the sisters' faces until we've
switched cars and I catch a quick glimpse of the Camry's new
driver, adjusting her hoodie and cracking her neck.

Our new car is a black Mercedes S-Class with heated leather
bucket seats that are as warm and welcoming as a lover's embrace. "Hot damn," says Wendy as she starts up the car and
pulls away from the curb, her tone chipper as ever. "I wonder
who belongs to this beauty." Wendy loves luxury cars. She told
me this early on in our ride, by way of excusing her "depend-
able but dull-as-a-post" Camry. She's got a Mercedes of her

own at home—a 1963 300 SL she tinkers with every weekend but loves too much to subject to the road. "This must be your dream assignment," I tell her.

She grins. "You bet your ass." There's a noise at the back of the car—a loud thud that makes me jump.

"Shit," Wendy says.

"You think we ran something over?"

She inhales sharply. "I hope not. Jesus. I hit a raccoon once. Wrecked my whole week."

"I'm sure it was just—"

Another thud.

"*Shit.*"

It sounds as though it's coming from within the trunk—something heavy, thumping around in there—and I tell Wendy as much.

"Yeah?" She actually sounds relieved.

"What do you think it is?"

She shrugs. "Equipment for the assignment?"

"That makes sense, I guess." I open up the envelope. There is a folded-up piece of printer paper inside, and when I smooth it out, I see the instructions typed out in twelve-point Calibri. I shine my phone on it and read it out loud.

Make a U-turn. Right on Chestnut. Drive 3.1 miles to Crestwood Ave. in Hollandville. Make a right. Two miles down is the Hollandville Village Green. At the center of the green, next to the flagpole, you will see a free library.

Pull out *A Tree Grows in Brooklyn*. You will find another envelope inside. Follow the instructions within.

Wendy lets out a theatrical yawn. "And, ladies and gentlemen, we still don't know what the fuck we're doing." She screeches into a U-turn, the thing in the trunk clanging again. Neither one of us mentions it. "Talk to me some more, Camille," she says. "I need to stay awake."

BY THE TIME we reach Hollandville, we're back to *The Bachelor*. I really do enjoy discussing the show, especially now that it's close to three a.m. and I'm sleep-deprived and edgy. When you're in a place you've never been with a person you've just met, following a long list of instructions sent by someone whose name you don't even know, there's something uniquely comforting in talking about a reality show that's been on the air for more than twenty seasons.

Wendy says, "You know what my favorite thing about the show is? None of the girls give a damn about Pilot Pete."

"*Why?*"

"Well, would you give a damn about him?"

"No, I mean why is that your favorite thing about the show? It's pretty obvious they all just want fame—but that's the part that makes me ashamed for watching."

Wendy smiles. "Ah, but you see, it's not fame they're after," she says. "It's winning."

"Winning *what?*"

"It doesn't matter. That's the genius of it. Poor Pete's just a maypole they all dance around, and all each of them wants is to be the last one standing. He could be anybody. Anything."

"Any*thing*?"

"Yep."

"Anything. Like . . . say the Bachelor was a bowl of chili."

She snorts. "They'd fight just as hard to be the future Mrs. Hormel."

"Wow."

"Imagine *that* rose ceremony."

"Oh my God."

"Camille, will you accept this bad case of gas?"

"Stop!" We both erupt in giggles, and soon we're laughing so hard, we can barely breathe.

"The wedding!" Wendy shrieks. "You'd throw rice. And cheese. And onions."

"And that's all fine, until the groom spends the whole honeymoon in the can!"

"I can't believe you said that out loud."

Tears are rolling down my face. My stomach hurts from laughing, and Wendy is making little squeaking noises. It's very impressive to me how she's able to drive so carefully and at the speed limit when she's completely losing it. "Okay," she says. "Okay, we have to . . . Oh my God."

"Deep breaths." I wipe a tear from my cheek, and Wendy and I breathe together, in and out. Once we're calm, we sit in silence, collecting ourselves.

"This is one crazy-ass night."

"Understatement of the year."

We gaze out the window, this tiny town with its clapped-together houses, the one old-fashioned gas station, everything dark and abandoned-looking.

"There it is," she says.

Within seconds we've reached the town square. She pulls up to the curb right next to it and stops the car, and without a word I step out into the night, my hoodie pulled past the sides of my face. Next to the flagpole is a squat little bookcase with a hand-painted sign at the top that says FREE LIBRARY. I shine my flashlight on it, and a noise erupts behind me—a muffled animal wail. *Bear.* I spin around to look, but the street is still. Quiet. The sound must have come from inside my mind, some primal fear making itself known. . . .

From behind the wheel of the Mercedes, Wendy gives me a tentative wave and only then do I realize I've been staring at her, frozen. I flash her a thumbs-up, turn back to the book-case. *Keep yourself together.*

It's just four shelves, all of them stocked with weathered tomes that are probably rejects from the real library. I find it quickly. *A Tree Grows in Brooklyn* is on the top shelf, third from the left. I pull it out and flip through the pages until I find a sealed legal-sized envelope, which I bring back to the car.

Once I'm inside, I start to open the envelope, but Wendy puts her hand on mine. "Camille, before we do this next part, I should tell you something." She says it very quietly.

"What?"

"I know who you are."

"Oh."

"It took me a little while, with your new hair and all. But when you were taking me out of the bar, everything snapped into place. The video. The trial. Your daughter."

I exhale.

"For what it's worth, I hate that Blanchard kid. I've always hated him. Never believed that bullshit story in *Rolling Stone*."

"Thanks," I tell her. I mean it.

"So, that being said . . ." Her voice trails off.

"You sound like you're going to ask me to accept this rose."

She doesn't laugh. She doesn't even smile. "I want to tell you about my son."

"Oh, Wendy, you don't have to—"

"I know I don't. But I want to. It's only fair."

I put the envelope down. Turn to her. "I would like to hear about him."

She takes a breath. "Okay," she says. "So first of all, our son Tyler was what we used to call a 'change-of-life baby.' I was told I couldn't have children, but then surprise, surprise . . . I was forty-seven years old."

"Wow."

"He was a miracle," she says. "He was also born a girl."

I nod.

"He knew from pretty early on that he was different, and so my husband and I . . . Well, Carl wasn't as on board with it as I was at first, but he came around. We let him live the way he wanted to. He went from Taylor to Tyler. And even though this was some years ago and our town isn't exactly San Francisco, his elementary school was understanding. He had friends. Played sports with the other boys. It was nice."

"Uh-huh."

"Then came junior high."

Another thumping noise from the back of the car. Neither one of us pays attention.

"Junior high is hell under the best of circumstances," I tell her.

"Exactly. And for Tyler, it was the darkest pit of it. The kids there bullied him, emotionally, physically. He'd come home with bruises, pink paint thrown on his clothes, in his hair. It was relentless."

"Did you talk to the principal?"

"Oh yeah. Repeatedly. We got a lot of lip service, but no action. She seemed to think Tyler brought it on himself."

"Seriously?"

Wendy shrugs. "What are you gonna do? It's a small upstate, redneck town."

"Did you homeschool?"

"Yep. Which would have been fine. But those assholes kept it up online. I'd go into his room. Catch him looking at his laptop, crying."

"Did he ever show you what they were saying? Talk to you about it?"

She gives me a side-eyed glance. "*You* had a teenager. What do you think?"

I swallow hard. Emily's secret Instagram accounts. The photographs. The poses. *No fucks left to give.* And we never would have known about any of it. *Never . . .*

"So this one boy. He was the leader, the douchebag in chief, and one time he followed Tyler home from his piano lesson and he . . . God, all these years, I still can't say it. . . ." A tear trickles down her cheek. She swipes it away. "He . . . Jesus. I can't . . ."

She brushes off another tear, takes a shuddering breath, and clears her throat. "He took away Tyler's innocence. How's that?"

I open my mouth, but I can't speak. *The things they do to our children. Our babies.*

"It wasn't something that our son could easily recover from. But maybe . . . if we'd been able to get him help. The thing is, he never told anybody."

"You didn't know?"

"Not until we read it in his suicide note."

My breath catches. "Oh my God. Oh, Wendy."

"The police said there were no witnesses. They said Tyler was deeply troubled. He could have lied in the note. . . ."

"No. Awful."

"King Douchebag never spent a day in court."

Several seconds pass. I shake my head. I can't find anything to say. We drive for a while, the Mercedes's engine soft as a whisper.

Wendy says, "Douchebag must have felt guilty about it, though. Deep down."

"What happened?"

"He flung himself off a bridge six months ago. Imagine that. Ten years after the fact, the asshole finally finds his conscience."

I turn and look at her. She's beaming.

I feel my face flushing. *The collective.* "Imagine."

"I am so fucking grateful to those who helped him find that conscience of his."

"Me too." I put my hand on hers and squeeze, my energy coming back. I think, *I'm ready to do this.* For Tyler. For Emily. For whoever it is whose child's death Wendy and I will soon be avenging. I tear open the envelope, unfold the note. There are two pages—the first consists of a map of the area and an address to plug into the Mercedes's GPS: 2 Lake Road, Bird Hollow, New York.

On the next page, there are instructions:

Once you reach the dock, remove the lighter and the fully charged burner from the glove compartment. Put the Mercedes in neutral, exit the car, and push it into the lake. You will then take the lighter and safely burn these sets of instructions. When this is all complete, turn on the burner. Go to texts. You will see one text that simply says: READY? Reply YES to receive info as to where to meet your ride.

We are working in unison, Wendy and I. Reading the same words at the same time. ("The burner. That's the flip phone, right?" I ask. She nods.) And once we've made it through the final sentence at the bottom of the page, we turn to each other at the same second, the same look in our eyes, and there is no doubt in my mind that we share the same thoughts.

The sentence reads:

DO NOT OPEN THE TRUNK.

TWELVE

We drive in silence for most of the ride, Wendy following the orders of the GPS's calm female voice, her eyes clear and open and alert as the clock edges closer to four a.m.

My eyes are bleary, my thoughts slow, but my pulse races. I feel as though I'm in a dream. *Almost there.* The thought chugs through my brain. *Almost there, almost there, almost there . . .*

According to the GPS, we're just five minutes from our destination, and this last part of the ride feels like the end of a fireworks show, Wendy plowing down a series of narrow unpaved roads through thick woods, one sharp turn, then another, then another, the sleek car bucking and leaping, releasing puffs of dirt. The thing in the trunk thuds and clangs with each turn, but I don't say a word about it. *We're not supposed to open it. We'll never know what it is. Or who it is.*

Finally Wendy says, "What do you think is back there?"

"No idea."

Wendy glances at me, then turns back to her driving.

The GPS says, *"Turn right on Lake Road,"* and we emerge from the wooded area, a shimmering lake spreading out before us, reflecting the stars. At the same time, we gasp. It's beautiful. Snow-dusted evergreen trees, a row of log cabins, boarded up and abandoned for the season, traces of powdery snow on their roofs and windowsills, light as confectioners' sugar on a gingerbread house. It's as though we've driven into a painting, everything perfect and peaceful and absolutely still.

"Would you look at that?" Wendy says as the headlights hit a large sign up ahead that reads CAMP ACACIA. "A summer camp," she says. "What better place to get rid of something in the winter?"

"Good thing the lake isn't frozen."

The GPS tells us to drive seventy-five feet. And then: *"Your destination is on the right."*

Wendy turns onto a long, sloping concrete dock—a boat launch—stopping just shy of the edge. There are no boats hitched to it, of course. Like the rest of this summer camp, the canoes and kayaks and rowboats are hibernating somewhere, making the permanent structures like this dock feel ghostly and strange.

Our destination.

I open the glove compartment, where the lighter and the flip phone have been placed side by side. I take them out. Two burners. There's something poetic in that, isn't there? The synonymnity of it all. *Is that a word? Are these real thoughts? Is this a dream?*

Wendy puts the car into neutral, and we both get out. We walk around to the back, one on each side, our eyes on the trunk. Wendy says it again. "What do you think is in there?"

"I don't know."

Something pounds against the metal.

Wendy says, "Should we open it?"

"The note said—"

"I know." She turns to me. "But we weren't supposed to talk, either, and we've been talking all night."

"Yeah, but—"

"I know."

"This warning feels more important. Doesn't it?"

"Yes."

We move toward the trunk and place our gloved hands against it, side by side, but a noise erupts from the metal—an animal sound, much like the one I heard when we stopped at the free library in Hollandville. We stare at each other.

Bear, I'd thought the first time I heard this, then chalked it up to my mind, to my exhausted imagination playing tricks on me. But no. This is real. Wendy hears it too.

"Wow."

I hear myself say, "Give me the key."

Wendy gapes at me. "You really think we should?"

We hear it again. A muffled cry. Human.

Wendy is balancing the keys in the palm of her hand. I pluck them away from her, more out of reflex than legitimate decision making.

"Wait. I don't think we should . . ."

I can't help it. I am unable to continue without seeing, without knowing.

"Oh my God," Wendy says.

I've done it. I've clicked the trunk icon on the key fob and it's sailed open. I pull my flashlight out of the pocket of my hoodie and shine it on the figure inside.

"It's him," Wendy says. "It's *him*. Holy shit. *Holy fucking shit*."

He's been gagged with what looks like dark pantyhose, face contorted, arms tied behind his back, legs lashed together. He writhes like a giant bug, and then he is still, his face shifting into focus. Bright blue eyes in the flashlight beam. His shirt, ripped and sweat-stained, but tailored. Expensive. The square jaw. The salt-and-pepper hair. Fake hair. Fake tan. I know him. *I know you.*

"Holy shit," Wendy says again.

It's the billionaire who killed 2223's daughter. Three months in a Club Fed. A mansion on Long Island. He raped her repeatedly. Passed her around to his friends. *He broke her spirit,* 2223 typed. *He killed her soul.*

I've seen pictures of him in the papers, online. At charity events, yukking it up with politicians, his beautiful age-appropriate wife at his side. That smugness radiating from his flat, fake smile. We've both seen him. We both know him. He is the type of person everyone knows, because he is so shallow, you can fully know from a picture.

But still . . .

His eyes lock with mine. The pain in them. The fear.

I make myself think about 2223. Her daughter. Did he show her mercy? Did he think about how young she was, how easily hurt? Did he ever view her parents as anything more than a nuisance? *Your pain is not human. Your fear is not human. You are a monster. You deserve to die.*

He moans out a word. It's muffled by the gag. There's blood on his face, across the front of his shirt. He has a wound under his eye. Scratches across his neck. What they did to him. What we did to him. "Help. Please help."

I can't move.

He says something else. It sounds like, "Sorry."

Wendy marches up to the car and slams the trunk shut. When she turns to look at me, I'm still frozen, the beam of my flashlight hitting the rear bumper.

"Come on," Wendy says.

"I shouldn't have opened it."

"It's over and done. It doesn't matter." Her eyes are shining, her face calm. She raises one hand to me, beckoning. "Join me. Sister." She turns toward the trunk and braces herself against it. I can hear him from within, sobbing now. "Justice for 2223's daughter," Wendy says, loud enough to drown him out. *"Justice for the girls."*

And the spell is broken. *The girls. Those poor, disposable girls.* Hate warms my blood, strengthens me. *Who the fuck cares if he said he was sorry?* I let out a sound—a wild animal cry. I throw myself against the car, and we both push and push, the wheels pressing forward—until, at last, the car is free of the dock.

Wendy and I jump back. For one suspended moment the Mercedes seems to float, the billionaire's sobs echoing in the air around us. But then the bottom drops out from under the chassis and it sinks fast. The tailgate, then the rear windshield, then the roof, the whole car swallowed up, the lake's surface awash with bubbles. I double over, breathing hard, sweat pouring down my rib cage, the backs of my legs. I'm shivering. I'm not sure whether it's the cold or the exhaustion, both physical and emotional, but it's difficult to catch my breath. Wendy puts an arm around me, and I straighten up and lean into her, my breath steadying itself at last. I rest my head on her shoulder.

Wendy and I watch the lake until the water is smooth again, and it's as though nothing ever happened, the only sound the whoosh of wind, the creak of tree branches, a crow shrieking, probably dozens of miles away.

I want to ask Wendy if she saw it, too, the car resting atop the water for such an impossibly long stretch of time, and if she heard the billionaire's cries as I heard them, clearer than when the trunk was open. But I decide not to mention it, because I don't think the moment was real. As I look back now, it feels imagined, the way most last chances do.

"Camille," Wendy says.

We are standing near a sign that reads CAMPFIRE AREA, having just burned the two sets of directions to ash. I'm still thinking about what we've done—the car sinking into the water, the billionaire's wails escaping from the trunk. If this were a movie, he'd make it out of there for real and swim to shore. I'd see his shadow behind me—the unvanquished killer rising up, dripping mud and seaweed, bringing an ax down on my skull as Wendy screams. And in a summer camp, no less. But it's no movie. It's real. We've ended him. He's gone.

"Hello? Earth to Camille."

"Sorry. What?"

She holds up the burner. "They sent the directions to where we're supposed to meet our ride, and we're supposed to head 'due north' at a certain point."

"How do we do that?" We have no cell phones, as specified by 0001. Our only GPS is at the bottom of the lake.

Wendy tosses me a piece of plastic, and I shine my flashlight on it. A compass.

"Found that in my mailbox two days ago," Wendy says. "The collective thinks of everything."

I give her a weak smile.

Wendy stomps out the rest of the embers, and we head up the road on foot, due north half a mile, according to the text. "Haven't used one of these since Girl Scouts," Wendy says, "which, by the way, was the last all-female organization I joined."

I laugh a little.

"Camille?"

"Yeah?"

"You okay?"

I nod.

"You don't feel sorry for that motherfucker, do you?"

I turn to her. That determined soldier's gait. I remember what she said in the car, how she claimed killing for the collective was easy, and for the first time tonight, I'm too ashamed to respond truthfully. "No," I tell Wendy. "I was just thinking about what you said . . . about being in all-female organizations."

"And . . ."

"I was in a sorority."

"No shit. I wouldn't have pegged you as a Greek gal."

"Oh you'd be surprised," I say. "A few of us even posed for *Playboy*. 'Women of the Pac-10.'"

"Really?"

I shrug, the billionaire's screams still loud in my mind. "I had different priorities back then." I glance over at her. "Different boobs, too."

She smiles, and that gets me thinking about it for real. The *Playboy* photo shoot, when I stood in a cold studio, wearing nothing but a pair of USC Trojan boxer shorts, grinning like an idiot for some sweaty, hairy, middle-aged photographer in a cargo vest and matching pants who kept telling me to arch my back. And the worst part was, I wanted his approval. I craved it. When he said, "Yeah, that's hot," I was *thrilled*. . . .

"Sometimes I worry I passed it on to Emily."

"Passed what on to her?"

"I don't know. . . . Vanity? Insecurity? Kardashianism?"

"There's nothing wrong," Wendy says, "with being proud of your body. Hell, I wish I had *Playboy* photos of myself at twenty."

"Yeah, but . . ."

"Nothing. There are no buts. That kind of attitude—that guilt. Blaming yourself in any way for the actions of horrible men—or boy, in your case. It's what allows that *thing* we just dumped in the river to survive and flourish."

I stare at her. She sounds exactly like Joan. And, in the moonlight, she almost looks like her.

"I'm not kidding, Camille."

"I know."

"Then why are you looking at me like that?"

"You just remind me of someone I once knew," I say quietly. "Someone who helped me."

"Did she pose for *Playboy* too?"

"I don't think so."

Wendy snorts, goes back to the compass. "Then I don't want to hear about her," she says.

WE FOLLOW THE rest of the instructions—sixty degrees southeast one mile, a quarter of a mile southwest, the cold air pinching our faces until finally we reach a small hill that leads up to a road, where a solitary car is parked. "That's gotta be the ride, right?"

I nod, but Wendy grabs my arm.

"Okay, so since we aren't going to be able to talk once we get there, I'm thinking we should have like . . . a code."

"Huh?"

"In case something happens. If someone saw us on the dock . . . if one of us gets in trouble."

I look at her, my face reflected in her glasses. I've thought about this during the walk. But I haven't brought it up. I was the one who opened the trunk, after all. I've broken enough rules for the night. "You're right," I tell Wendy.

"I mean, I know we can't talk after this, or see each other again. But . . ."

"Just for emergencies."

"Yes."

"I think we should."

"Okay, good," she says. "Because I have an idea. If there's any trouble . . . we post on *The Bachelor* Reddit thread."

"And then what?"

"Nothing. We just know something's gone down."

"But what if it's a warning that needs to be explained?"

"Right . . ." She chews her lip, thinking. "Okay. *Anti-Alayah* means 'shut up and lie low.' *Pro-Alayah* means 'we need to talk,' and if it's safe—only if it's safe—we meet."

I nod slowly. "That works."

"Right?"

"I'll check the thread first thing in the morning and at

five p.m. every day. You do the same. We can meet at the Exit 19 park and ride. Same place your Camry is, so we'll both know how to get there."

"Perfect. I feel better now." She smiles, her teeth chattering. "That had better be our ride. It's freezing out here."

We both power walk up the hill, to where the car waits, its headlights flicking on.

The window rolls down. "I'm Susan," says the driver—a square-jawed, middle-aged woman who also wears all-black, her salt-and-pepper hair in a messy bun.

It's not her real name, but one devised by 0001—code, more or less, for *I'm the one. I'm a sister. It's safe to get in.* When I picked up the frantic young woman in the Bridgeport parking lot, I was Susan too.

Wendy gets in the front passenger seat. I slide into the back.

Susan starts up the car without speaking—a sister who plays by the rules. The radio is tuned to a country station, some yodeling sad sack whining about his "stupid heart" getting broken.

Wendy closes her eyes. Within minutes she's snoring, and it makes me feel as though she's been holding this entire night together. And now, at long last, she can finally let go.

I gaze out the window. The sky is clear and dark, with a sparkling sliver of a moon, stars spread out around it like bubbles on the surface of a still black lake. I close my eyes and time my breathing with Wendy's, that awful scene in my mind again, the trunk drifting open, the man inside. . . . Only, now I see that the scene isn't awful, because he isn't a man. He's a *thing*, as Wendy said. An evil thing.

And what we did wasn't murder. It was justice.

"SO?" LUKE SAYS.

I'm still half-asleep, "Barracuda" having jolted me awake, but I try not to sound that way. The clock by my bedside says it's seven o'clock, and it's dark outside. *Seven p.m.? Seven a.m.?* "So . . . how was last night?"

"What are you talking about?"

"*The Bachelor* watch party?"

"Oh . . . right. That." Last night. So it must be seven p.m. A whole day gone.

"Camille?"

"Yeah?"

"You okay?"

"Yeah. I'm fine. I just woke up. I mean . . . I took a little nap." I squeeze my eyes shut, fragments of my dream floating around in my head. *Blood. Wide-open blue eyes. A machete in my hands. Wendy laughing.*

"You sound . . . How can I put this tactfully? Unbelievably hungover."

I exhale hard. "I'm fine."

"Should I call back another time?"

"No." I pull myself out of bed, phone at my ear. "No. I can talk." I switch on the bedside lamp, move over to my desk, flip open my laptop, and put him on speaker. "You want to know the truth?" I tell him, the alibi coming back. "I had a really rough night."

"Meaning . . ."

As I speak, I open the web browser, then google the billionaire's name. "My new friend from the Reddit group turned out to be a crazier drunk than I am."

"Wow. Really?"

"I'm not going to take that personally."

"You know what I mean."

I click on news, check for his disappearance. *Nothing. Of course there's nothing. It hasn't even been twenty-four hours and that car sunk like a stone.* "Yeah, well, she downed probably half a dozen drinks and picked a fight with some ladies at the next table."

"Over *The Bachelor*? Are you kidding me?"

"Apparently, some of us take our dating reality shows very seriously. . . ."

I stand up, and there's a whoosh in my ears. Sparks dance in front of my eyes. I hear Luke's voice over the speakerphone, but I don't know what he's saying.

"Cam?"

"Yeah. Sorry . . . I was just . . . Man." It's the antianxiety meds. The lack of them, rather. I usually take them first thing in the morning, meaning I've basically skipped a day. "What did you say?"

"I said, you didn't get punched in the head, did you?"

"No, no. I emerged unscathed." I sit down on the bed, rub my temples. I need to take my meds. But first I need to make it into the bathroom without passing out.

"You didn't let her drive home."

"Hold on a sec." I lurch down the hall and into the bathroom, drop the phone in the sink. I can hear Luke asking if I'm okay, and it makes me angry. *"I said hold on."* It comes out a growl. Just one day without my pills and I'm like this. Joan prescribed them when she was alive and she died a year ago. I need to see another shrink. Get weaned off. It's awful to be this dependent on anyone or anything. I pop two pills into my mouth, gulp water from the faucet, and close my eyes until I'm me again. "Sorry, Luke." I say it to the mirror once I feel steadier. I catch my own gaze, stare into my eyes, and remember *him* staring into them, the last eyes he ever saw. *Sorry*, he had said. Too little, too late. What was it Violet Langford told me, about them begging and pleading? "I just . . . I just needed a drink of water."

"Better now?"

"Much."

"Good."

"So, anyway . . . I drove her home myself. In her car."

"Wow. Above and beyond."

"Well, I didn't want to subject some poor Uber driver to her."

"Not to mention their upholstery."

"Exactly. Even when I got her there, I felt like I had to hang out with her for a little while. Just to make sure she didn't die of alcohol poisoning. . . ."

Luke says, "When did you get home?"

"All I can tell you is that by the time I Ubered back to where I'd parked, the sun was rising. I guess I'm lucky I didn't get towed." Amazing how easily the story comes out. My alibi. And with my back to the mirror, I believe it all. *I haven't killed anyone. I just had a rough night, taking care of a friend.*

Luke says, "And here I thought the big news was Alayah coming back."

"Who?"

He says nothing for several seconds. "Alayah. From *The Bachelor.* The reason why you met your Reddit friend in the first place."

"Oh right. Yeah." I wince. "That was quite a plot twist."

"So," he says. "The reason why I'm calling has nothing to do with Pilot Pete."

I frown. "It doesn't?"

"Nope." I don't like the tone in his voice. It feels cheerful but forced, as though he's in character and about to lower the boom on some bad-apple cop in his precinct. "I'm calling," he says, "to let you know that Nora and I decided to take you up on your offer."

"What?"

"The invite? To your place?"

Slowly, it comes back to me. The morning after my arrest. Standing in his doorway. The sadness in his face. The pity as he looked down on me, into my eyes. *And please thank Nora for me. It can't be easy, sleeping alone. . . .* The way I'd felt. Like something more trouble than it's worth. The words had spilled out. *I wish you guys would come up and visit me sometime. I have a big house. Lots of room. I'd like to return the favor.*

It feels like so long ago. "Great!" I say it with a cheer that sounds more forced than Luke's. "When?"

We settle on next Wednesday. Luke tells me that he isn't shooting that day or the following, and he's pretty sure Nora can take those days off too. "We'll get there in time for *The Bachelor*," he says.

As he speaks, I walk down the hallway to my one spare bedroom, Emily's old room. The shut door. I try to remember the last time I opened it. Then I do.

Luke is talking about how great it will be to get out of the city and I'm saying how wonderful it will be to have him and Nora see my place and it feels like we're both reciting lines from a script, neither one of us very convincingly.

"Cam," he says finally.

"Yes?"

"You think I'm keeping something from you, don't you?"

I frown. "Well, I—"

"You know me too well."

"Well . . . what are you keeping from me?"

"I'll tell you when we get to your place," he says. "It's good news, I promise."

"Okay . . ."

"We can't keep secrets from each other, can we?" His voice is so warm, like arms wrapped around me. Or heated seats in a Mercedes S-Class. "Not even good ones."

I wince. "You have my heart." It's a bad pun and one I use with him a lot. It also happens to be true.

"I know I do," Luke says. "See you soon."

When we finally hang up, I put my hand on Emily's door-knob. I don't want to open it, but I have to—the couch downstairs doesn't pull out, and so this is my one guest room. I have to get it ready.

To give myself strength, I remember Wendy and me, side by side, pushing the car into the lake.

I am capable. I am capable. I am capable.

I turn the knob, push open Emily's door, and switch the light on. The last time I was in here, it was daylight, and with the sun streaming in, the dust motes were so thick in the air, they looked like a solid path to the sky. I had dusted then. Cleaned the whole room. But that was more than a year ago. I haven't been in since.

In one of the support groups I tried going to following Emily's death, a lot of the parents spoke of their children's bed-rooms, how they'd closed them off for years and turned them into time capsules, the teenage posters still on the wall, baby clothes hanging from puffy pink satin hangers, stuffed animals lined up on the bed, endlessly waiting for their owners' returns.

You'd think I'd be one of those parents—a time-capsule cre-ator. But I'm not. Emily's room holds nothing of hers. Nothing at all of anyone's, save for a full-sized mattress on a box spring at the center of the room—the last piece of furniture I bought for this house, if you can call a mattress furniture. I ordered it after Emily's death but before the trial, to replace the old one.

A year ago, when I came into this room and dusted it, my goal had been to turn it into something else—a guest room/ office space that would be wholly mine and memory-free. I had all sorts of decor ideas. I'd bought potted plants, a midcentury floor lamp, and some framed pulp fiction covers I'd found at a yard sale. I planned to move my desk out of the bedroom and into this one, order some build-it-yourself bookshelves for the window-facing wall, maybe even paint the walls a new color—robin's-egg blue, I was thinking. But I never even got as far as making the bed.

Maybe I can put a few things in this room by the time Luke and Nora get here—a bouquet of flowers on one of my nightstands, the lamp I bought for it, which now resides in the living room downstairs. A little something to make it feel less like an interrogation chamber.

I walk over to the closet, grab the packages of bedding to bring down to the wash—a sheet set, pillowcases, and a down-filled comforter, all of it cream-colored, as neutral as it gets. Emily's comforter had been black, dotted with glow-in-the-dark stars and planets. She'd wanted to paint the walls black too—black suddenly became her favorite color when she turned fourteen—but Matt and I had said no, not now, you don't understand how small and sad the room will feel. (*I'm small and sad, so that works.* She'd said it without a hint of a smile, yet I still convinced myself she was just pulling my chain. *It's her dark sense of humor.*)

Forced to keep the walls the pale yellow of her childhood, Emily had covered them in posters of her favorite band, My Chemical Romance. The posters bore ghoulish illustrations, and from the little I heard of their gothic, melodramatic music, I didn't understand their appeal. How had she shifted loyalties from the adorable One Direction to these creeps in less than two years? I had wondered. But puberty is a powerful thing, and parents aren't supposed to understand what their teenagers listen to. That's how I reasoned it back then, and it still makes sense. A kid's music should be her own. I just wish Matt and I hadn't given her the privacy that we did. . . .

I sit down on the bare mattress. After she died, Matt wanted to go the time-capsule route. "We don't need the room anyway," he said. "We never have guests."

But I protested. Told Matt he could—and should—move his office up there, even though the one he'd created in the basement was spacious, soundproofed, more suited to his telecommuting needs. Plus, he said, he didn't want to clean out Emily's room. He thought getting rid of her things felt like another violation, and he didn't want to hurt her any more than she'd already been hurt. *Just leave her be,* he pleaded, his eyes glistening. *Leave her be.* . . .

But as consuming as his need may have been to keep that room the same, mine bordered on obsession—the need to clean it. So I went into the room myself, threw open the door early one morning while Matt was still snoring in our bed. Dusting was what I told myself I wanted to do, but before I knew it, I'd ripped all the My Chemical Romance posters off her walls and ceiling, and there was no turning back. I cleared the knickknacks off her desk, emptied her drawers and shelves into black plastic garbage bags—her clothes, her books, her jewelry. The more I got rid of, the better I felt. And so I moved fast. I didn't think. I saved nothing.

The whole time, I told myself that I was doing something therapeutic. But deep down, I knew where this urge was coming from, why it trumped Matt's very valid feelings.

I wanted to destroy evidence.

Three weeks before Emily went to the frat party where she was killed, it was Matt's and my seventeenth anniversary. We wanted to celebrate it in a special way, and so we spent the night at a lodge on Hunter Mountain. It was the first time we'd trusted Emily to be alone in the house overnight, and I'd been a little nervous about it. Fifteen is, after all, the most duplicitous age.

But Emily assured me she'd be responsible, and she seemed to make good on her word, responding to our frequent texts, calling before bedtime and in the morning, even texting us a picture of herself in her bedroom, just before lights-out. We'd come home to a neat house, our daughter assuring us she'd spent an uneventful night playing *The Simms*, chatting with friends, and watching TV. *See?* Matt had said. *She's a good kid. There was never anything to worry about.*

I was worried, though, still. There was something a little too perfect about the way the house looked upon our return, something evasive in the way Emily met my gaze. And a few days later, when she told me about the college boy she'd met "at Brie's party"—which had taken place a full week before our anniversary trip—her words felt hollow and rehearsed. *His name is Harris, Mom. He's really nice.* And I thought: *Why did she wait so long to tell me?*

I put it out of my mind. Called myself suspicious and cynical, looking for lies when there were none to be found. *If you would just relax and let her grow up,* I told myself, *you might be able to enjoy your own life.*

And then she went with him to that frat party.

It was the *Rolling Stone* article that made me go into her room. All those lies Harris Blanchard told about how "mature" and "worldly" Emily had been. How she'd lied to him that she was eighteen, claimed to go to community college, told him she lived on her own in a mountain house she shared with a group of roommates. He said the sex was consensual—that she was drunk, yes, they both were. But this was no innocent schoolgirl. She knew what she was doing. He said, *It wasn't the first time we'd been together.*

Matt never read the article. *I have no desire,* he said, *to know what that prick has to say.* He didn't even want to hear about what was in it, with the trial just weeks away. And the thing was, he had that luxury. Matt wasn't getting stares at his office, because he worked out of the home, and as is the case with so many brainy people—make that brainy *men*—his co-workers were interested in his skills, not his home life. Not me. I had to read that article and find out what we were up against. And after I did, I needed to see if any of it was true.

Emily's phone had gotten lost that night in the woods, but I opened her laptop, looked through what few photos she kept on it—a few friends laughing, a dog, the sun setting over the Ashokan Reservoir, dresses she wanted to buy . . . Nothing worldly or mature. But still, I bagged the laptop, along with her pajamas and bathing suits and schoolbooks, her YA novels and old teen magazines. There was no evidence here, nothing to back up anything Harris Blanchard had said in the article, but I still wanted to get rid of it all. I'm not sure why—maybe I was afraid there were secret codes scratched into the schoolbooks or encrypted into the innocent-looking photos she took. Maybe the bathing suits and thong underwear would be judged as too revealing for a girl her age. Whatever it was, I just had this feeling that I couldn't trust my own instincts and there was something I was missing, something she'd been hiding in plain sight that I was too dense and self-absorbed to understand. I was best off getting rid of everything.

And that's what I did. It took around two hours, Matt asleep the whole time. I got to the bed and folded up her starry black comforter, the matching sheets and pillowcases . . . and that's when I saw the mattress.

By the time Matt woke up, I'd lugged everything outside and into the garbage bin behind the garage. The room was completely empty except for the dust. He asked me why I'd done it, and I couldn't explain. Couldn't tell him what was running through my mind or what I'd seen or why it was even important when all teenagers have secrets and a blood spot on a girl's mattress could mean any number of things.

I told him I just wanted to give her some privacy. It was the truth.

I lie back on the new mattress, the springs pressing into my spine. Joan once told me she thought compartmentalizing gets a bad rap—especially when it comes to people like us, who have been through something so traumatic; ignoring it for long periods of time can be a means of survival. *When you've been through fire, you can't feel that burn every day*, she explained. *You have to go on with your life.*

As perceptive as she was about so many things, Joan thought she was teaching me something new. But the truth is, I'm a pro at compartmentalizing. I've been doing it since Emily was alive, glossing up the cookie-baking, keyboard-playing honors student part of her and locking away the other parts—the ones that made her not just my sweet child but a separate human being beyond my understanding. It took extra work to shut away that morning and never think of it again. But, pro that I am, I managed to.

On the ceiling, I can still see a few stubborn remnants of the double-sided sticky tape Emily used to put up her posters. They cling to the plaster like blisters. Like scars.

THIRTEEN

The billionaire's name was Gary Kimball. I've known this all along, of course, but I haven't really thought of him as having a name until now. In fact, when I hear the name over the radio at Analog, I don't recognize it for a few seconds. *"Financier Gary Kimball,"* the announcer says, during a brief news break on the classical station, *"was reported missing yesterday morning by his wife, Marietta."*

So much to unpack here. *Financier,* for one thing. That's how they're identifying him, as opposed to rapist, child abuser. Murderer. It bothers me so much, it doesn't even register at first that Gary Kimball's beautiful age-appropriate wife is named Marietta. Or that he was reported missing, not dead. But then it does.

They haven't found the car yet. It's been three days.

I'm here to meet with a potential client—a jewelry designer named Xenia Hedges who also happens to be Glynne's ex-wife. On my screen is a folder full of potential website designs, from clean and simple to purply ethereal and several options in between, and I should be going over them, making final edits. But what I want to do is go online and deep-dive into Gary Kimball and his wife, Marietta, all the young girls he's ruined, with or without her knowledge.

I know I need to keep up appearances, to focus on the day-to-day rather than on my work for the collective. It's so hard, though, to care about website design when, three days ago, I got rid of the person who made 2223 wake up every day with her gut tied up in knots, with that all-the-time humming in her brain and the deafening, draining rage that I feel so often myself. I wish there was some way I could let her know that he's at the bottom of a lake. Not missing at all.

"Mr. Kimball was last seen leaving for Long Island Mac-Arthur Airport at six p.m. on January twenty-seventh," the announcer is saying. *"His wife told authorities that he was scheduled to board a private plane bound for Pennsylvania, where he planned to meet with an investor. But he never arrived at the airport. He was driving a black Mercedes S-Class."*

A memory flashes through my mind—my head resting against the plush leather, the heated seat, Wendy grinning behind the wheel. *I wonder who belongs to this beauty.* I wish I could talk to her about this.

My gaze rests on a youngish couple at the next table, both in jeans and flannels, laptops open in front of them. I'm guessing they're city people who can never truly escape their jobs—we get a lot of those up here, and true to form, the guy's been working his keyboard nonstop. But not the woman. She's been listening to the radio, just like I have.

"Bullshit," she says once she catches my eye.

"Excuse me?"

"Gary Kimball isn't missing." She spits out the words. "He escaped. And his wife's in on it."

I raise an eyebrow. "That's an interesting theory."

"It's what happened," she says. "Come on. It's obvious. He's probably in fucking Thailand right now."

"I don't get it. He did his time. I mean . . . what would he be escaping from?"

She puts down her coffee cup. "More girls were coming forward."

"What?"

"They were planning a civil suit." She gives me a bitter smile. "You haven't read about it?"

"No."

"It was on Jezebel a few weeks ago."

"I . . . I didn't see it."

She sighs heavily. "Not surprising. It'd be everywhere if they were rich white girls." Goes back to her keyboard. "Anyway . . . I hope they catch his sorry ass."

"Yeah. Me too."

I open the design folder on my screen and stare at it, my brain reeling. It doesn't matter. Their case doesn't matter. If he'd lived and if this went to trial, he'd hire the same expensive lawyers he had before, and they'd do the same number on these girls that they did on the victims in the criminal case and they would wind up broken and humiliated and none of them would see a dime. 0001 gets that. There's no way she didn't know about the civil case when she gave Wendy and me the assignment. And if I talked to Wendy, she'd agree. If I talked to her, just about the civil case and how it's been in the news. Just that.

Some rules can be broken, can't they? Look at how much it helped us to talk . . . I could find her. Her last name is unusual. Same as Iggy Pop's. Osterberg.

I look for Wendy Osterberg on Facebook, but the only one I find lives in Germany, and looks more like Iggy Pop than the woman I know. And when I search the member list in the Niobe group, she doesn't turn up there, either. It makes sense. After everything her son went through, why would she want anything to do with social media? I try googling her name and the tiny town of Jefferville, New York, where she told me she lives. A phone number pops up—just one, along with an address. Wendy Osterberg, on Dove Street. It has to be her. I pick up my phone. But as I start to tap in the number, I remember the last words we said to each other, Wendy rubbing sleep out of her eyes and joking, *This was like a really good one-night stand, only without the sex.*

I'd replied, *And without the pretending we'll keep in touch.*

Wendy cast a quick, meaningful glance at Susan, still waiting in the car, and put a shushing finger to her lips. *We'll always have Alayah.*

But that's only for emergencies.

I glance around. Besides the couple, there are only two other customers—a stoned-looking bearded kid with a sketch pad and an old hippie guy I've seen in here a lot. The kid's drawing furiously and the old guy is absorbed in a paperback. The couple are both clacking away on their laptops now, no one paying me any attention. I switch servers, call up Ağlayan Kaya, and click into the chat. My new world. My sisters . . .

Destroy him.

. . . rip her eyes out.

. . . make them feel the way my son did, only I want it to last longer. I want the pain to be unbearable. . . .

I open up my private messages, type a message to 0001. **I've been listening to the news about Gary Kimball. I heard there's a lawsuit planned against him. We didn't take him too early, did we?** But it feels strange, going into this much detail in a message. I delete most of it and just send the beginning.

0417: I've been listening to the news.

As I watch it disappear, I remember that Wendy and I weren't supposed to know who or what was in the trunk of the Mercedes, and my breathing gets too fast. *The make and model were mentioned on the news. If you hadn't looked in the trunk, you'd still be able to put two and two together. . . .*

The screen pulses with ellipses, and I rehearse responses in my head. *I had no idea until I heard it on the radio, I swear. They said Kimball was last seen in a Mercedes S-Class. Am I wrong? I just assumed. . . .*

0001: It feels good, doesn't it?

My eyes widen. No defense needed, I guess.

"Camille?"

I minimize the screen quickly and look up. Xenia Hedges. I recognize her from her publicity shots—broad, photogenic smile; high cheekbones; a buzz cut that's blue now (it used to be pink). She's easily twenty years younger than Glynne, but they still look like they belong together—cut from the same fine cloth. Too bad they aren't a couple anymore. No doubt their wedding pictures were spectacular.

I stand up to shake Xenia's hand, and it's only then that I notice the odd look on her face—the tightness in her deep red lips, the concern in her onyx eyes.

Xenia takes my hand in both of hers and grasps it. I try to pull away, but she keeps holding on. *What is going on? Did she see my screen?*

She says, "Are you all right?"

I take a step back. "What do you mean?"

"News reports are one thing, but when it's real people . . ."

"What?"

"There's got to be a lot. To, um, process. Did you just find out, or . . ." There's an edge to her voice, a tremor. As though she knows I've killed a man. But how could she? Did she get here earlier than I thought? Did she read what I deleted?

I take a deep breath. "I'm sorry. I don't understand."

"Oh God," Xenia says. "I mean . . . I just *assumed* you knew."

She says it too loudly. I can feel the old hippie putting his book down to look at us, the young couple turning from their laptops.

What the fuck are you talking about? I want to say.

But she doesn't give me the chance. She says it quietly, with the forced, professional calm of a hostage negotiator, and in that slice of time before I fully understand the meaning of the words, I feel sorry for her, a complete stranger, tasked with delivering news that sends shapes swirling in front of my eyes. "Harris Blanchard," she says. "He's dead."

IF I HAD no idea that the collective existed, the details of Harris Blanchard's death would have struck me as too perfect to be real. I would have assumed Xenia was lying—that she wasn't a jewelry designer but a reporter or an internet troll, or maybe a friend of the Blanchards playing a cruel prank in order to get a reaction out of me.

Even knowing what I do, it seems crazy: Harris Blanchard dies nearly five years to the day after Emily, the cause of death the same: hypothermia and probable alcohol poisoning.

"You're serious." I actually say it at one point. I can't help myself. "This isn't some sick joke?"

Xenia slides her phone across the table. "It's all over Twitter," she says. "I have an article open. Go ahead. Look."

I shake my head. "That's okay. I believe you. It's just . . ."

"I know."

"It's a lot."

"Of course it is."

I take her phone after all and read the article on her screen, just so I can have something to do with my eyes. It's hard to get past the accompanying picture: Harris Blanchard, Martha L. Koch Humanitarian Award in hand, posing by himself in front of the Christmas tree at the Brayburn Club. The photo was taken after my arrest, and I'm a little surprised by the look on his face—that shaky, uncertain smile. I enlarge it until the smile fills the screen, then make it bigger, even bigger, until it looks like something that was never human to begin with.

According to the article, Harris Blanchard had been in Vermont on a ski trip with a group of Brayburn friends, enjoying the tail end of the last winter break of his college career. He had been drinking with them the night of January 27 and was last seen leaving a bar in Burlington at eleven thirty p.m. "very, very drunk," according to one witness. Some at the bar said he called an Uber and left on his own, while others insisted they saw him leaving with a girl—a stranger. The indisputable fact is that he died that night. His frozen body was found the afternoon of the twenty-eighth, two miles away from the bar, in the woods surrounding a ski trail.

"Who was the girl?" I whisper.

Xenia just looks at me.

I skim through the article again. He died the twenty-seventh. That was Monday. The same night I was in Pough-keepsie at *The Bachelor* watch party with Wendy. I knew at the time we were building an alibi—that was obvious. What I didn't know was that it would cover two separate murders.

Xenia says, "Are you sure you're okay?"

"I don't know."

"Believe me, I know how you feel."

No, Xenia, you don't. It's as though I've been trapped in a dark cell for five years, and now I'm finally out—but it's because the floorboards have given way beneath me.

Maybe the collective didn't kill him. Maybe it's just a bizarre coincidence.

What a ridiculous thought. When the man who killed Rachel Ruley's son accidentally shot himself, was that a bizarre coincidence? How about when Ashley Shawger blew himself up on the thirtieth anniversary of his victim's death? And when Gary Kimball is finally found dead in the trunk of his own rapemobile, will that be a bizarre coincidence too?

I hear myself say, "It's very sad."

Her eyes narrow. "It is? Really? I mean, after everything you've been through . . ."

"I wouldn't wish it on any mother. Including Harris

Blanchard's." It feels true. It's what I feel. I grit my teeth. *Stop it, stop it, stop it.*

Xenia reaches across the table, places a cool hand on mine. "You're a very good person, Camille."

My cheeks heat up. "I don't know about that."

I open my laptop, Xenia's website folder filling the screen, the private conversation with 0001 long gone. I open one of the layouts—the purply ethereal one—and turn the laptop so that she can see it. "I'm a very good designer, though."

LUKE CALLS ME on the way home from Analog, and I don't need to ask why. I accept the call over the Bluetooth. "News travels fast," I tell him.

"So does karma."

I smile a little. "Yes."

"Listen, Cam. I just wanted to let you know that when I told you to let it go, that was for you, not Blanchard."

I take a breath. "I know that."

"You don't have to forgive him, okay? You never had to forgive him."

"Uh-huh."

"And now that he's dead, you have every right to feel the way you do."

My stomach tightens. "Can I call you back in a little bit?"

I hang up before he can answer. I feel nauseous, my head swimmy. When I reach the stoplight, I open the driver's-side window all the way and lean out of it, taking gulps of cold air. A car passes me across the road, and I can feel the driver staring at me. *I'm okay*, I tell myself over and over, until I'm steadier and my head clears and I can close the window again. *I'm okay, I'm okay, I'm okay.*

"I'm okay," I whisper. The light changes, and I ease my foot off the brake. "Everything's going to be okay."

As I'm passing the Mount Shady Library, 0001's message flashes through my mind. ***It feels good, doesn't it?*** She'd obviously assumed that by "news," I'd meant Blanchard's death, not Kimball's. But if I were to answer her question truthfully . . .

Maybe it's that I didn't get to see Harris Blanchard die or that I heard about it secondhand or maybe I'm still in shock. But I don't think it's that simple. I think the reason why I feel the way I do is that when it all comes down to it, yes, Harris Blanchard was a terrible human being. But he was also a kid like Emily was, with a mother and a father. And his death hasn't changed my life for the better. It hasn't made Emily any more alive.

I turn up the road that leads to my house, a steep uphill drive. My ears click. I drive in silence, trying to think about nothing, but I can't stop picturing Lisette and Tom Blanchard hearing the news that their son has died, collapsing onto each other the way Matt and I did when we heard about Emily, our bones giving way. They're like me now, the Blanchards. They're like all of us in the collective. They are parents whose son was taken from them. They have nothing.

When I reach my driveway and pull in, I call Luke again.

"I'm going to be honest with you," I tell him. "I don't know how I'm supposed to feel."

"You should feel vindicated," he says.

My eyes burn. I shut them tight. A hot tear slips down my cheek. Then another. "Why?"

"Because," he says. "Harris Blanchard left this world trying to do to another girl what he did to Emily."

"What?"

"People are talking about it, Cam. They're calling him a rapist. They're saying 'Justice for Emily' again."

"Who's saying that?"

"Lots of people. There were so many comments on Lisette Blanchard's Instagram, she closed down her account."

I exhale. "Come on, Luke. You know better than to believe online gossip. Think about what they were saying about *me* a few weeks ago."

"I know," he says. "But this stuff is true. And he was escalating."

My hand freezes on the door handle.

"Jim Grady told me. He knows a detective in the Burlington area, so I asked him to do some digging."

"Is that . . . Is that kosher?"

"He's a friend. You've met him. He knows where my heart comes from. He wanted to find out himself."

"Okay, fine."

"When did you get so concerned over the sharing of police information?"

I clear my throat. "What did Jim say?"

"A lot," he says. "For one thing, the reason why the cops were looking for Harris Blanchard in the first place wasn't because his friends reported him missing."

"I don't understand."

"They only found out he was missing after they went to his Airbnb to question him, and his friends said he never came home. A girl had been in the station that morning. . . . Apparently, she had left the bar with him and they went for a walk. They were both drunk, but he was blasted. He got violent."

"Oh . . ."

"She managed to fight him off and get away and leave him there in the woods, where he passed out. But her clothes were torn. She had cuts. She was very shaken up. I know I'm not a real cop. But I've done tons of research, and I've learned a lot from Jim over the years, and if there's one thing I know, it's that guys like this don't just mellow out on their own. They get a charge off hurting people and getting away with it. And the more they get away with it, the more dangerous they become."

"She had cuts? This girl?"

"Yes. She said he held a knife on her."

My throat closes up. "A knife."

"It was a deer-hunting knife, Cam," he says quietly. "A big one. They found it on his body."

FOURTEEN

It was a Buck 119. I actually have to bite my tongue not to say it out loud. Luke starts talking about the recidivism rate among rapists, but all I can think about is Ashley Shawger removing it from the glass display case and showing it to me, the long blade gleaming. *This is the Buck 119. Nothing fancy, but a good, solid, versatile knife.*

After I left his store, I'd driven eighty-one miles, as instructed, to the post office in Ellenville, where I'd disguised myself for the security cameras, slipped the Buck 119 into a padded envelope, and mailed it to a PO box in Burlington, Vermont.

0001 knew what would happen. If everything went the way she planned it to go and if each part of this giant machine she's assembled performed her role effectively, she knew very well where the knife would wind up, but how did she know Harris Blanchard would be there?

Luke says, "You're so quiet, Cam."

"Did Harris post on Instagram about going to Burlington?"

"He always posts about it. He and that group of friends go there every winter break. Why?"

"Nothing. I guess I'm just processing everything."

"He's gone," Luke says. "He'll never hurt another girl again."

"I know."

"And he did it to himself."

I don't say anything.

"When Nora and I come up, we can all toast to the future."

"I'd like that," I tell him, just to get off the phone. "I'd like that a lot."

I HAVE A landline at home, but I don't remember the last time I used it. It's one of those things I keep telling myself I should get rid of, but there's something that keeps me from doing it—my last tie to the past, I suppose. Plus, the turquoise rotary phone in the living room—a Salvation Army find from my college days—would be dead without it, and I don't like that thought. I never sprung for landline voicemail. Instead the phone is attached to an answering machine that's nearly as ancient as it is. At one point, there was a recorded message on it featuring Matt, four-year-old Emily, and me, but it got erased when she was around nine—I think by Emily herself—and it's been the default robot voice answering that phone ever since.

That is, on the rare times it needs to be answered. Telemarketers call it on occasion, but I can't remember the last time the red message light read anything other than *0*. Once I get into my house, though, and set my laptop case down on the coffee table, that glaring light is the first thing I notice: 23. Twenty-three messages.

I push the button. *"Hi, Camille."* The voice is chipper, female, and unfamiliar. *"How are you feeling? This is Katie Mitchell from the* Daily News, *and I just wanted to see if I could talk to you about Harris Blanch—"*

I press delete. The next message is almost identical, except that it's from a *New York Post* reporter named Daphne something or other, and besides wanting to know how I'm feeling, she's also *"wondering if I plan to attend Harris Blanchard's funeral."* Delete.

A serious-sounding young male voice follows, this time from the *Times Union,* calling me "Mrs. Gardener" and wondering how I *"feel about everything."* Next up is a man from the *Daily Freeman* in Kingston and then there's a producer from some radio show I've never heard of and then a guy calling from TMZ (*Must be a really slow day for celebrity news . . .*), each and every one of them posing different variants of the same question: *How do you feel?* As though, after five years, a light's been switched on, and how Camille Gardener feels is the only thing that matters.

I know I stoked this interest with my Brayburn Club outburst, but still. *Still.* I delete the reporters' messages, one after another after another, until it becomes reflexive and rather satisfying. I don't let them speak long enough to learn their names or where they're calling from. I just listen for the

hello and push delete . . . until I'm twenty messages in and
for the first time, I recognize the voice of the person leaving
the message.

"Hi, Cammy. It's Matt."

I lift my finger from the button.

*"I was hoping to catch you at home. I'm sure you've heard
the news about Blanchard."*

"Heard it?" I whisper. "I made it."

*"I don't want to say I told you so about karma, but . . .
actually, maybe I do."* Matt makes a noise—half-laugh, half-
cough. *"It's going to be weird, don't you think? Not waking up
every morning knowing he's still alive? What are we going to
do with ourselves, without all that hate?"* A dog barks in the
background, the sound of it echoing against the walls of Matt's
house—a house I've never seen, never even imagined. A dog I
never knew he had. *"Anyway, I'm free now, and you are too.
And I hope you know that. I hope the reason why you're not
around to pick up the phone is that you are running down
that mountain with the wind in your hair, feeling everything
it is to be alive when he's not. I mean . . . if it isn't too cold out."*

I place my hand on the machine, my eyes hot from the
threat of tears.

"You don't have to call back," Matt says. *"Just . . . take care
of yourself, Cammy."*

I delete the message.

I wish I hadn't done that. But it doesn't matter. I don't think
I'd ever be able to listen to it again anyway.

I lift my laptop bag from the chair and lug it upstairs to my bedroom, set it on my desk, open up the Tor server, navigate my way back to Kaya, and start a new private chat with 0001.

0417: I'm troubled by a few things.

The line disappears, and she answers immediately. It makes me wonder what her life is like, what she is like—always in front of her computer, all-knowing. Always ready.

0001: What are you troubled by?

0417: The knife. The girl going to the police.

0001: Why do those things trouble you? They're exactly what you wanted.

I start to type, *No, I didn't want those things. I only wanted him gone*. But before I can finish, 0001 has re-sent me the screenshot from weeks ago.

0417: I don't just want him killed off. I want his soul destroyed, his memory ripped to shreds, just like he and his family and their lawyers did to my daughter. After he's dead, I want the whole world to see him for what he truly was. I want his parents to have to live for the rest of their lives knowing what a mistake it was to bring him into the world.

"What he truly was," I whisper.

0001: Ask of the collective, and you shall receive. ☺

I stare at the screen, that smiley-face emoji, then watch it all fade to white.

She's right. She's absolutely right. So why am I not celebrating? I can't put it into words because they are words I don't want to think about.

0417: You're right. I am very grateful.

0001 is typing . . .

I watch the screen, the ellipses disappearing, then appearing again until a reply finally appears.

0001: You're not being honest.

"Because I don't know how."

0001 is typing . . .

0001: I'm going to tell you what you're REALLY thinking.

"Fine."

0417: Fine.

0001 is typing . . .

0001: You feel guilty. Not because of what happened to Harris Blanchard but because you're now doubting yourself for wanting it to happen. You're questioning everything you've said, everything you've thought all these years. What if the sex was consensual? What if he really did lose her to some shaggy stranger and she lied to you in her dying breath in order to spare your feelings? What if they were just two stupid kids and now they've both lost their lives and their legacies because of their parents' misconceptions about them? Am I correct?

I feel like I've been kicked in the gut. And when the words fade, it's as though they've seeped into my skin and become part of me. "No." I say it to the screen.

0417: Yes.

0001: That's weak.

0417: I know.

0001: And you're feeling sorry for his parents, which is even weaker. Do you think that family worried about whether or not

they were telling the truth when they gave that interview to
Rolling Stone?

I say it first. Then I remember she can't hear me, that we're
not in the same room.

0417: No. They lied about her to save themselves.

0001: And they've continued lying to themselves, all these
years. They've told themselves pretty lies about their "perfect"
son and they've been thoroughly, shamelessly happy. Your
instincts were correct. We gave him—we gave THEM—exactly
what they deserved: the truth.

My eyes are welling up. Sometimes in therapy with Joan I
would get this feeling—as though I were underwater, but so
close to the surface, just about to break through and breathe. . . .

0417: I drowned a man in his own car.

0001: WE did.

0417: I drugged a boy and froze him to death and planted a
knife on his body.

0001: WE did. Not you. We did those things and so much more.
What does that make us?

The words blur. Tears spill down my cheeks.

0417: It makes us monsters.

0001: YES.

0001 is typing . . .

0001: Think about monsters you've seen in movies. Frankenstein's monster. King Kong. Godzilla.

I blink at the screen.

0417: I'm not sure I'm following.

0001: None of these monsters are evil. It's the evil of others that makes them powerful. Beaten down by the world, shunned, robbed of what they love, they don't curl up and die. They don't apologize. They fight back. They get bigger, stronger, more terrifying. You are a monster. We all are. Be grateful for THAT.

"Yes." I say it out loud, close as I've ever felt to breaking the surface. A gust of wind rattles my bedroom window, then another. I get up from my desk to make sure the window's locked, and catch sight of the darkening sky, swirling snow-flakes. Out of nowhere, as though to punctuate 0001's point.

I move back to my computer and type out the thought as it enters my mind.

0417: But what if I'm a different type of monster? What if I'm more like the monster in *Alien*?

Her response is so quick, my words barely have the chance to vanish.

0001: She was a mother. That space crew fucked with her kids. She gave them exactly what they deserved.

THE SNOWSTORM IS over in just under an hour, leaving strewn branches in its wake and a light, slippery coat on my walkway, like spray paint. One of those "juvenile delinquent storms," as Matt used to call them. *They show up, vandalize your house, and get out of town.* I'm surprised I haven't lost power—a blessing, considering I haven't stoked the woodstove.

I put on my coat and gloves, wool scarf and hat. I head outside and salt my walkway. Then I survey the driveway for branches, pulling the bigger ones out of the path of my car and dragging them over to the woodshed out back to saw up later for the stove. Once I'm done, I walk out to the main road and head up the mountain, the cold air biting my face.

Trying to feel the way she did at the end, Joan would say. But this time I'm trying to feel the way *he* did, stumbling drunk or pumped full of GHB or whatever it was she slipped into his drink, the girl—one of us, a sister—like a ghost beside him, fading in and then out of his line of vision, then multiplying into other girls, other women. Did a group of them drag him? Was there a gun at his back?

I want to know who he thought of in those last moments of consciousness, before the knife I bought was slipped into his pocket, before he passed out in the snow, same as my daughter did. Did he think of Emily? I want to believe he did—that without his parents there to protect him from the truth, he finally understood what he had done to my daughter, to my family. To me. I want to believe he was sorry.

After my private chat with 0001, I switched back to my regular server and checked my email. There were two new ones in my inbox: one from Xenia Hedges, confirming our contract and telling me how much she enjoyed our meeting, and one from Brayburn College. I'm still not sure how I got on their mailing list, but the email is a newsletter, the main story Harris Blanchard's untimely death and his funeral, tomorrow, on the Brayburn campus. They're going to bury him next to Tom's mother, his grandmother. Harris Blanchard was a Brayburn double legacy whose parents had met there during freshman orientation week, whose grandmother had been a Brayburn Angel—meaning she donated more than five hundred thousand dollars a year to the college, right up until her death. And the newsletter had read that way.

Our community is devastated by the loss of senior and

Martha L. Koch Humanitarian Award–winner Harris Blanch-
ard, it read. *An extraordinary student, son, friend, and hu-*
man being.

If your family gives enough money to a school, that school
will defend you to the death, no matter what the facts are behind that death. They're like cults you pay to be the leader of.
And Brayburn, as I learned from Xenia, of all people, has been
serving its devotees an especially potent strain of Kool-Aid.
"Your daughter—what happened to her—was one of the rea-
sons Glynne and I split," she had told me. *"It wasn't the first*
time they'd tried to gloss over the bad actions of a privileged
student, and to see her siding with the school, over and over,
just because she was an alum and Dean Waverly liked her
artwork. . . ."

I'm angry all over again—a monster, created by Brayburn.
If anyone from the school had bothered reaching out to Matt
and me rather than to the press, if they'd shut up about the
dangers of fraternity culture and just once offered us a real
apology, treated us like human beings rather than something
bad that had happened to their reputation.

At least they invited me to Harris Blanchard's funeral.

By the time I reach the trail that leads to Unicorn River,
my eyes are watering from the cold. My teeth chatter and my
fingers are frostbitten, even in my heavy wool gloves. I can't
feel the tip of my nose. But I keep moving until I catch sight of
the big smooth rock, the stream frozen solid, just as it was five
years ago, after Emily was taken from me.

As I reach the rock, I imagine Emily at six on a sunny spring day, smiling up from the red-checked blanket we used to use for our picnics, cookie crumbs all over her face. Unicorn River wasn't frozen back then. It was a whooshing stream we pretended we discovered ourselves, and for all we knew, we could have. In all the times I've visited this spot, I've never encountered another person.

We had a funeral here of our own, for Emily's goldfish Jub-Jub. It was close to fifteen years ago. But when I kneel beside the rock and brush the light layer of snow away with my glove, the grave marker is still there—a *J* formed from seashells we picked up from Shelter Island, stuck into the earth by Emily, Matt, and me.

So much has changed since then, so many things caving in and crumbling and falling apart. Yet the universe has chosen to leave a goldfish's grave unmarred. I run my fingers over the dull shells, remembering the little wooden box Matt had made for JubJub's body, the prayer Emily wrote on construction paper to bury along with him:

PLEASE BLESS THIS FISH.

I was the gravedigger—a job that I took seriously. When planting bulbs, you want to dig a hole that's twice as deep as the bulb is tall, but I figured a fish in a wooden box should be buried much deeper than that, to keep it safe from stray cats and forest creatures. I took my garden spade up here early and started digging, so that by the time Emily and Matt arrived, I'd made a hole that was wide enough for a shoebox and four

times too deep for an amaryllis. After we buried the late Jub-
Jub and paid our respects, we pressed the shells into the moist
earth—a sweet, sad family activity. *Now God knows where we
put him*, Emily had said.

Last year, after Joan died, I bought a shotgun from the
Walmart at the Hudson Valley Mall—the same place where I
bought the hat, notebook, pen, and gloves for my first assignment for the collective, and probably the reason why the store
makes me nervous. I bought ammo at a hunting store, loaded
the gun, and took it here to Unicorn River one morning at
dawn, the goal being to join JubJub.

I sat on this big smooth rock with the safety unlocked and
the barrel aimed up, into my mouth, the pink sunrise all
around me, begging myself to pull the trigger. But I was unable to do it. I told myself I couldn't leave this earth as long
as Harris Blanchard was still on it; that if I did, it would mean
he and his family had won.

I wound up wrapping the gun in a garbage bag and burying
it next to JubJub so that I'd never be tempted to do it again.
Joan would want me to live, I told myself. *She would want
me to win.*

And now I have won. I'm alive on an earth that no longer
sustains my daughter's murderer. I stand up and stretch and
head back down the trail, thinking, *Sometimes the monster
outlives her creators.*

I am going to Harris Blanchard's funeral tomorrow. I need
to see him buried.

FIFTEEN

I dress carefully for the funeral—black suit, white blouse, low heels. Long black overcoat and shades. It's the first time I've worn a skirt in I-don't-know-how-long, and the suit, which harkens back to my glass tower, fashion magazine days in NYC, hangs on me. Whereas it used to hug my curves back when I had them, it now gives me a severe Secret Service agent look, which I guess isn't that bad a thing.

I debated getting dressed up for the Blanchard funeral. It felt like a strange, disingenuous thing to be doing—putting on a mourner's costume, essentially. But when I reach Brayburn College's main gates, I'm glad I did it. The guard turns away the car in front of me—something I've never seen done here before. When I drive up and open my window, though, he nods at me like we're friends. The guard is a big, bored-looking man with a neatly trimmed beard, dark circles under his eyes, and a uniform—black pants, white shirt, black tie, black jacket—that makes us look as though we work for the same company.

He seems to appreciate that on some level. "Funeral?" His voice is deep, nasal, and devoid of inflection—he sounds even more bored than he looks.

"Yes."

He asks to see my invitation, and I hand it to him through the open window. "Make a left and then go past the quad," he says, after giving it a quick once-over. "You'll see an open field and then a parking lot on your right. Park there. The cemetery is across from the lot, on Cornell Road. Can't miss it. The gate's open."

I ease my foot off the brake, then press it back down. "Out of curiosity," I ask, "why did you turn away that other car?"

He rolls his tired eyes. "Reporters."

"Ah."

"That reminds me. The family is requesting you leave your phone in your car. No pictures. Not saying you were planning on taking 'em. But . . ."

"I get it."

"Sure you do. You got a brain." He waves me through.

With winter break winding down, the campus is busier than the last time I was here. Clusters of students hurry through the quad as I drive by, some of them hauling suitcases into their dorms, some assisted by parents. That steady, joyful march forward, those suitcases stuffed full of shorts and T-shirts, a warm spring to look toward and the knowledge that, no matter how cold it is now, there will be outdoor keg parties, music blasting from open windows, and classes held on dewy lawns. Even as they shiver in their heavy coats, these kids—these blessed, protected kids—can smile knowing that there will be a spring of 2020, and that, for them, it will be a glorious one.

I'm sure Harris Blanchard felt the same way.

As I stop at a crosswalk and let a group of them pass, I think back to just two weeks ago, how one of these kids had made me so angry—just by existing—that I almost ran him down. Maybe the collective is a form of therapy after all, because I don't feel that way anymore. The reality is, everything changes, and anything can end on a dime. And no matter how young and healthy and privileged you are, you're made of breakable parts just like the rest of us, and so there isn't a single thing you can depend on. Not even spring.

I reach the parking lot just as the ceremony is supposed to begin. There aren't as many cars here as I expected there would be—just around a dozen.

I wind up parking at the same time as another car—a pale blue Audi, an elderly couple inside. I wait for them to lock up and make their way out of the lot before I get out of my car, then follow behind them at a safe distance as they walk in. His coat is black and luxuriant—probably cashmere. She wears an ankle-length fur, and her hair is the color of cultured pearls. I assume they're relatives of the Blanchards, and so I stay far back, for fear they'll sense I'm watching them and turn and recognize me. I don't want to be noticed.

As the guard said, you can't miss the cemetery, and that's mainly because of the gate—a huge, imposing wrought-iron thing that looks foreboding even when it's open.

The gate was donated thirty years ago by the class of 1990. Before that, there was just a simple wooden fence marking Brayburn College Cemetery, which houses the graves of a Pulitzer Prize–winning poet and a Nobel Laureate, as well as some of the oldest and largest maple trees in the Hudson Valley. I learned all of this last night, researching the cemetery online, though I'm not sure why I need to know all or, for that matter, any of that. Knowledge breeds confidence. I guess that's what I was thinking.

My plan is to fade into the scenery throughout the ceremony. Once the crowd starts to disperse, though, I will step forward and remove my dark glasses. I want Lisette to see my face, but more important, I want to see hers. I want to see if she's changed, as I have.

I follow the couple until I catch sight of the funeral, then move in behind the group of mourners—again, much smaller than I expected. From where I'm standing, I catch a glimpse of Lisette and Tom Blanchard in the first of just three rows. I watch their blond heads as they face the grave, and even from the back they look different. Smaller.

". . . lay his body to rest," the priest says in a honeyed voice, "and see his soul off to its eternal home."

As he launches into Psalm 23, I hear footsteps behind me, more people settling in. I keep my eyes on the group of young men standing next to the Blanchards, their heads bowed. I recognize one of them—a dark-haired, square-jawed, broad-shouldered boy with a profile that looks as though it were carved from granite. It's the fraternity president—the one who claimed he saw Emily heading into the woods with a bearded stranger. His first name is Braddock, and I remember him so well from five years ago, not so much for his testimony as for the way he'd acted outside the courthouse, after Harris was found not guilty. A big athletic slab with pink cheeks and a tiny Pilgrim's nose, he had pulled Harris into a hug, clapping him on the back as though he'd just scored the winning touchdown.

What is wrong with you? I had shouted, Matt leading me away, ducking my head and protecting me from the cameras, both arms around me as he whisked me back to my car, and I felt myself sinking, drowning. . . .

The priest says, "'Surely goodness and mercy shall follow me all the days of my life,'" and Braddock surveys the crowd, almost as though he expects an objection. I take a step back, but his gaze moves past me, through me. I'm glad for the dyed hair and sunglasses, though most likely, he wouldn't remember me anyway. For some of us, life moves on with ease.

But then he stops, stares. He puts a hand on Tom Blanchard's shoulder, and Blanchard turns, too, his jaw clenched.

Do they see me?

Tom Blanchard slowly turns back and wraps an arm around his wife, but the fraternity president keeps staring, his eyes hard, the color gone from his cheeks. He's not seeing me, though, but past me, and when I turn in the direction of his gaze, I see a group of girls standing in a line about twenty feet back from the rest of the mourners. They look like college students and could have easily come from the quad, but they stand stock-still, their arms locked. The one in the middle holds a homemade sign. Red block letters:

RAPIST

Tom Blanchard says something to Braddock. I expect a scene, and brace myself, but the two of them just turn back around. The girls remain motionless. The ceremony continues as though they aren't even there, Lisette Blanchard leaning against her husband, weeping silently into his coat.

NEITHER TOM NOR Lisette speaks at the funeral, which isn't surprising. It's hard, if not impossible, to make a speech at the burial of your child. Matt did make an attempt at Emily's, but he only got through a sentence or two. We did have a lot of people wanting to speak, though—teachers and neighbors and family friends—and we accommodated all of them. A few girls from her class performed Joni Mitchell's "River," one of them on acoustic guitar, and I still can't hear the song without tearing up. This was before the trial, of course. It was when Emily's death was just a death—the simple tragedy of a young girl taken from the world too soon. Her funeral was crowded, and it lasted a long time.

Harris's funeral is markedly different—the ceremony brief

and apologetic. The priest seems as though he's searching for good things to say, managing a few well-chosen words about how Harris was a work in progress, a seed that still hadn't reached its full maturity. "Who knows what good he could have accomplished," he says, and I can practically feel the contempt of the protesters behind me. When he mentions Harris's Martha L. Koch Humanitarian Award, one of them actually hisses.

Braddock is next, and his voice is so different than how I remember it in court, all the confidence gone. He reads from a crumpled piece of paper clutched in trembling hands, and I almost feel for him, until I recall once again what he said about my daughter. "Harris was a loyal friend," he says. "I was proud to call him my pledge son."

One of the girls coughs loudly, and a few people turn around, and I can no longer focus on the rest of whatever Braddock is attempting to say. I keep thinking instead about what Luke told me over the phone. *They're calling him a rapist. They're saying "Justice for Emily" again.* Would these girls feel different if they knew what really happened in Vermont?

Outside of the protesters, there are no other young women at Harris Blanchard's funeral. There are Lisette's polished middle-aged friends, and elegant-looking elderly women. But no girlfriends or female cousins or classmates wanting to speak. It also goes without saying that all of the mourners are white and expensively dressed, and it makes me think about how wrong I've been all this time, believing that the whole world was on Harris's side and that they'd stay there, no matter what. This is a small, frail group. And it's fading fast.

"Thank you all for coming," the priest says. Lisette collapses into Tom's arms and starts to sob—deep, anguished cries that seem to weaken her entire body. The white-haired woman in the fur rushes up and takes Lisette in her arms, as the other mourners, Braddock included, stand there helplessly. A cold wind whooshes through, and the trees around us creak like haunted house doors, the sky growing darker, threatening snow.

I imagine myself stepping forward as I planned, but I find myself turning around instead. *I want to leave before it starts snowing*, I tell myself. But the truth is, I don't have the stomach for the plan anymore. I've seen enough of Lisette Blanchard. I know that she's changed.

I leave the funeral quickly, but I'm not as fast as the protesters. I trail behind them, trying to overhear their whispered comments. As I pass through those big, threatening gates, an older woman in sunglasses bumps into me, and the two of us stand there for an awkwardly long time, apologizing to each other like women tend to do.

She smiles. It's a familiar smile. "Camille?" She removes her glasses, her eyes a piercing, shimmering blue. "What are you doing here?"

In frames, I remember her. The silver hair. Those bright blue eyes in the light from the streetlamp. The card pressed into my hand. *Niobe.* "It's you. Listen, thank you for the card. I really—"

She puts a finger to her lips. "You shouldn't be here, Camille. Leave quickly. Before anybody sees you."

I stare at her.

She shakes her head—a scold—then moves away.

"Who are you to tell me where I should and shouldn't be?" I ask, but she's already joined a group of older women piling into a van. I hear her say, "Oh, she was just asking for directions."

Is she a Brayburn alum? A family friend? Perhaps she thought she was doing the Blanchards a favor—by introducing me to the Niobe group, she might give me enough closure to leave Harris alone.

No good deed goes unpunished, as they say.

My attention returns to the group of girls, who have reached the field by now. I hurry to catch up with them. "Excuse me," I call out, once I'm within shouting distance. "Excuse me!"

The one with the sign turns around. She's a light-skinned Black girl with golden hair and freckles across her nose. She looks a lot younger and more delicate now that her arms aren't locked with the other protesters, and it makes me think about what 0001 told me, about there not just being safety in numbers, but also a great deal of power. "Yes?" she says.

"I'm just wondering about the meaning behind your sign." I keep my sunglasses on so she won't recognize me, but I say it gently.

"The meaning?"

"Is this because of Emily Gardener?"

My daughter's name sounds strange and formal coming out of my mouth—almost as though I've pronounced it wrong. I feel guilty for not telling the girl that I'm Emily's mother, but I want an unvarnished answer. My heart pounds.

The girl blinks at me. "Well," she says quietly, "she was the first."

I swallow hard. "You mean . . . before the girl in Burlington."

She shakes her head slowly, her gaze pinned to the sidewalk. Then she looks up. "I knew him. Personally. A few of us knew him personally."

"He hurt you?"

She nods. "I was too scared to say anything." She gestures at a fellow protester, a tiny red-haired girl with big blue eyes like Emily's, watching from a few feet away. "It happened to Hannah too. She complained to the university. They said they would look into it. Then she lost her work-study job."

I shake my head. "I am so, so sorry . . ."

"Jen." She sticks out her hand.

"Camille." I don't tell her I'm Emily's mom. I don't know why. We shake, then hug, and it feels strange and natural at the same time, like distant relatives meeting.

"I did read about the girl in Burlington," Jen says. "I'm glad she got away."

"Me too."

"And I'm really glad she told the cops. I wish I could write her a thank-you letter or something."

"Me too."

She waves, then hurries off to catch up with the rest of the group.

Around the time of the trial, I said it to anyone who would listen. *This isn't just because of my daughter. I want to make sure it doesn't happen to other young girls.* But I don't know that I ever truly believed that it would happen to anyone else, weakened as I was by my own guilt—the idea that it was my fault, that if I'd only raised Emily differently, if I'd paid her more attention, if I hadn't criticized her so much, if I hadn't been so strict or so permissive or such a failure as a parent, she would never have died the way she did.

But what happened to Emily wasn't my fault. I know that now. If any parents were to blame, they were Harris Blanchard's, who had raised him to believe that his feelings were the only ones that mattered, that compassion and empathy were just words people printed on awards, that the world was his for the taking, literally.

We gave him exactly what he deserved.

As I head back to the parking lot, the wind dies down. The sun starts to burn through the heavy clouds, and while it doesn't make me feel any warmer, everything looks a lot brighter than before.

SIXTEEN

0001: I have another assignment for you, but it is time-sensitive.

I see this once I've changed out of my funeral suit and into sweats and made a fresh pot of coffee, and even though I'm exhausted, both physically and emotionally, I answer quickly.

0417: I'm available.

I see the ellipses as my reply fades, and again it makes me wonder about 0001's setup. How is it that she's always available for a private chat? And how many people is she chatting with at once? I don't have time to think about it long, though, because 0001's reply comes as a rapid-fire series, and I have to read each message as carefully as possible before it disappears.

0001: Grab a pen and a piece of paper to take notes on the following.

0001: Drive to Tarry Ridge tonight. Write down this address: Beth Shalom Cemetery. 1561 Woodlawn Ave.

0001: Park across the street from the cemetery NO LATER THAN EIGHT THIRTY P.M. TONIGHT, and watch the entrance.

0001: A bald white man—approx. 5'9"—will leave the cemetery and cross the street between 8:40 and 9:00. Do not leave your car until you see him exit the cemetery. Act as if you are making a call. When he is in the middle of the crosswalk, look up. MAKE SURE THAT HE SEES YOU. Then SAY HELLO.

I wait, but the screen stays blank. Free of ellipses. Finally I type.

0417: Then what?

0001: That's all.

0417: Just hello? That's all I'm supposed to say?

0001: DO NOT speak to him until he is crossing the street. Understood?

0417: Yes.

0001: And do not move from where you are standing.

0417: OK.

As soon as my message is gone, this pops onto my screen:

0001: SCRIPT: You're going to a grief-counseling group that meets at 9:00 p.m. It's at St. Frederick's Church on Peach Tree St. You saw an announcement for the group on an online forum. You are a first-time attendee. Use your real name.

I check the time on my phone. I have just about two hours to get to Tarry Ridge. I change out of my sweats and into a pair of jeans and boots and a dark turtleneck sweater. Then I throw on my coat, pour some coffee into my to-go cup, and grab a bottle of water, a banana, and a bag of chips on my way out the door so that I can eat dinner behind the wheel. I stopped for gas on the way home from the funeral, and I'm glad for that. I can hit the thruway right away and, barring unforeseen tie-ups, I'll make it there with plenty of time to spare.

As I start up the car, I think about how I haven't had an assignment since the night of Gary Kimball—not even a random purchase at a hardware store or a quick trip to a post office— and even though it's only been four days, it's made me feel a bit anxious and adrift. There's a weight to having a destination and a purpose, even if that purpose is saying hi to a stranger as he's leaving a cemetery. It tethers me, the way being a mother used to. It makes me feel as though I'm part of something more important than myself.

When I'm leaving Mount Shady and pulling onto Route 28, the sun is setting. It's beautiful, the sky shot through with veins of purple and orange. I turn on the radio, but I don't search for the news this time. I want music. I find a song I used to love in high school and start to mouth the words. "Just like heaven," I whisper, my pulse quickening, that gorgeous bloodshot sky above me, the thruway entrance so close, I can nearly read the signs.

THE OLDIES STATION loses its novelty before it loses its signal, and so by the time I reach the exit for Tarry Ridge, I've been shifting back and forth between three commercial news stations, and an ad for an incontinence clinic is stuck in my head. I've been listening for information about Gary Kimball and Harris Blanchard, but I've heard nothing. Nothing new, anyway—just the same story about the search for Kimball continuing, played on two of the three stations twice within the hour. Harris Blanchard, it seems, is no longer big enough for radio news.

I drive past a row of Tarry Ridge businesses—a bagel place, a Mexican restaurant, a high-end boutique, a gym. What strikes me most about this ride is the loneliness of it—an entirely different experience than my ride with Wendy. It makes me long for her company, for company of any sort, really, even texts on a burner. Now that I know the collective is real, there's something anxiety-producing about doing the work solo, and when I turn the radio off, the silence roars at me. I took my pills this morning; I'm sure of it. But it feels as though I haven't, as though I'm not living but *reliving* this moment and there's something inside me clamoring to escape. . . .

"Call Luke." I say it without thinking. My phone dials his number, and he answers before I have time to think better of it, the warmth of his voice lassoing me back.

"You're a mind reader," he says. "Grady and I were just talking about you."

Jim Grady. His police consultant. My nerves roil again. I take a breath, deep into my lungs, then let it out slowly. It's what Joan used to call a cleansing breath, and it works, somewhat. The world around me shifts back into focus, and when I speak, I sound normal and relaxed. "Actually, I butt-dialed you."

"Then I guess your butt is a mind reader."

I force out a laugh. Make myself ask it, because if I were innocent in the matter, it's what I would ask. "Anything new about Harris Blanchard?"

"No, no. Nothing like that. I was just telling Grady how much I admire you."

"Okay, what do you want?"

"I'm not kidding. I've been thinking a lot lately about everything you've been through as a parent. It would have killed most people. But you're still here. You've survived."

"That's debatable."

"I mean it, Cam. I don't think I've ever told you this. You're the toughest person I know."

The GPS tells me to turn left on the next street, and as I do it, I feel myself smiling. "I survive," I tell Luke, "because I have a friend who's worth living for."

"Aw."

"Not kidding," I tell him. "You and Nora had better take care of yourselves. Roll yourselves up in Bubble Wrap or something—"

"Hey, where are you?"

"Huh?"

"I just heard your GPS," he says. "You're not doing another *Bachelor* thing, are you? It's not even Monday."

I take another cleansing breath, recite the script 0001 sent me. "I'm actually going to a grief-counseling group I saw an announcement for online," I tell him. "Rest assured, no Final Roses will be served."

"I'll let you go, Cam," he says. "See you soon."

After I hang up, I think about him and Nora coming to visit in just four days. I wonder if he'll notice anything different about me and, if he does, what lies I can tell to keep him from learning what that thing is. I've never lied to Luke before. I don't know if I'll be able.

I ARRIVE AT Beth Shalom Cemetery at 8:20, then drive twice around the block before finally parking my car directly across the street from the cemetery's entrance at 8:28.

There's a large vacant lot here, with a sign that reads, FU-
TURE HOME OF FOX GLENN ASSISTED CARE FACILITY. I
hope that when the place is built, all the windows face in the
other direction.

There are very few cars besides mine along this street—a
Tesla and a Porsche, their drivers nowhere in sight. It must be
a safe area, people trusting cars like that across from a lonely
cemetery this late. There is no crosswalk, but the street isn't
busy. One car passes, then another, and then there's no one for
a long while. I settle in and watch the entrance, sipping some
of the bitter, lukewarm coffee from the to-go cup.

Even on such a dark, quiet night, this cemetery seems more
welcoming than the one at Brayburn College, I imagine because there's no imposing gate outside—no gate at all, actually. Just a simple illuminated sign out front—gold letters on a
pale marble background.

My second cemetery today. I replay the funeral in my
mind. Those two weak speeches, the girls with their sign,
Lisette Blanchard sobbing into her husband's lapel. The flip
side of the Martha L. Koch Humanitarian Award ceremony
at the Brayburn Club, as though a sparkling curtain had been
pulled, revealing something sad and rotting behind it.

What would Luke say if I told him I'd been one of the people to pull back that curtain—that I bought the knife that was
found on Blanchard's body? I want to think he'd still admire
me, but I know he would be horrified. Unlike me, Luke Charlebois is not a monster.

I switch off my radio. It's 8:40 now. I aim my eyes at the cemetery's entrance.

Five minutes later I see a shifting form moving up the walkway, a shadow playing on the illuminated sign, and then on the path out front. *Right on schedule.*

He wears a long dark coat and moves quickly. He's a giant. A freak. My hands ball into fists. This feels like a nightmare—an enormous ghoul emerging from a cemetery, flying straight at me.

But when he steps into the dim light, he's much smaller than his shadow had led me to believe. It's not a nightmare. He's just a man, approximately five nine.

A car passes, and it feels like a screen wipe. I'm back to business now. I can see 0001's words in my mind: *Do not leave your car until you see him exit the cemetery. Act as if you are making a call. . . . DO NOT speak to him until he is crossing the street.* I get out of my car. I step into the streetlight and start playing with my phone. I sense him stepping off the curb, but my gaze doesn't lift until I hear his footsteps jogging across the macadam.

And that's when I see his face.

"Oh my God," I whisper. The clean-shaven head, the hollow cheeks, eyes peering out from beneath a low brow, just as they'd glared into his rearview mirror and through my windshield two weeks ago. That purposeful Manhattan stride. That expensive coat. That shiny Porsche, parked up the street, behind the Tesla. It's his Porsche. *I know you.* His name escapes my lips. "Dr. Duval."

He stops jogging. "You."

He did see me that night. I wasn't imagining it.

"Who are you? Why are you following me?"

I don't know what to say. For a second I'm embarrassed, but then I remember who he is. I think of that woman on our page, a sister. *My* sister, her daughter killed by this plastic surgeon's carelessness—a cruel, callous man, she said, who had never apologized, never paid. Her daughter gone forever. *Cancer didn't get her. But you did.* I hear myself say, "Were you visiting her grave?"

He stands perfectly still. "You're one of them. You're sick. You're all—"

A big pickup truck roars through the intersection and runs down Dr. Duval, crushing him beneath its wheels.

My throat feels very sore, which tells me I screamed. But I can't remember doing it.

I can't move, and when I finally am able to take a step, it's as though I'm pushing through water. My legs shake. My lips tremble. It's very hard to breathe.

By the time I make it to the middle of the road, the driver has backed up and gotten out of the truck, and she's kneeling beside Dr. Duval. He seems to have gone between the truck's wheels rather than under them, but it doesn't matter. Blood pools beneath his body. His mouth forms a word. *"Cla . . ."* And then his eyes go as still as glass.

The pickup truck driver has gray-streaked dark hair that

hangs in her face, and she wears tan corduroy pants, now stained with Duval's blood. Her build is sturdy, her movements practical. She puts two fingers to his neck, feeling for a pulse. Thumps his broken chest hard with both hands, then feels for a pulse again. She shakes her head. "I didn't see him coming." She says it like an incantation, her voice low and melodic. "I didn't see him coming."

My own voice returns, but it sounds weak and tinny, as though it's coming from somewhere else. "We have to . . . Don't we have to . . . to call . . ."

"He just jumped in front of my car. I didn't have time to move out of the way. You saw it." She brushes her hair out of her eyes and turns her face to me, and it's as though we're all members of the same repertory theater, Dr. Duval and me and this steely-eyed woman—*I'm Susan*, she had said to Wendy and me—and we're all starting work on a new play. The one about the plastic surgeon stepping into traffic. "You saw it, sister."

"Yes." I feel numb, but I know my role. I understand. "I'm the witness. I saw it happen."

Susan removes a phone from her pocket. "Where were you going?" she says. Running lines.

"A grief-counseling support group. At St. Frederick's. It was supposed to start at nine."

"You pulled over to make sure you got the address right?"

"Yes."

"Then you see this crazy man, running into the middle of the street."

"I . . . I saw him . . . walk right in front of your truck." My gaze travels up the length of the streetlight, the security camera at the top. What did it capture? A woman on her phone. A man hurrying into the middle of a two-way street then stopping abruptly. A truck driving through an intersection on a dark quiet night. A woman rushing out of the driver's side, doing everything she can to help . . .

"I wasn't even speeding," Susan says. "Speed limit is forty-five. I was going forty-four."

I look at his face. He had mouthed a word, just as the truck made contact with his body. A name, I think. His mouth is still open from the end of it. *Claire.*

He killed a woman's daughter and got away with it. This is what needed to happen.

Just like Shawger and Kimball and Blanchard and Krakowski. He was no better than they were. He was no more human.

Susan dials 911, and when the operator answers, her voice goes an octave higher. "Oh my God. Oh my God. Oh my God. I think I killed him. Help me. Help me, please. Please let him be alive."

I can hear the operator's voice through the phone, asking the woman who exactly she killed.

"I don't know. He just . . . Oh my God." She starts to wheeze. "I . . . I have asthma."

"It's okay, ma'am. Take a moment. Now tell us your location."

She grabs an inhaler from her coat pocket and puffs on it

audibly. "I'm on . . . on Woodlawn Ave. . . . in front of Beth Shalom Cemetery. He just . . . He ran out in front of my car. I can't believe this. *Hurry, please!*"

"Can he speak?"

"No."

"Is he breathing?"

"I don't know!"

"We are on the way."

"Okay . . . Okay . . ."

"Is there anybody there with you?"

She takes a deep, shuddering breath. "Yes," she says. "Yes. I . . . A woman. She's still here. She saw the whole thing happen." She bursts into sobs, then glances up at me. Her eyes are flat gray dimes.

DR. DUVAL IS dead. The paramedics know that instantly. As we wait for the police, they turn their attention to Susan, who tells them haltingly that her name is Vicky, but can't seem to get out much more. "I . . . I think she's in shock," I tell them as Vicky starts to shiver. One of them grabs a blanket from the ambulance and wraps it tightly around her shoulders, talking to her in measured tones. "Can you breathe all right?" he says as two cop cars arrive, sirens blaring.

She nods, twirling the inhaler between trembling fingers.

"I'm Officer Dunne," says the cop from the second car—a young guy with a powerful build and a military-style haircut. He's speaking to me.

"Hello."

"You saw all this happen, ma'am?"

"Yes."

He leads me away from the scene to where his squad car is parked, and asks me questions. I recite to him the words from the script I was given—about the grief-counseling group at St. Frederick's Church on Peach Tree Street. How my car's GPS had confused me and I'd gotten lost and stopped to get my bearings. I add in a bit about how I was programming the Peach Tree Street address into my phone when the man had rushed into the street etcetera, etcetera. Through it all, he scribbles on his notepad and nods at me with sympathy and understanding. He takes my driver's license and looks at it.

"Can I get your phone number, ma'am, please?" he says, and I give it to him, Dr. Duval's words still in my mind. *You're one of them.*

"Wait," Officer Dunne says. He peers at my face. "Camille Gardener?"

I swallow. "Yes."

"You're . . . um . . . I know you. I mean, I don't *know* you, but—"

"You saw the video."

"Yeah. And . . . uh . . . I'm sure you know that the guy . . ."

"Harris Blanchard. He's dead. Yes. It's . . . a lot to process." I clear my throat. "It's actually why I was looking for a support group."

"Sorry you weren't able to make it."

"Oh . . . I'll find another one."

He says, "Interesting you came all the way down here for a support group. I mean . . . isn't this town far from where you live?"

"It's about two hours."

"But instead of going to a local church or whatever, you drove two hours to Tarry Ridge. And then you got lost. . . ."

My face flushes. I hope he doesn't notice. "Someone was talking about this particular group in an online forum I'm in. Plus, I didn't want to go where people might know me." I give him what I think is a pointed glare. "I'm not sure what it is that you're implying."

"I'm just saying it's weird, you coming down here and seeing what you did."

"Why?"

"Dr. Duval lost his child too. It was three years ago, when I was graduating high school—big local news story. A hit-and-run."

I stare at him. "Oh my God. Did they ever catch the driver?"

"Yeah," he says. "Turned out to be some billionaire's teenage daughter. Wound up with a suspended sentence. Community service or something, I don't know."

My jaw tightens. "Not fair."

"Not fair at all," he says. "Anyway, their kid is buried in

that cemetery. The Duvals moved to Croton, and I heard his wife died last week. So, it makes sense in a super-sad way . . . him walking into traffic."

My ears start to ring. *You're one of them.* "How did she die?"

"Suicide," he says. "Like I said, it's super sad."

SEVENTEEN

It's past midnight by the time I get home, but I can't sleep. I spend more than an hour online, finding out everything I can about Edward and Natalie Duval and their twelve-year-old daughter, who was killed walking home from school in a hit-and-run.

Their daughter's name was Claire.

I learn about the fifteen-year-old girl who hit Claire—Berry Wright, who was truly Tarry Ridge royalty, her father tech magnate Reynolds Wright. Her uncle Roger Wright is the real estate developer who basically created Tarry Ridge—but that's an entirely different story. (Suffice it to say, there are questionable genes in that family.) At any rate, despite the fact that the Duvals were relatively well off, the Wrights' wealth and local celebrity more than eclipsed their own. And so, even though Berry was too young to have a license, left the scene of the accident, and waited forty-five crucial minutes before telling anyone about it—during which Claire Duval's life might have been saved—she received that infuriating plea deal.

Edward and Natalie did win a sizable wrongful death suit against the family. But, while it surely enabled Edward to buy that big fuck-you of a shiny Porsche he was driving around, money is no substitute for justice.

Here's what I don't find: a single word about Edward botching a breast reconstruction, much less killing a patient as a result. Not even on the website for the New York State Department of Health, which lists all legal actions taken against doctors. Did the victim's mother decide not to sue for malpractice or wrongful death? I can't be sure, but on our page, it would have been unusual for her not to have at least tried, and Dr. Duval's record appears spotless.

You share a mindset when you're part of a group like mine. And that shared mindset makes you feel as though you know everything about people, without even having to ask. For weeks I've assumed Dr. Duval was a soulless, lip-injecting prick who took the life of a cancer survivor and lived to drive around in his Porsche without a care in the world. Which brings me to the next thing I figure out in the course of my research: There may be both safety and power in numbers, but safety and power do not equal insight.

I return to the open Kaya chat and scroll back until I find the posts from the breast reconstruction victim's mother. Her number is 0517, which, when you think about it, is quite close to my own. But she doesn't *live* close to me. Nor does she live close to Edward Duval, who spent his entire professional life in New York State. In her earlier posts, which date back to months before I joined the group, there are references to a hospital in Huntington Beach, to a shady lawyer from San Pedro, to her daughter's ashes scattered just off Catalina Island. 0517, her daughter, that horrible plastic surgeon. All of them are from Southern California.

Maybe Duval did something else, something I haven't been able to find information about, and his own child's killing had been a tragic coincidence. Maybe his wife honestly did commit suicide, and it was out of guilt over the bad thing her husband did or she did or they did together. Maybe Edward meant something else when he said, *You're one of them.* I have learned at this point not to always trust my instincts.

But then, again, it all seems pretty obvious.

I open a private message thread with 0001, but I don't know what to say to her. I decide to start with the facts.

0417: Assignment completed.

I stare at the screen for a long time, expecting her to explain, or at least to say something. But she doesn't. I open another thread.

0417: What did Edward Duval do to deserve that?

0001: What did I tell you when you asked me the same thing about Richard Ashley Shawger?

I shake my head. "This is different," I say. As though she can hear me.

0001: The collective targets no one who doesn't deserve to be targeted.

0417: That doesn't answer my question.

0001 is typing . . .

0001: Have you not learned enough to trust us by now?

I pound my fist against my desk. I don't know how much more of this I can take. I type very quickly, my fingers slamming into the keys.

0417: Here's what I think. I think Natalie Duval was in the collective. She told her husband. You killed them both because he was going to go to the police.

0001: No.

0417: Then tell me what he did. Tell me what she did. Whose child did they kill to deserve what you gave them?

0001: What WE gave them.

"Stop it!"

0001 is typing . . .

Her response appears on the screen, and I read it once, twice, three times, my jaw dropped open, my eyes salty from not blinking.

0001: On January 18, you followed Duval from the train station. That wasn't part of your assignment. And if he saw you and identified you, it could have endangered the collective.

My hands are shaking so much, I can barely get the words out.

0417: How do you know I followed him?

0001: Instead of punishing you, I made it so that your misstep worked in our favor.

"How do you know I followed him?!" I shout it at the screen. A new message appears.

0001: That's how this collective works. We gain strength from our weaknesses. Unless they are the type of weakness that cannot be forgiven.

"Are you watching me?"

0001 is typing . . .

0001: I value you as a member of the collective. So I share more with you than I should. I can't think of anyone else I would have told about Shawger. But I told you—in order to assure you that you can put your faith in us. And now it seems I have to do it again.

Ellipses pulse on my screen. I sit perfectly still, waiting. *She knows I followed Duval. Does she know I met with Violet Langford? Does she know how much information Wendy and I exchanged?* Does she have me bugged? Chipped? Has she installed cameras in my house? It makes me want to close the laptop, get rid of the Tor server, slam the door on the collective entirely. But how could I do that? I've drowned a man. Played a part in the deaths of three more that I know of and still more that I don't. I am invested.

0001: I know about Claire Duval. I am sorry for her parents' loss. But experiencing personal tragedy doesn't exempt you if you've caused someone else's and have gone unpunished by the system.

I take a deep breath, count to ten. . . .

0417: I researched Edward Duval. I can't find one instance of malpractice.

0001: MEDICAL malpractice.

0417: ?

0001: Go to the main chat. Search for 1225.

I close my private messages, go to the main chat page, and type "1225" into the search box. It takes me a while to find what 0001 is talking about because, as it turns out, 1225 posts on this page *a lot*, empathizing with the mothers as they tell their stories in particularly graphic, visceral ways. She did it with me when I told mine . . . 1225: Or try a cut to the carotid, in front of a mirror. Make it shallow so he can see it happen. Then chop off his head.

Of the many angry women on this page—and I am one of them—1225 stands out. We are all full of rage, yes. But she seems consumed by it.

I scroll back several months before I finally find the post where 1225 tells her own story. Like the rest of us, she doesn't mention names or a specific time frame. But she's very clear about what happened. Her eight-year-old son was bullied to death—chased to the edge of a cliff by a group of older boys, who scattered and ran when he fell over the edge. It was deemed an accident, with none of the boys even standing trial, let alone going to jail. But most all of them apologized. *Most all of them.*

I open a new private chat and message 0001.

0417: Edward Duval was the ringleader. The one who didn't apologize.

0001: Yes.

0417: This had to be at least forty years ago. How can you be sure you found the right man?

0001: We always do. No matter how long it takes.

0417: Why did you kill Natalie?

0001: We didn't.

0417: I don't believe you.

0001: Believe what you want.

I feel exhausted. Drained. She makes sense. She always does. But why should I believe someone who has been watching me without my knowledge?

0001: After his wife's death, he took one day off. But other than that, Edward Duval was a creature of habit. He arrived home from work at the same time every day. And every Saturday at 7:30 p.m., he would drive from his home to Tarry Ridge, and spend between half an hour and forty-five minutes at his daughter's grave. We learned this by watching him for close to a month. You were part of this. YOU are part of US.

Then why were you watching me when I followed the Porsche out of the train station? Why didn't you trust me, the way you're asking me to trust you?

I type, *I need to think on this,* and send it.

0001: It would help if you stopped saying I and YOU and started saying WE. It's always WE who do things. It's always US. WE need to think on this. Say it out loud.

I grit my teeth, flick on the caps lock.

0417: WE NEED TO THINK ON THIS.

0001 replies with a screenshot from our first exchange.

0001: Can we trust you?

0417: Yes.

0001: Do you swear on your daughter's memory that you will never betray us?

0417: Yes, I swear.

I start to reply, but she leaves the conversation.

"Define *betray*," I whisper.

I shut down my computer, thinking back to just days before 0001 and I met—the morning I visited Emily's grave and found a bouquet of flowers, the card attached that read *Ağlayan Kaya*. At the time, I felt embraced, supported, protected—not stalked, even though the bouquet of flowers was fresh and even though, as I bent down to take the card, I had the distinct sense that someone was watching me. . . .

"How do you know I followed Duval that night?" I say it aloud in my empty house, half-expecting an answer. *"How the fuck do you know?"*

I run downstairs to the kitchen, grab my flashlight out of the junk drawer and my car keys out of my purse, and step outside into the cold, misty night. For a few moments, I put my hands on my hips and gaze up at the stars—the same stars shining on 0001, wherever she is, whoever she is. Then I unlock my car, open all four doors, and start searching every inch of it.

AT TWO IN the morning I find a small black plastic disk affixed deep inside the right rear wheel well like a malignant growth. After I yank it off my car, I take a picture of it and blow it up big enough to see the tiny white brand name: *Linix*. After dropping the picture into Google Images, I see dozens of discs exactly like this one, most of them for sale in spy shops. It's a tracking chip. Of course it is.

Carefully, I attach the chip to the garage door and head back inside, shivering from too much stress and winter air. I pop an extra antianxiety pill before going to sleep.

I DON'T GO online again till the following morning, when I search neighborhood Facebook groups for Croton and Tarry Ridge, then public pages of individual members, until I find out, on the page of one of the Croton administrators, that friends and family are currently sitting shiva for Natalie Duval at the home of Edward's sister, Olivia Weiss, and, while his burial won't take place until Sunday, those close to the recently deceased may observe his loss at the Weiss home as well.

After I shower, eat a few slices of bread, and chug enough coffee to feel semi-human again, I find another suit from my magazine days—navy blue with black velvet lapels, a onetime favorite. I put it on over a black silk blouse, hose, and sensible black heels and pose in front of my full-length mirror, appraising the look. Not bad. With a couple of barrettes and a little makeup, I will be ready to sit shiva for the stranger I killed.

OLIVIA WEISS LIVES on the outskirts of Croton, in a white ranch house with a screened-in porch and a beautiful blue spruce in her yard that makes me wish I could ask for cuttings.

There are several cars parked outside, spilling down her driveway and then bumper to bumper down half the length of her quiet street, so I feel reasonably comfortable as I park behind one of them and make my way toward the house. As I walk, I feel that same sensation I'd felt at my daughter's grave and at Harris Blanchard's funeral—that prickling of the skin at the back of my neck, the chill across my shoulders, as though I'm being watched.

I feel it even though I've removed the chip from my car, which makes me think that it's not 0001 or the collective who have been watching me at these sad places; it's the dead.

No one answers when I ring the bell, so I try the handle on the front door and find it unlocked. There's a mirror next to the door, a black cloth thrown over it, as is the custom at a shiva. There's also a coat tree lurking somewhere beneath a mountain of high-tech fabrics and fur-lined hoods. I don't take my coat off, but I do unbutton it and follow the muffled voices I hear to my right, through a small sitting area, pushing open a door to a living room buzzing with people, all wearing dark colors and speaking softly to each other, or milling around with paper plates full of cold cuts and stunned expressions on their faces. None of them turn to look at me as I enter, and I'm able to scan the group freely, until I catch sight of a drawn-looking dark-haired woman in a black sweater and pants, leaving the kitchen with a full plate and handing it to an elderly man sitting alone on the couch. "You should be sitting," he says to the woman. "You should be resting, not me."

Olivia Weiss. It has to be.

She wears no makeup, and her complexion is chalky, her eyes a dull, watery gray. We catch sight of each other before a woman in a navy-blue sweater dress approaches her and hugs her tightly, the two of them locked together for a long while. I wait until they separate and the woman in the sweater dress makes her way past me and out of the room, trailing expensive perfume and cigarette smoke.

The dark-haired woman is now standing alone, and so I approach her, my hand outstretched awkwardly, as though I'm trying to sell her something. A weird gesture, but she takes my hand anyway.

"Olivia Weiss?" I ask.

Her hand is very cold. "Have we met?" Her speech has a slight slur to it and her lids look heavy, the way mine do if I take an extra antianxiety pill. I'm sure it's for the same reason. Who could blame her for self-medicating? Her brother and her sister-in-law, both dead of apparent suicides, in a span of three days.

"No," I tell her. "But I'm sorry for your loss."

She frowns, then twists her face into a weak smile. It's easy to read her thoughts: *Then what the hell are you doing here?*

"My name is Camille Gardener," I say. "I was the witness. I saw Dr. Duval . . . I was across the street from the cemetery when it happened."

Her eyes sharpen up a little. "You saw him?"

"I wish I could have stopped it from happening." It's only

after I've said the words that I realize how deeply I mean them, and I want to leave her to her grief, to give up this idea of mine and go home. But if I did, where would that leave me? Trapped in a powerful group I'm not sure I can trust with my own life, let alone with my daughter's memory. *(And what did that mean, anyway, that oath 0001 made me take, back when I'd convinced myself this was just a game? Did it mean that if I go against the group, it will destroy Emily's memory, all over again?)* I need to know who I've been dealing with. And for that to happen, I need to find out if 0001 was telling the truth about Duval. "I really do."

"I do too." She gazes at my face for a long time, reading the pain in my eyes, taking the bait. "You want a glass of wine?"

"Sure."

I follow her into her kitchen—an airy space with shabby-chic cupboards and an enormous granite-topped island. A recent remodel, probably. If I were to walk in here under different circumstances, I'd have envied the owner—not so much for her money as for her desire to create a kitchen like this, so perfect for big family gatherings.

She opens the stainless-steel fridge, grabs a bottle of chardonnay that's half-empty, divvies up the remainder into two red Solo cups, and hands me one. I don't know that I've ever been offered an entire Solo cup full of wine—not since college, anyway. I take a few sips from my cup while she takes a long pull off hers. She says, "You were the last person to see my brother alive."

"Yes."

"He just stepped out into traffic, in front of a truck."

I nod.

"He visits Claire and then he . . ." She takes another huge swallow. "He went through so much. First Claire, and then Natalie. I mean . . . God. He must have been hurting so bad."

"I know."

"Well . . . thank you for coming."

"No, I mean that's why I came here. Because I think I know how he felt."

She glances around the room. "I'm not sure I understand."

"I lost my daughter too," I tell her. "My husband left me. I've thought about doing what your brother and sister-in-law did." Her eyes are dulled but kind. She puts a hand on my shoulder. This is easier than I thought it would be, but then again, all I'm doing is telling the truth. "I nearly did do it once."

She sips her wine, her eyes narrowing. "I'm so sorry."

"It happens to some of us. You know how certain people with missing limbs say that it hurts even more after the amputation? That's what it's like for some of us who lose children. There's nothing you can do to make that pain go away and you know that. It'll just get worse and worse until you can't feel anything at all." I take a sip of wine. It's very sweet, but at least it calms me a little. "There's nothing you could have done for them. I wanted you to know that. That's why I came."

Tears brighten her eyes. She grasps one of my hands in hers. "I'm so sorry for your loss, but you don't know how much that means," she says. "They were both acting so strange, and I keep thinking about missed warning signs and . . . God."

"They were acting strange?"

She gulps down the rest of her wine, sets the cup on the counter, then grasps it for balance as a man walks in. He's about a foot taller than Olivia, big and broad-shouldered with one of those faces that look as though they're always smiling. He pulls her into a hug, kisses her forehead. "You okay?"

She looks at me. "This is my husband, Jake," she says.

"Hey."

"I'm Camille."

He scrunches up his face and looks at me for too long. I'm worried he's about to recognize me from the viral video. "Have we met?"

Olivia says, "She was the witness."

His eyes widen.

"Not the driver." She says it as though she can read his mind.

Jake clears his throat. "Did it happen . . . the way they said it did?"

He says it to Olivia, not me, and so thankfully I don't have to answer.

She gives him a terse nod and big eyes—more couples' shorthand for, *I'm fine. Let me finish this conversation. I'll fill you in later.*

Jake squeezes his wife's shoulder. "Take good care of her," he says to me. Which makes no sense, but it doesn't matter. He loves her very much.

Once he's safely out of the room, I ask Olivia what she means by acting strange, and she says, "I heard them arguing."

"They didn't ever argue?"

"No, I mean . . . Really shouting at each other. Which wasn't like them at all. They came here for dinner a few weeks ago, and we could hear them outside the door."

"Could you tell what it was about?"

"I heard Natalie say, 'I never should have told you.' And then Ed said, 'Why the fuck would you expect me to understand?'" She closes her eyes. "Ed never swears." She pours herself more wine and takes a swallow. "Swore. Ed never swore. Anyway . . . there was something going on with them. And I felt like . . . I don't know. If I had only thought to ask Ed what was going on. Or if I'd called him about it later and asked if he wanted to talk . . ."

She starts to cry. I hand her a Kleenex from my purse. She takes it quickly, pressing it against her eyes. "I can't . . ."

"It's okay. It's okay. . . ."

She blows her nose, then opens one of the cupboards—a built-in trash can—and tosses the Kleenex in, these actions taking all of her concentration, as though she's fighting to do each of them without collapsing. "When I first heard about what happened to Natalie," she says, "before I learned that she'd done it when he was at work, and so he couldn't have . . ."

"You thought your brother killed his wife?"

She nods. "I thought maybe the fight was because she told him she was having an affair. I thought maybe she was leaving him, and she was all he had. Because . . . I know people say this all the time. But Natalie was not the type of person to hang herself. She was trying to get help. She was in therapy— some kind of support group, I think? She didn't tell me very many details about it. But she called me on Claire's birthday and told me she finally felt a sense of hope. And then one month later, practically to the day . . ."

I can't speak.

"She's gone. And then Ed . . ."

Olivia wipes her face, then goes to the refrigerator for more wine. "I guess you don't really know what anybody is capable of doing," she says. "Even people you love."

"Especially people you love."

She takes another pull off the Solo cup. I wait till she stops. "When was Claire's birthday?"

"December nineteenth."

"1219," I whisper, my mind racing back three weeks, to when I believed the Kaya chat was nothing more than role-play.

Olivia says, "Excuse me?"

"That's my birthday too."

To be a member of this group is to take an oath of secrecy, 0001 wrote to 1219. *If you tell a soul, Kaya will dissolve. It will lose its magic. Telling one non-member ruins everything for us all.*

And all 1219 had wanted to do was tell her husband.

I put both hands on Olivia's shoulders. Make myself look into those foggy eyes. How long after 1219's chat room comment had Natalie argued with Ed outside Olivia's door? How long after that argument was I assigned to surveil him? Natalie was 1219. She told her husband. They both paid the price. "It was beyond your control," I tell Olivia. The absolute truth. "There is nothing you could have done."

In my thoughts, the scene unfolds again, each moment like pages in a flip book: Ed Duval stopping in the middle of the crosswalk. His name on my lips. The gleam in those eyes. The same eyes as Olivia's. *You're one of them.* The screech of tires . . .

"Walking in front of a truck," Olivia says. "I wish I knew what he was thinking."

No, you don't. I take a sip of wine, desperate to change the subject. "Jake seems like a nice guy."

"He is."

"You have kids?"

Her eyes brighten a little. "My boy is sixteen, and my two girls are in college."

"Be with them. Go to dinner at your favorite restaurant. FaceTime your daughters. Plan a family vacation. Take a drive. Grab on to every moment you have with them and don't let go."

"It's so hard now, though."

"Nothing's guaranteed, Olivia. Trust me. I know."

"I miss my brother," she says quietly.

"Of course you do."

She gives me a tight hug that takes me by surprise. When she releases me, I feel the warmth of her tears on the collar of my silk blouse. "Thank you," she says. "I think I just needed to get that out."

My stomach churns. *You were part of this. YOU are part of US.* We killed your brother. We killed your sister-in-law.

A question is on my mind—the question I've come here intending to ask. But now I'm not sure the answer matters. "People change. Kids grow up. Life tosses them around and wears them down and sometimes they learn from it and don't need to be punished any more than they've already punished themselves."

Olivia is giving me a strange look. "What?"

I didn't mean to say any of that out loud. "Oh . . . I was just thinking about . . . Okay, to tell the truth," I try, "I was a mean girl in school. A bully. There was a girl we used to tease relentlessly. And I didn't just join in. I was the ringleader."

"Yeah?" There's no spark in Olivia's eyes, no nod of recognition. If her brother was a bully who chased a boy to his death, she's either in denial about it, or she didn't know him as well as she claims to.

"Sometimes I think about that girl, and whether what's happened in my life might be some kind of karma."

I watch Olivia's face. It still doesn't change.

"I'm sorry. It's nothing. I was thinking out loud."

"I get it," she says. "But I don't believe in karma."

"You don't?"

"Nope," she says. "My brother was a very sad, very sick kid. Leukemia. He was eventually cured, but once he got out of the hospital, he had a weakened immune system, and my mom was so scared he might catch something, she homeschooled him till he was eighteen."

"He didn't play with other kids, ever?"

"Camille," she says. "He hardly ever left the house."

He wasn't a bully. He wasn't a ringleader. He didn't chase a boy to his death. 0001 lied.

"He was awkward in college. Never had any friends. Not until Natalie. And look at what happened to both of them."

My heart sinks. "They didn't deserve it."

"If you're a karma person, then Ed and Natalie deserved nothing but sunshine and rainbows for the next hundred years. But all they got was enough happiness to know how awful it is to lose it." She polishes off the rest of her wine, then lifts her glass to me. "It's like you said, Camille. Nothing's guaranteed."

EIGHTEEN

Nothing's guaranteed—not future plans or justice or love or goodwill or the integrity of groups to whom you swear your allegiance. Not the good guys winning or the truth prevailing and certainly not life, the least guaranteed thing of all. As I walk up the street to my car, I'm crumbling, these thoughts a swirling storm cloud in my head. . . .

The collective killed the Duvals. *We* killed the Duvals. Innocent grieving parents, one of whom was a member of our group. We didn't kill them to avenge a child's murder from more than forty years ago. We killed them because 1219 told her husband about us and he was probably going to talk. This is the organization I've entrusted with my life, my conscience, my daughter's memory.

I start up my car and pull away from the curb, a parked black Prius starting up as I pass it, its headlights blinking on like an animal waking up. I listen to my phone's GPS as I drive—it's a little tricky, getting back to the thruway—but my mind isn't on the road. In my head, I'm flicking through my options, all of them bad: I can confront 0001 with what I know. But what good would that do? She'll either come up with some other clever lie I can't refute, or set the other numbers against me and I'll wind up like the Duvals. I can't go to the police—I'm a murderer. And even if I were willing to turn myself in, spend the rest of my life in jail, and get Wendy charged as well (which I'm not), what evidence do I have that I killed Gary Kimball as part of a group, beyond a site on the dark web that can be taken down on a dime?

Oh, and I'm dependent on antianxiety meds, the only therapist I ever had died from a fall down a flight of stairs, and there's a viral video of me losing my mind at a public event, taken just before my own arrest. I'm not what anyone would call a reliable witness.

I could message 0001 when I get home and tell her I want to leave the group—no hard feelings, no secrets revealed. *I just want to move on with my life*, I could say. *I'm ready now.*

But can I? How can I move on after all I've done and knowing what I do now? How could 0001 allow me to do that? When I first joined the collective, she had been very clear about the rules: 1) we must commit fully to our cause, and 2) tell no one about it. If Natalie had been killed for breaking the second rule, I'd surely meet the same fate for breaking the first. . . .

"Help," I whisper. And like an answer, an idea comes to me, the thinnest shred of one, anyway. I know someone with FBI connections. And she also happens to be the only person in the world who might understand. . . .

I make a right onto a quiet residential road and pull over to the side, turn on my hazard lights in case it's illegal to park here, and open the Reddit app on my phone. I go to the Alayah subreddit and think. It takes me a while to recall what Wendy and my code blue message is—it feels like a million years ago—but then I remember: *Anti-Alayah* means watch your back. *Pro-Alayah* means meet at the Exit 19 park and ride. I thumb in the words, and post:

Queen Alayah is too good for Pilot Pete and she always will be! YAAAASSSS!!

That's about as pro as it gets.

The Kingston park and ride is two hours away, and if she gets the message and it's safe for her to do so, Wendy will be there within an hour of my arrival. "Here's hoping," I whisper.

It's not until I've crossed the Mario Cuomo Bridge and I've been driving at least a half hour on the thruway that I really take notice of the car in my rearview mirror—a black Prius. It's been in my line of vision since Croton. And not only do I believe that it's been following me, I'm nearly positive it's the same Prius I saw leaving the Weisses' house at the same time I did.

I suppose it isn't just the dead that have been watching me.

There's a lot of traffic around the Prius and me—it's been stop and go since the bridge. The late-afternoon light being the way it is, I can only see the driver's outline in my rearview, but once I get an opening, I move into the left lane and make a point of staring into the car as I pull alongside it. The driver's wearing enormous sunglasses, bright red lipstick, a red scarf around her neck, and she has a big head of yellow-blond hair that could easily be a wig. *I've clocked you, bitch. I see you.* And even though I have no idea what she looks like underneath this strange disguise, I say it out loud, clear enough for her to read my lips. "I see you."

The red lipstick stretches into a toothy smile—a rictus joker grin. *I see you too,* she mouths. *Sister.*

I turn back to the road, my heart crashing into my ribs. Anxiety kicking in. *Okay. Point well taken.*

I push forward, and the Prius slides in behind me.

I see the glint off her sunglasses in my rearview, and it replays in my head, that bloodred mouth, that baring of teeth. "Get away from me."

When I turn back to the road, I'm racing for the bumper of the car in front of me. I pull to the right and switch lanes just in time, avoiding hitting it but cutting off a truck. Its horn blares, and I shift into the right lane, and then the one next to it, my eyes peeled for the Prius. *Lost you, you psychotic . . .* But there she is again, maybe a car length back, two lanes to the left.

How can a Prius go that fast?

It's now in the lane next to me, the bumper parallel to my own. "What the hell?"

There's a clear stretch ahead of me, and it feels like a gift.

I jam my foot into the accelerator, taking my Subaru up to eighty-five, then ninety, shifting lanes whenever I can. In my rearview, I can see the Prius surging forward. I move into the fast lane and take it up to ninety-five.

I'm scaring myself. This isn't me. Emily and Matt used to tease me about what a boring, by-the-book driver I was, hands always at ten and two, never more than five miles over the speed limit, and though I've certainly been a lot more reckless in recent years, a car chase is not me.

Is it? I flash on three weeks ago, riding the bumper of Edward Duval's Porsche, pulsing with anger at a man I didn't know, then five days ago, on the steadiness of my hands as I pushed the Mercedes into the lake. *It is me. Now it is.* The collective changes you to suit its needs, magnifying the ugliest parts of your broken faith, weaponizing you. Who knows what Rictus Grin was like before she gave into her grief and rage and became a monster? *She was somebody's mother once. That much, I know.*

I'm going close to one hundred. I can't look for the Prius. I have to keep my eyes on the road. I shift one lane to the right and swerve around an eighteen-wheeler like this is just some big video game. Its horn wails.

Once I reach a less congested area of the thruway, I search for the Prius in my rearview, then in both of the side mirrors and through the windshields, front and back, my breathing shallow until finally, finally I feel as though I've escaped it.

"Thank you," I whisper.

I slow down to seventy and take the center lane, as though none of this had ever happened. As I pass the Harriman exit, Woodbury Commons spread out beyond the trees, I let my mind travel back to the time I first met Luke there, at Applebee's—a simpler, sweeter time, when my marriage was still on life support and I had never played a role in anyone's murder.

How can I fix this? Can I fix this? Can Wendy help me? *Please, Wendy. Please show up at the park and ride. . . .*

The short burst of a police siren slaps me out of my thoughts, the flashing lights in my rearview like some maniacal Christmas toy.

Oh sure, now I get pulled over.

I shift into the right lane, then onto the shoulder, making sure to put my blinker on as I do it. *By the book. Thoroughly respectable middle-aged lady in a suit.* I'm not sure when this cop started following me, but I feel like I've been going seventy long enough to merit acting confused when he asks if I know why he pulled me over.

It's worth a try anyway, though I don't really care. Traffic tickets used to give me serious agita, but considering everything else I've been through today, this feels like a muchneeded time-out. I roll my shoulders and crack my neck, and when the trooper's uniform fills my peripheral vision, I open my window readily.

"Yes, Officer?"

"License and registration, please," says the cop—a powerfully built woman in mirrored aviator glasses that cover most of her face.

I think about asking her why she pulled me over as I get my driver's license out of my wallet and then open my glove compartment for the registration. But then I figure, what's the point? There's something almost welcoming about the normalcy of a speeding ticket. And my record is spotless—well, outside of my drunk and disorderly and disturbing the peace charges of earlier this month. And those were mere violations.

As I hand it all over, I try a cheery smile. "Here you go, Officer."

She takes them in a gloved hand, gives the license a quick read. "Get out of the car."

"Wait, what?"

"Get out of the car."

She opens my door and steps back, her hand resting on her holstered gun. "No sudden movements," she says.

What is happening? I get out of the car slowly, my hands spread and raised. My knees feel weak and wobbly. I may fall. *Don't fall, don't fall.*

"Move around to the back of the car."

"Officer, I'm sorry. There must be some—"

"Not going to ask you again."

I start to move.

"Not so fast."

I do as she says. Must have seen me speeding. Must have been following me for a while. *Or else . . . Oh God . . .*

"Do exactly as I say. Place your hands on the left rear bumper. Wide stance. Legs three feet apart."

They found Kimball. They must have. I feel her gloved hands at my neck, my shoulders, down the length of my back, around my waist. She pulls at my hair, jams her hands in the pockets of my coat. She tells me to take off my shoes.

"What?"

"Kick off your shoes. Do not move your hands."

Does she think I keep a stiletto in my heel like some James Bond villain? But I say nothing. I do as I'm told, my head bowed, my stockinged feet on the icy road, the cold burning into my bones.

She stands behind me for a long time, saying nothing. I start to shiver uncontrollably. *Do something. Arrest me. Read me my fucking rights.* I want to say it. To scream it. Flag down a car. Run into traffic.

I feel her moving closer, her boots scuffing the macadam.

Then I hear another sound. The snap of a holster. The release of a safety.

"Please," I whisper.

She says, "Why did you go to Olivia Weiss's house?"

"What?"

"Stay still or I shoot."

My teeth chatter. I can't form words.

"Why did you go to Olivia Weiss's house?"

"I . . . I was . . . Her brother . . . I was a wit—"

"We know what you were," she says. "We know what you are." And it all comes together, the pieces arranging themselves in my head. *We.*

"Did you tell Olivia Weiss about the collective?"

I close my eyes. "No."

"We'll find out if you're lying."

"I swear I didn't."

"Then why did you go to her house?"

"I . . . I wanted to . . . I was just . . ."

"What?"

"Curious."

"Curious?"

A car whooshes by, the sound of it lingering in my ears. Then another whoosh, and another. The roar of silence. My breathing is shallow. *Panic attack. Stop. Calm down. Think.* "Yes."

"What the hell were you curious about?"

"Her brother." My voice quavers. "He lost a child. Like I did. *Like we did.*"

The trooper doesn't speak. I keep my eyes shut, holding my breath, until finally I hear the safety clicking back on.

"If you don't do what you're told to do," she says, "it ruins things. Not just for us. But for the memories of our children. All of our children. Do you get that?" I hear her take a step back. "Look at me."

I do. I turn around and look straight at her, my face stretched and distorted in her fun house–mirror glasses, her hand resting on the holstered gun at her hip. "Do you?"

"Yes. Yes, I get it."

She watches me for a while, then places my license and registration on the trunk of my car and gives me a sweet, pearly smile. "We're letting you off with a warning, ma'am." She thwacks a finger against the broad brim of her hat as I stare at her, frozen. "Please try to be more careful next time."

After she leaves, the panic attack revs up. I spend several minutes doubled over on the macadam, my veins throbbing, threatening to explode.

NINETEEN

We're everywhere, Camille, Wendy had said to me when we were leaving the Wild Rose, just after we got the send-off from the bartender, that virgin-serving sister in the sparkly dress, our alibis achieved. At the time, it thrilled me, the idea of being part of something so big and effective and strong. But now I find it terrifying, like an impenetrable dome over my head that I'm only just discovering.

When I reach Exit 19, which is my exit, I'm still shivering from my encounter with the cop. My hands have been gripping the wheel so hard, they ache, and I haven't been able to think of anything but those mirrored glasses, the sound of her gun's safety, the dry calm of her voice.

We'll find out if you're lying.

As I pull off at the exit, I catch a glimpse of a shadow in the tollbooth, and I could swear the woman in the Prius is standing there in her enormous sunglasses, grinning at me through her painted red lips. *We're everywhere. . . .*

My breath sticks in my throat, and I tell myself to calm down, keep it together. It's not her. It's an elderly man. . . . I think about skipping the park and ride, driving home, barring the doors to my house, and never leaving. But then I remind myself: They're not everywhere. How can they be? They just want me to believe they are so they can scare me into submission.

Not they. We.

Past the tollbooth is a traffic circle, the park and ride just off the second exit. Once I reach the park and ride, I head in slowly, my gaze darting from space to space, checking for stationary drivers who might be staking me out the way the woman in the Prius did, the way I staked out Edward Duval for a solid week at the Croton-on-Hudson train station.

I complete a full sweep of the lot, passing every empty car and satisfying myself that no one is waiting here for me. Then I find a space close to the entrance, with an empty one next to it, and wait. It's six p.m., and this park and ride is about an hour away from Wendy's town of Jefferville. I'll give her an hour, and if she doesn't show by then, I can assume she isn't going to. Probably best for her if she doesn't. If I allow myself to need certain people in my life, bad things happen to them. My mother died too young, of cancer. And then of course there was Emily. Matt changed so much as a person, he no longer became necessary, and thus got out of "us" alive. What's saved Luke, I'm convinced, is the distance between us—the fact that we live more than two hours apart, and his life is too busy and full for me to rely on him the way I'd like to. . . .

And here's something I try very hard not to think about: I was the last person to speak to my therapist, Joan. She had told me a few days earlier that she didn't think analysis was helping me anymore—that I hadn't made much progress in the past three years, and she felt it was her fault. She was holding me back by being so available to me, and as a result, she was keeping me from forming meaningful relationships. *You're not my mother,* she had said, meaning she didn't want me to turn into someone like her mother—friendless, joyless, ruined forever by the death of her child. . . .

I didn't care what she meant. I went off my meds for those three days, and took it worse than I've ever taken a breakup. I called Joan at two in the morning like some obsessed, spurned lover, waking her from a deep sleep and begging her to reconsider. *You need help, Camille,* she had said. And I had replied, *That's why I'm calling you!*

I don't remember exactly how the conversation ended, but I do remember dissolving into tears. She was found at the bottom of her staircase a week later, her phone near her body, mine the last on her recent calls list.

Would she have fallen down her stairs in the middle of the night if my call hadn't awakened her? Who knows? But I'm wondering if that's what drew me to the collective in the first place—the idea of forming connections with people I'll never know well enough to kill.

I check the clock on my dashboard. It's close to six thirty. My brain is going places I don't want it to, spinning stories about 0001 finding out about our plan and reading my post on *The Bachelor* subreddit and siccing the collective on Wendy. . . . *Please no*, I think, over and over and over again. *Please no.* And then, fifteen minutes later, when my heart is beating so hard that it hurts to breathe, I see a silver Camry pulling in and its headlights flashing and then Wendy behind the wheel. I'm relieved, of course, but the relief is tinged with dread. It feels too much like the answer to a final wish—one that I'm selfish to have made in the first place.

Wendy pulls into the empty space next to mine, and we both open our windows. "Did they find the car?" she says. "Did the cops—"

I shake my head.

"Then what?"

I say it between my teeth. "It's not about Kimball."

I point at the exit to the park and ride, and she nods. I close my window, and she follows me into Kingston, up and down a series of one-way streets until I'm certain no one else is tailing us. I pull into the parking lot of a small strip mall, an open grocery store at one end, the other end much deader, most of the businesses closed for the night.

We park in two spaces between a physical therapy center and a pizza parlor, both of them dark and empty. I unlock my doors and push open the one on the passenger side.

After she's safely in the passenger seat, both doors closed

and locked, I ask Wendy one of the few questions I didn't ask her during the night we killed Kimball. "How long have you been with the collective?"

"About three years," she says. "Why?"

"Have you ever played a part in the murder of someone who didn't deserve it?"

"What? No, they all deserve it. Kimball—"

"I told you. This isn't about him."

I turn and face her—the clear-framed glasses, the sensible cap of light brown hair. She's wearing yoga pants, pink Skechers, and a sweatshirt with a cat on it. She's holding a drugstore bag in her hand, like she stopped on her way here to pick up a prescription, and I don't know that I've ever seen anyone look less threatening. "Then what are you talking about?" she says.

I just say it. "Edward Duval." Saying the name out loud is like jumping into cold water—a shock at first, but then I'm in.

"Who's that?" Wendy says.

And I tell her everything.

THE STORY I tell starts with my spur-of-the-moment decision to follow Edward Duval out of the Croton-on-Hudson train station and finishes half an hour ago, with me waiting for Wendy at the park and ride. Throughout it all, Wendy doesn't say anything—no prompting questions, no expressions of shock, not even a nod. She just stares at me, her arms folded over her chest, like someone watching a movie. When

I'm done, she doesn't speak right away, and I start making bets in my head on what she'll say first, just to calm myself down.

When she does finally say something, it's this: "The collective chipped your car?"

"That's your first question?"

"I thought I'd start small."

"Okay."

Neither one of us says anything for a long while.

"It's weird," Wendy says finally. "When I first joined, 0001 said that one of the rules of the collective was to tell no one about it. I assumed she just meant that the collective wouldn't continue to work if anyone talked. That our efforts would be for nothing, that people would get found out. Do you know what I mean? I didn't take it as a *threat*."

"Me neither."

She lets out a heavy sigh. "You miss a lot of nuance when you're private messaging."

"Yep."

More silence. Then . . . "Camille?"

"Yeah?"

"I don't think we can do anything about this."

I look at her.

"I mean, we're both involved. People have been killed. This isn't something we can just walk away from."

I swallow hard. "We can talk to your sister-in-law."

Her eyes go huge.

"You don't even have to be involved. You can just say I'm

your friend. Your fellow *Bachelor* fan, and we went out for drinks and I told you about this thing, you know it sounds crazy, but your friend can show her the website. I'll take it from there."

"You really want to do that?"

"I don't *want* to. But what I want doesn't matter."

"You're going to shut this whole thing down. After everything it's given us."

I stare at her. "Are you serious?"

"I heard about Harris Blanchard, Camille. I was at work and some people were talking about how he died—*the way he died*—and I had to do everything I could to keep from cheering. It was fucking poetic. And you never would have lived to see that happen if it weren't for the collective."

"Listen, Wendy—"

"I knew exactly how you felt about Blanchard, because a year ago I got to feel that way too. I told you what a blessing that was. I can sleep at night now. That . . . thing who raped my son. He got what he deserved." She puts her hand on mine and gives me big, expectant eyes. "Gary Kimball won't destroy another young girl. And it's because of *us*."

For a few seconds I'm with her. The collective has given Wendy and me so much, not to mention Rachel Ruley, Violet Langford, all the mothers of Gary Kimball's victims. . . . The collective has succeeded where the system failed all of us. Couldn't I forgive it collateral damage? Wouldn't it be so

much easier to heed that trooper's warning, to forget everything Olivia Weiss said to me, to compartmentalize what I did
to the Duvals like I've done with so many other things I've
done wrong in my life. . . .

But then I recall 0001's own words, and I'm back to where I
started. *Harris Blanchard just won a humanitarian award at
school. Do you feel the good deeds he racked up to win that
award outweigh what he did to your daughter?* "Good acts
can't erase unspeakable ones," I say. "I killed a grieving father,
Wendy. As he was leaving his daughter's grave."

She turns away from me, her forehead resting against the
passenger-side window. "You did," she says quietly. "Not me."

She puts her hand on the car door handle. I push the auto-
matic lock.

She laughs a little. "You're trying to trap me in here?"

"Do you know the details behind any of the deaths you con-
tributed to? Do you know the identities of all your victims?
How do you know that one of them wasn't someone like Natalie Duval—someone whose husband found out? How do you
know you haven't killed a decent human being just because
they said or did something that 0001 didn't like? I've been in
the collective for three weeks. You've been in it for three years.
What are the odds you haven't killed an innocent person?"

Wendy says nothing, and she won't look at me. I wish I
could see her face.

"I'm scared," she says.

"Me too."

"I swore my loyalty. On Tyler's memory."

"I swore mine on Emily's."

She pulls away from the window and levels her eyes at me, her voice low and angry. "Why did you look up Duval's name?"

"I don't know."

"Why do you have to keep asking so many questions?"

"Wendy," I say, "if I didn't ask questions, the truth would still be the truth."

She opens her mouth, then closes it again.

"I know it's hard. . . ."

"I have to think."

"Okay." There's nothing else I can say.

She puts her hand on the door handle again, and this time I release the lock.

"I strangled a woman to death."

She says it the way you might tell someone you're going out for groceries, and I don't say anything in response. I don't think she wants me to.

"It was about three in the morning. An empty parking lot at a strip mall, a lot like this one. She was in the front seat. I was in the back. She was older than I was. A lot smaller. I used a scarf that turned out to be her own. Stolen off her purse, I think, by another sister. Sent to a PO box down in Larchmont. Anyway . . . Turns out she owned a dry cleaner's in the strip mall, and she was found in there the next morning. I heard on the news that she hanged herself in her place of business, so, obviously, she got moved after I left."

Hanged herself. Just like Natalie Duval.

"It's the worst assignment I've ever done. The only thing that got me through it was thinking of Tyler. And how this woman must have killed someone's child, just like that animal killed him."

I put a hand on her shoulder. "I'm sorry, Wendy."

"Duval could have been an aberration. A onetime thing."

"Yes. It could have been. But it's still something that happened."

She pulls something out of the drugstore bag—a white box with bold red letters on it—and hands it to me. "It's a burner," she says. "I bought one for each of us, back when I thought that this was about Kimball and we might need a way to communicate."

I watch her open the car door. "What do I do with it now?"

"I don't know." She doesn't look at me when she says it. She just leaves my car, gets into her Camry, and drives away.

I open the box, flip on my dome light, and follow the instructions to activate the phone. I'm not sure why I do, why I don't just throw it out. A tiny speck of hope, I guess. After all, Wendy could have thrown the phone out too.

IT'S A BLEAK, starless night when I get home. I forgot to leave my outside light on when I left the house this morning and it's now so dark, I have to use the flashlight on my phone to get from the driveway to my front door.

The night smothers me. I walk stiffly, my shoulders nearly touching my ears, that feeling coursing through me, as though there are a million eyes in the trees around my house, shadowy hunched figures lurking in what's left of my garden, following my every move. It's paranoia, I know. I also know I'll be feeling this way for a while. Even if you don't suffer from anxiety issues, you don't have a day like I did and emerge from it unscathed.

I've just about reached my doorstep when something near me shrieks, something shrill and mechanical.

"Shit." I whirl around, shining my flashlight into the trees, around my car . . . until I realize that the sound is coming from my bag, and that it's the burner phone Wendy gave me. I catch my breath enough to answer it. "What's up?"

"If I were to decide to introduce you to my sister-in-law, Sheila, what would you be able to tell her?"

"What do you mean?"

"Well, we don't have any names other than our own. Outside of her giving me assignments, I've only had one conversation with Triple-Oh-One. I know nothing about her."

"Only one conversation? In three years?"

"Yeah. Is it different for you?"

I unlock my front door, push it open. I'm not sure how much to tell her. All this time I've wondered how 0001 could be available to all of us at any hour on a moment's notice, but now I'm wondering if it might just be me. And if that's true . . . why me?

I tell her, "I don't know much about her either."

"I can't just go to Sheila with nothing. You get that, right?"

"Of course."

"Good."

"Wendy?"

"Yeah?"

"Does this mean you're with me?"

"It means I'm thinking about it."

"Okay. Thanks." We end the conversation, and I go into my house, my shoulders relaxing. I flick on the lights, and settle into the warmth of the kitchen, the comfort of the burner phone in my hand. I'm glad I didn't throw it out. And I feel like, maybe, I'm a better judge of character than I thought.

0417: I got your message loud and clear.

It's 10:45 p.m. I've waited to private message her until I've eaten something, taken a hot shower, and changed into sweats, and yet still, like always, I see ellipses immediately.

0001: You could have put us in real danger.

I rest my hands on the keys, thinking of everything I'd like to say. But I have my own personal script now, and if I'm going to find out anything about 0001, I need to stick to it.

0417: I didn't put us in danger. I didn't tell her anything. I just wanted to express my condolences as the witness to her brother's death.

0001 is typing . . .

0417: I let my feelings get the best of me.

0001: That isn't an option. Not in war and not here.

0417: I shouldn't have done it.

0001: I need to know that you won't do anything like that again.

0417: I won't. I promise.

0001: You are on notice.

0417: What does that mean?

0001: What do you think it means?

I get the feeling she's about to leave the private chat. I type very quickly.

0417: Are you a mother?

0001: Of course I am.

0417: Tell me about the death of your child.

I wait a full minute after my message disappears. But there are no ellipses. No reply.

0417: My point is, you know so much about me. You know where I'm from and what I look like and who my daughter was and the first and last name of the person who killed her and made me into the monster that I am. You know that about every member of our collective, but we know nothing about you.

0001: I understand your loss, your pain, your rage.

0417: But I don't understand yours. I private messaged you the first and last name of my daughter's killer. Could you do the same for me?

Ellipses appear on the screen. But only briefly. What I wouldn't give to see what she typed, then erased.

0417: All I'm trying to say is that I can't see you.

0001: That's because your eyes are closed. OPEN THEM. When my children were killed, I changed like Niobe did. I walked through fire and it turned me to rock. That's all you need to know about me. I cannot be destroyed. Do not test me.

0001 has left the private chat.

I stand up, my eyes fixed on the screen as the private message thread disappears, my breathing shallow. "Well, that didn't go very well."

Thinking about it now, I'm not sure what I expected to get out of 0001. She barely told me anything about herself back when I had her trust. Why should I expect her to identify herself to me now that I don't?

I head into the bathroom, brush my teeth, take my nighttime meds, along with half a Xanax. I need to sleep. I need to escape, even if it's only for a few hours.

I exit the Kaya page, so many women still on it, repeating those phrases that just a few days ago I used to find exhilarating. ***Make him pay. . . . Cut out his heart. . . . Give that bitch a death as miserable as my baby's. . . .*** The comments used to feel like witches' spells; they were that magical and empowering. But now they read like groupthink, the chants of cult members, 0001 the charismatic, invisible leader. ***Your eyes are closed***, she had said to me. ***OPEN THEM.***

And now that I'm remembering, she also said something else. . . .

0001 said she changed like Niobe did when her children were killed. Not *child*. *Children. In the plural.*

Of course, she could have just been trying to throw me off.

But she could also be a woman who has lost two sons. . . . Someone like Violet Langford—a sweet librarian with three cats whose mind immediately went to surveillance cameras when I introduced myself to her at her workplace. A woman whose eyes lit up when she spoke of killing, and who explained the act of taking part in a murder with such contagious energy, she sold me almost instantly. A woman who had described herself as having "walked through fire"—exactly the way 0001 just did.

Your eyes are closed. OPEN THEM. . . .

I do. And as I do, it strikes me that when I drove to Haven-kill to talk to Violet, my car was chipped—same as it was when, motivated by a similar curiosity, I followed Edward Duval out of the train station. We're not supposed to see other members in person unless specifically instructed. Yet while 0001 had been all over the Duval incident, she never mentioned my visit to Violet's workplace.

OPEN THEM.

Other details are coming to me now—how both Violet and 0001 had referred to Ashley Shawger by his given first name of Richard, and how, of all the deaths I'd known of since join-ing the collective, none had been as baroque and intricate as Shawger's had been—a collar bomb strapped to his body, detonated in his own house. As though 0001 saved the most theatrical revenge for herself . . .

Something explodes outside my window, making me dive

for the floor and cover my head. It takes me time to register that it's only the roar of an engine, a car winding up my road too fast, gunning it. It passes my house, and I calm down a little bit, but still. Still. There are a couple of houses past mine toward the top of the mountain, but they're second homes—summer homes. Cars hardly ever drive by my house at this time of year, especially this late. It's nearly midnight.

I can't help but think it's intended for me, how the driver leaned into the accelerator like that, like the punctuation at the end of an angry note.

I'm so alone in this old house. So isolated. It would be so easy to make me disappear.

TWENTY

At eight in the morning I call Wendy on the burner phone. "Camille," she says in a hushed, nervous voice. "I'm at work."

"Okay. Well . . . can I talk to you? It won't take long."

"Wait a second," she says. "Just hang on."

The line goes staticky, then I hear muffled voices, as though she dropped her phone into her pocket. After a period of time where I can hear nothing but the sound of rustling clothes, she's back at last. "I was on my way into a meeting. What is it?"

"I think I might know who 0001 is."

"Wow. Really?"

"Well, I'm not positive by a long shot. But I do have a theory."

"I can't call Sheila on a theory."

"I know that," I tell her. "But I also think I have a way we can test the theory."

She doesn't say anything, but I can almost hear her measuring pros and cons in her head. "I don't want to get you in any more trouble," she says after a moment.

"You won't."

"And to be honest, I don't want to get in trouble either."

"This is totally safe."

"Are you sure?"

"As sure as I am of anything."

More silence from Wendy. I think I can make out traffic noises in the background. She must be talking to me from the parking lot. "What do I have to do?"

I exhale. "Okay, first of all, when do you get off work?"

"I have a client coming in at one. I can probably leave by one thirty. Is that early enough?"

"It depends," I tell her. "How far are you from Havenkill?"

I'VE GOT THE website for Havenkill Library up on my computer screen when Wendy calls on the burner phone. "I'm here," she says.

I check the clock at the bottom of my screen: 2:00 p.m. Earlier than we discussed. "I thought you said you were an hour away from Havenkill."

"I rescheduled with my client," she says. "Faked a stomachache. Since I wasn't really faking, it wasn't that hard."

"You ready?"

"Yep."

"Okay. I'll wait for your text."

She hangs up, and I take one last look at the home screen picture—Head Librarian Violet Langford reading to kinder-gartners from Havenkill Elementary just yesterday, at the weekly story hour. Violet sits in a throne-like chair, her eye-brows raised, coppery hair shining, her frosted coral lips mak-ing a delighted O as she reads to the rapt group of children, the pages opened for all to see. *Where the Wild Things Are.* The wild rumpus. The big creatures dancing. The monsters.

I close the page, then go to Kaya. I read the chat screen while I'm waiting—a new member telling her story, her shy fourteen-year-old daughter prodded into suicide by two popular girls who went on to become homecoming queen and student body president, who headed off to college, got married. . . . Like me, she says she's chosen her number after her daughter's birthday: 0203. Today.

The other women post their replies, about spiking the girls' skinny tea with rat poison, drowning them in acid, trapping them in their husbands' fancy cars and feeding them to trash compactors.

I wish that could happen, 0203 types. I want it so badly, it would be worth my own life.

I want it for her too. It's been years since she lost her daugh-ter. Those girls will never be punished. They've probably never even lost a night's sleep. For a brief moment I forget why I'm on the page, and all I want to do is to open a package, remove an unregistered gun and an address, and blow at least one of these bitches away. But first I'd force her to say on tape that she killed a young girl so I could make it into a GIF.

Do I really want to take that possibility away from 0203?

The burner phone vibrates in my lap. I check the small screen, and sure enough Wendy has texted me two asterisks— our code, meaning she's made contact with Violet Langford— and I do my best to put 0203 out of my mind and replace her with Olivia Weiss, the family she's lost.

I open up my private messages, and I write to 0001.

0417: I need to talk to you.

The line disappears, and I wait for ellipses, my gaze shifting back and forth between the private messages box and the time at the corner of my laptop. One minute passes, then two. Five minutes, and still no ellipses, not even a check mark, to indicate that 0001 has read my message.

Five more have passed when I get another text from Wendy—two ampersands, meaning she and Violet have finished their conversation. Around thirty seconds later I glance at the screen again and the skin prickles at the back of my neck.

0001 is typing . . .

"Hello, Violet," I whisper.

As soon as I finish my private chat with 0001—which consists of me asking her when I can be taken off probation or notice or however she'd phrased it, and her replying, **Whenever I feel like I can trust you again**—I call Wendy.

"It's her," I tell her.

"You're positive?"

"I can't be positive of anything anymore," I say. "But the two of them were not in the same place at the same time, so I'm sure enough to tell Sheila."

"Okay."

"What did you and Violet talk about?"

"I asked her why the library doesn't have any L. Ron Hubbard books."

"Seriously?"

"I figured that would make her not want to look me in the eye."

"Ah. Good thinking, actually."

"Not that she'd know my face," she says. "Tyler's story wasn't in the news the way Emily's was. But still. I have a lot of tells. And if she's really 0001 . . ."

"She's smart enough to catch on."

"Yeah." She clears her throat. "Anyway, I'll call you back after I talk to Sheila."

"Great." My eyes go back to the screen, to the dozens of women replying to 0203, crafting elaborate deaths for her enemies, weaving their spells to make her feel whole again. . . .

Wendy says, "I'm just going to do what you said—tell Sheila

I met you through *The Bachelor* Reddit, and that you've been talking about this group, and you think this librarian . . . Do you really think that sweet old lady is running the whole operation?"

"There's nothing cleverer or more terrifying than a sweet old lady. Ask Hansel and Gretel."

"Camille?"

"Yeah?"

"Are you sure you want me to do this?"

My gaze rests on the screen, on 0203's latest comment: You are all giving me hope. You feel like sisters.

"You have a say in this too. . . ."

"I know," she says. "I'm going to talk to Sheila. It's the right thing to do."

"Good." I say it another time, more to convince myself than anything else: "Good."

Wendy and I work out a new code for texting. After we hang up, I close the page and my laptop before I can read any more.

AN HOUR PASSES with no text from Wendy, and it dawns on me that while she did say she'd call after talking to Sheila, we never discussed when that would be. Pretty dumb to be sitting at home waiting for a call that could easily take hours, if not days.

I decide to go grocery shopping while it's still light out, and spend close to an hour and a half at the Mount Shady A&P, walking up and down the aisles, loading up my cart with cleaning supplies and garbage bags, paper towels I find on sale, a stack of frozen meals, a loaf of bread. I listen to the soft rock music playing over the speaker system, singing along with that song about those stupid sailors who won't marry poor Brandy because they love the ocean more—as if a barmaid and a body of water were mutually exclusive. I'm not sure that I've ever found an activity so soothing for its familiarity, the bright lights and normalcy of this place, the lack of strange people staring or stalking. I'd like to stay in the grocery store forever.

The checkout line is pretty long, and it isn't until I get outside and the voicemail tone dings on my cell phone that I remember that our local A&P, for some strange reason, is a dead zone. I check my voicemail—just one call from Luke, telling me that he and Nora can't wait to come visit me in two days, something I seem to have forgotten about. *"We have so many things to tell you,"* he says on the message, and I think, *That's interesting, because I have so many things not to tell you.* Will my life be back to normal by the time Luke and Nora get here? Or will I still be waiting for Wendy to call? I never activated voicemail on the burner, but I do check the texts—nothing from Wendy since the two ampersands this afternoon. It's five p.m. and the sky's a darkening lavender—the last gasp of sunset, twilight starting to bloom.

I wonder if Wendy plans on speaking to her sister-in-law tonight, or if she's saving it for tomorrow. To tell the truth, I'm kind of hoping for the latter. As selfish as it sounds, I could really use one boring night.

THE SKY DARKENS quickly—a matter of minutes, it seems, and twilight has already slipped into night. I'm nearly done unloading my cart when I hear my name called out, and as soon as I look up, Glynne Barrett is slamming her trunk shut and heading toward me, a colorful scarf tied around her hair, a red wool cape flaring all around her. I can't think of anything more on-brand for Glynne Barrett than wearing a cape to shop for groceries. "Camille!" She smiles. "I was just talking about you."

"You were?"

"Yes, with Xenia Hedges," she says. I suppose it's also on-brand for her to call her ex-wife by her first and last name. "She's thrilled with your designs, really."

I smile back at her. "I'm glad," I say. "I like Xenia. Thank you for recommending me." Then I wait.

"I also wanted to tell you, Camille . . ."

Here we go . . .

"I'm sure you've heard the news."

"About Harris Blanchard."

"Yes." She puts a purple leather-gloved hand on my shoulder. "You must feel vindicated."

"I haven't been paying that much attention to the news, Glynne." I take a step back. Her hand falls away. "And I've never had any need to feel vindicated. I've always known what he was and that's enough." It's a lie. But it still feels good to watch her face flush as I say it.

"I'm so sorry about the way I was after the Brayburn Club.

It's obvious you were in great pain, and I was . . . Well, *insensitive* is probably too kind a word."

"That's okay," I tell her, and it isn't a lie this time. So much has happened in these past few weeks, what happened at the Brayburn Club feels like decades ago, when I was a different person, when I had never killed anyone intentionally and I truly was in great pain every day of my life. How things have changed since then, and for better or worse, I have the collective to thank. "Really."

As I load my last bag into my trunk, I spot a car two spaces away, its dome light on, someone behind the wheel. The dome light switches off, then on, then off again, and I hear another car pulling away behind me. I whirl around as a small black car—is it a Prius?—screeches out of the parking lot, and when I turn my attention back to the dome light car, its headlights switch on.

"Are you all right?" Glynne says.

"Yeah . . . I'm . . . just"—*surrounded*—"a little tired, I guess." Something vibrates against my side. The burner phone in my purse. A text message from Wendy.

The dome light car is moving now. It's a Subaru like mine, only silver rather than black and a much newer model. And as it passes us on its way out, I catch a glimpse of shiny hair, a smile, and then a hand waving, a jeweled ring catching the light.

"Bye!" Glynne calls out to the driver, and then the car passes under one of the parking lot lamps and I see her face in full.

"Who is that?" My gaze is glued to the bumper. The license plate. *Who are you?*

"Old classmate of mine from Brayburn," Glynne says. "I ran into her on my way in. She hasn't changed a bit."

"What's her name?"

"Do you know her?"

"I might."

And even though that's a rather strange response, Glynne answers amiably. "Penelope Chambers," she says.

I nod. "Sounds familiar." But really, it's the face that I know—the silver-haired woman who gave me the Niobe card. I'm this close to saying out loud that I ran into her at Harris's funeral and she warned me to leave and that now I'm quite certain she's been part of a coordinated effort to stalk my every move.

But what if Glynne, too, is part of that effort? How big is the collective? How much do they know?

"So strange to see Penelope here of all places," Glynne says mildly. "She was always such a city girl."

I wait until Glynne leaves and I'm alone in my car to read my burner phone text from Wendy—three asterisks, meaning call her back as soon as I can. I want to do it right away, but instead I wait until I'm home and in the kitchen, the groceries unloaded.

Wendy says, "What took you so long?"

"I'm being followed."

"Are you serious?"

"There were two cars watching me at the grocery store tonight—I even recognized one of the drivers."

"Oh my God."

"Not from an assignment. I didn't even think she was with the collective, actually. I thought she was just from Niobe."

"From where?" she says. "Forget it. It doesn't matter. Look. I think Sheila's going to need to meet you in person. She's skeptical about the story, as pretty much anybody would be. Is there a safe place?"

I remember the roar of the engine outside my house the previous night, how it seemed to come out of nowhere. "I think my car is chipped again."

"Ugh. Look. You stay put. I'm going to log on, private message 0001, see if I can get Violet to talk to me in front of Sheila."

"What? No."

"Why not? I'm obviously good at talking to people. Hell, look how much info I got out of you."

"You said you didn't want to get involved, Wendy. And you were right. It's not safe."

"Maybe I changed my mind," she says. "Maybe I don't care about what's safe or what isn't. My kid is dead. My marriage is over. And I've given three years of my life to something that wasn't what I thought it was. Oh, and Alayah's off the damn show again tonight. Did you see the spoiler on Reddit? What do I have to live for besides you?"

"Wendy."

"Okay, before you think I'm nuts, I was just kidding about Alayah, even though Peter really is going to kick her off again. And I wasn't planning on saying 'besides you' out loud."

I close my eyes, tilt my head back, and breathe, the burner phone pressed to my ear. Such a strange conversation to be having over any phone, especially a burner phone. Such a strange, important friendship. I remember her standing behind Kimball's car on the boat launch, her hand on the trunk I never should have opened. *It's over and done. It doesn't matter. Join me. Sister.* "Thank you, Wendy."

"I'd say you owe me one, but you don't, really," she says. "If everything goes okay, I'll call you tomorrow morning and we can all figure out a place to meet. Does eight o'clock work?"

"Sure, but . . ."

"Yeah?"

"What if everything doesn't go okay?"

She laughs a little. It sounds forced. "Then I guess we won't ever find out who gets Pete's final rose."

TWENTY-ONE

Unicorn River is no longer frozen. As cold as it's been, the stream still somehow melted, and as I try to dig up the gun I once tried to kill myself with, I can't hear anything above the din of rushing water. It drowns out all other sounds, which is a good thing because the ground is still frozen solid, and I am grunting and groaning from the effort it takes to make the tiniest of dents with my gardening spade. At this rate, it's going to take me all night before I even get close.

Give it all you've got, says a voice inside me. And so I do, raising the spade far above my head like a dagger, and plunging it into the ground with a shriek. It breaks. The ground breaks. From the spot where the spade pierced the earth, a red geyser erupts, drenching my hair, my eyes, my mouth.

It's blood, says the same voice.

But it isn't coming from inside my head; it belongs to Glynne Barrett. *"It's our blood."* The gardening spade turns into a beating heart. The river crests and tidal waves crash over my head, and I'm drowning, I'm drowning. . . .

I wake up in a sweat, my throat raw from screaming. I manage to catch my breath, but it takes me a while. I'm not going to fall asleep again without a Xanax, and I'm pretty sure it's too late in the morning for that.

I'm right. While it's dark outside, the clock on my phone reads 6:15 a.m.—a reasonable time to wake up, especially since Wendy is supposed to call in less than two hours.

What a dream that was—the kind that refuses to leave my head, even as I brush my teeth and take my morning pills and try to get myself ready for the day ahead of me.

What could it mean? If Joan were alive, she'd probably tell me the blood symbolizes my feelings of guilt, overflowing, unable to be stanched. The heart, of course, would be Emily's, beating inside the chest of Luke, who is supposedly driving up here tomorrow with Nora.

As for Glynne, she was probably in my head because she emailed me last night, telling me how "lovely" it had been to run in to me at the A&P—not to mention dear Penelope Chambers, her old college friend from the class of '74. *Perhaps the three of us can get together sometime*, Glynne wrote. *I know you'd like her.*

I didn't write her back. I probably never will.

I remember Penelope's face now, those piercing blue eyes as we left the cemetery after Harris Blanchard's funeral, the bizarre, knowing tone with which she'd said my name. I think of her in the A&P parking lot, her dome light flashing on and off. Has she been spying on me for 0001? Has Glynne? Are they both members of the collective, assigned to frighten me . . . or worse?

I could be jumping to conclusions. After all, Glynne is a local celebrity who has given a lot of open, revealing interviews— most of which I've linked to on her site—and if she'd ever been a mother, I'd have read about it in at least one of them. Plus, what self-respecting collective member would side with Dean Waverly over me? But then again . . . then again.

We're everywhere, Camille.

I brew a pot of coffee and eat some bread. By the time I'm done, it's after seven and I'm still worrying about Glynne. *If she is a collective member. If she's spying on me. If she hired me as part of an ongoing assignment . . .*

I head upstairs to my room and open up my laptop, go to Facebook, the Niobe group. I find Penelope Chambers on it, of course, though her page is private, and I can't see anything other than a profile pic of Penelope and three friends standing in front of the Las Vegas sign.

Glynne is not a Niobe member, but her personal page is accessible to me. We friended each other back when she hired me to do her website, and she encouraged me to look through her page and pull whatever photos I think would work.

I go to her page now. All the most recent posts are either paintings or pictures of Glynne posing in front of them. But once I scroll back a few months, I find more personal ones:

Glynne splashing around in a swimming hole back in August
with two male friends and a Jack Russell terrier. Glynne wish-
ing her deceased parents a happy anniversary by posting their
black-and-white wedding photo. A six-year-old "Facebook
Memory," reposted by Glynne last June for whatever reason,
of her and Xenia on their tenth anniversary. I skim through all
of them.

But when I hit her May 2019 posts, I slow down. In May,
Brayburn's class of 2019 graduated, and Glynne was there for it,
in a crimson-and-gold gown and mortarboard, next to her dear
friend Dean Waverly. Apparently, she was one of the speakers,
too, because she posted a picture of herself at a lectern, not to
mention several more with her former classmates, who were
celebrating their forty-fifth reunion that same sunny weekend.
I look at each picture carefully, taking in Glynne's body lan-
guage, the hugs and swoons, reading her gushy, emotive cap-
tions . . . until I find the one that makes me stop breathing.

The thing with the truth, it hides in plain sight. It crouches
in corners and pounces—but you have to look at it first. You
have to stop and face it head-on and then it will leap at you and
if you are not ready, you will fall. . . .

In Glynne's reunion pictures, there are then-and-now cast
shots of a play on which Glynne had served as the set designer.
I look at the "now" shot first—everyone smiling in front of
the Brayburn theater, Glynne included. And then the earlier
one, a black-and-white, taken in 1973 of just the cast, onstage
in flowing costumes and lined up for curtain call—the writer

and star at the center. *A life-changing experience!!!* Glynne has captioned it. *A devastating—and shocking—play about female empowerment by an actress/writer who embodies those two words!!!*

The writer and star is Penelope Chambers. The play is called *Ağlayan Kaya*.

CALM DOWN, I tell myself. *Calm, calm . . .*

The name of the play could be a coincidence. Life is full of coincidences. I need more. I need to know Penelope Chambers better, and so I go back to Niobe and type her name into the search bar. I read everything I can find that she's posted on the page, searching for clues as to who she is.

I don't find much. Penelope is not what you'd call an active poster. I scroll back weeks, months, a whole year, and find nothing but a few scattered supportive-but-generic comments to new members—odd for someone who actively sought me out, waiting outside a police station after midnight, just to make that connection. You'd think Penelope would be a hardcore Niobe zealot, but it appears she's more of an occasional visitor, which would make sense if she were spending all her screen time on Kaya.

At last I find what looks to be Penelope Chambers's only original post, dated April 10, 2016. My loss happened twenty years ago, but the pain is still fresh, it reads. And it details an accident I remember hearing about on the news—a summer camp bus that collided with a car on the New York Thruway and overturned, killing the bus driver and most of the campers, who ranged in age from seven to fourteen. The driver of the car, on a rubbery high from alcohol and pain pills, survived the crash. According to Penelope, he served just five years in jail—far too small a price to pay for her twin boys, who were ten at the time. Now they're gone and that driver is free somewhere, living his life. He claims the experience was an eye-opener for him. Made him give up drinking and find Jesus or some such nonsense. I don't care what my children's death taught him. I'll never forgive him.

In the responses, other members assure her that they would never judge her for having feelings, that she's justified in her anger, and if she wants to talk, this page is full of understanding people who are always available to listen. I only skim over them, because I don't care what they have to say. I've already found what I wanted to, and it's those two words: *my children*. Like 0001 and Violet, Penelope has lost more than one child to a killer who didn't pay. And when she finally responds to all of the commenters, it makes my spine straighten up.

Penelope Chambers: I DON'T WANT TO SHARE FEELINGS ABOUT HIM. I WANT HIM TO FUCKING DIE.

2016. Four years ago. Penelope's comment is the last in the thread, everyone else clearly too spooked to reply. I read it again, those capital letters, and feel a lump in my throat. It's like watching someone turn to stone, a mountain. I read it, and

I'm watching Ağlayan Kaya come to life—Penelope's play of "female empowerment," reborn on the dark web.

At some point, I know, I'll find the name of the drunk driver. And when I google it, I'll see a story about his untimely death—an accident with a gun or in a car, a heart medication overdose or a suicide by hanging, or something different, more creative. I know this. But for now, I have all the information I need on Penelope Chambers. I know who she is. And I need to get in touch with Wendy and tell her immediately.

I TEXT WENDY two percent signs—code for "emergency." But I don't hear from her. I check the time. It's close to eight a.m., the time she's supposed to call me anyway, to arrange a meeting place with Sheila. That's just about ten minutes from now. I try not to watch the clock.

But eight a.m. comes and goes, and the burner doesn't ring. She doesn't send a text, either. She probably just got held up somewhere, I figure. But then it's 8:30, 8:45. I text her two more percent signs and wait five minutes. Ten. Fifteen minutes.

"Okay," I tell myself. "It will be okay." But soon a million horrible scenarios flood my mind, the anxiety overriding the medication I've taken, and I'm drowning in a tidal wave, a geyser of blood. . . .

I stare at the burner phone, my heart racing, hands trembling. *Come on, phone. Ring.*

Eight more minutes pass. Nine. "Fuck it." I grab the phone

and call Wendy's burner number. But there's no answer—just a mechanical sound where the voicemail announcement should be, like an angel's harp. Then we're disconnected. Neither of these phones has voicemail.

"Wendy, Wendy . . ." I say her name like an incantation. "Please call me. Please . . ."

I remember the search I did on her back at Analog, and I do it again, my fingers shaking so horribly, it's hard to hit the keys. *Easy, easy* . . . I find her home phone number and address right away and call the number, my eyes on the burner the whole time, that silent, dead burner.

It rings once, twice, three times before the voicemail picks up—a husky young voice that makes my heart drop. *"Hi, this is Tyler. We're not here right now, but if you wanna leave a message . . . you know what to do!"*

I sit on the line, debating whether or not to say anything, before finally, I do, my eyes shut tight, tears seeping out the corners, trying to keep my voice calm. "Hi, Wendy, this is Camille. Too bad about Alayah and Pilot Pete, right? Anyway, I think I may have left something in your car when I . . . um . . . when I gave you a ride home last week. Can you call me, please? Thanks."

Five minutes pass, then ten. And then I can't wait any longer. I copy Wendy's Jefferville address onto a pad of paper, then throw on a pair of jeans, a clean sweatshirt, and my heavy coat and boots and run out to my car, burner phone in hand, cell phone in my bag. *Oh crap. It's probably chipped. . . .*

I open all the doors to search for the new chip. My plan is, if I don't find it right away, I'll hike to the bottom of the mountain and call an Uber from there. Ubers are very slow to show up in my town—half an hour at a minimum—but at least it beats getting followed.

After about ten minutes of searching the front of the car, I move to the rear. No luck. I slide under the chassis with my phone flashlight on, and find it at the center. It occurs to me that it might not be a new chip, that it could have been there all along—a backup for the more obvious one in the rear wheel well. And if that's true, there could be still more tracking chips on my car. But I don't want to think too hard about that. According to my phone, it's an hour and twenty minutes to Jefferville. I don't have enough time to think too hard about anything.

JEFFERVILLE IS ACROSS the river from where I live and close to fifty miles north. I make it there in just an hour and without getting pulled over, which is a small miracle, considering all the winding roads with twenty-something speed limits there are on the route.

In a way it's good, having to focus on driving as closely as I do. I need to be alert, and so my mind can't wander, and I'm unable to let this bubbling terror swell big enough to overtake me. As I hit the straightaway that leads into town, though, I glance at the clock and see that it's eleven already—three hours after Wendy said she'd call, and I haven't heard a word from her. Not even a texted ampersand.

I turn the radio on, then off, longing for a relaxation tape, an extra bottle of pills, those Belgian cigarettes I used to smoke in college, Corps Diplomatique, they were called, in their classy white package with the gold embossed print. How it used to soothe me, packing the box against the palm of my hand and taking a drag . . .

I see a sign that reads WELCOME TO JEFFERVILLE, and my heart smashes into my ribs, a small part of me wanting to turn around and drive home. I'm getting the worst type of déjà vu—that same swirling dread I felt while waiting up for Emily the night of her death, that tiny crystalline part of my brain working overtime, the part that knows everything. . . .

She's gone.

You beg and you plead and you bargain. *Please let her live. I'll be a better person, I promise.* . . . And that's what I feel myself doing now. *I'll give to charity. I'll never think bad thoughts. I'll move far away from here and devote myself to prayer; I will never want revenge on anyone, ever, if you let Wendy live.*

Downtown Jefferville consists of one street. I pass a CVS and a mom-and-pop hardware store, a diner-type place called the Kit-n-Caboodle, the post office, and the town hall, overlooking a village green with a flag waving in the wind and two teenage girls huddling on a stone bench, smoking a joint. I pass the junior high, which looks too big and industrial for this little town, and the high school, which is even bigger, electric scoreboards towering over a serious-looking football field, a red-and-white sign touting the Jefferville Wolverines. After the high school is an office complex with a big parking lot. I imagine that's where Wendy's accounting firm is, and I'm remembering her talking to me from there just yesterday, her hushed tones in the parking lot as I told her about Violet, and we went over our plan. Before hanging up, Wendy had said, "I guess nobody's perfect."

And I'd replied, "What do you mean?"

"Triple-Oh-One made a big mistake, introducing you and me."

My phone's GPS interrupts my thoughts, telling me to take a right on Dove Street, which I do. It's a wide street, lined with tidy ranch houses that look as though they were all dropped there at the same time, probably at the turn of the century. Wendy's house is a pale pink, with neatly trimmed azalea bushes lining the front entrance.

I park my car on the street, and as I make my way to the front door, I notice that there's only one car parked in the driveway—a red Honda Civic. Wendy's silver Camry is no-where in sight, and she never mentioned a Honda Civic. Just the Camry and the Mercedes she tinkers with and never takes out . . . *Don't jump to conclusions*, I tell myself, though I'm afraid to even think about what conclusions I'm jumping to. I press the doorbell—a screeching buzz that makes me jump back. I'd expected something more melodic.

I hear a deep voice say, "Just a minute," and then the door opens and a tall black man with horn-rimmed glasses, chinos, and a yellow polo shirt stands there, eying me warily. "Carl Osterberg?" I say, because he does look like an accountant.

"Yes?"

"I'm sorry. I guess . . . I didn't expect you to be here."

"Who are you?"

"My name is Camille," I tell him. "I'm . . . um . . . a friend of Wendy's. From her *Bachelor* Reddit?"

"Wait. You're the one who called?"

"Yes." I let out some breath. "Is Wendy around? I think I might have left something—"

"What's your deal?"

"Excuse me?"

"Why would you make a call like that? Why would you say you left something in her car?"

"Because I did."

He stares at me for a long time. And then finally he speaks. "Wendy's dead."

"*What* . . . no." My knees buckle. He catches me gently by the arm, and I feel woozy, my head light. "No, that couldn't . . . It couldn't have happened. Please." Tears spill down my cheeks. "Please tell me this is a joke, or . . . or a mistake or . . ."

"It's not."

"I don't believe you. You're just trying to get rid of me. If she died, then where are the police? Where are the other cars? Why are you alone? *How can you be so calm?*"

He opens the door slightly, and I can see into his house—a neat, well-lit living room, a row of pictures on a fireplace mantel, family pictures. Vacation and school photos, all combinations of the same three people. And as he speaks, my gaze rests on the big one at the center: Carl in a suit, a curly-haired black woman in a wedding dress posing next to him. "I'm alone because my wife, Wendy, died six months ago," he says. "And she never watched *The Bachelor.*"

TWENTY-TWO

Wendy Osterberg—the *real* Wendy Osterberg—died of an apparent suicide. According to her husband, Carl, from whom she was briefly separated but never actually divorced, it was sadly in character for Wendy to jump from the Kingston-Rhinecliff Bridge at three thirty in the morning. "She never was the same since our son died," he explained. "But in those last few months, she really went off the deep end. One night, she had a lot to drink and started rambling about some plot to kill this kid we used to know years ago—a classmate of our son's who was mean to him. Crazy, paranoid stuff. She was going to find the kid and warn him about the plot because two wrongs don't make a right and it's the worst sin to kill a child, even an evil one. . . . I couldn't get her to calm down. Next day, she was fine, said she didn't even remember saying any of it. . . ."

As he spoke, I remembered the woman I knew as Wendy, the spark of joy in her eyes as she told me what happened to the boy who had raped Tyler. *He flung himself off a bridge six months ago. Imagine that.*

"Imagine that," I whisper.

I'm back in Mount Shady now, driving through the center of town, past Analog and the community center, past Brilliance Jewelry Store, where Matt used to buy most of my birthday presents, and the ice cream shop, Sprinkles, where we held Emily's sixth-birthday party. It all looks fake to me—like an old-fashioned movie set, a plywood false front I could have pushed over years ago.

I reach Mountain, the street that leads up to my home, and as I turn on it, I think about how many different turns I could have made in life—staying in New York rather than moving here, especially. Mount Shady is a lovely town, but it's also homogenous and boring, and boredom dulls your ability to make the right decisions. Boredom creeps up on you slowly, wraps its tendrils around you and tugs at you in such a subtle yet constant way, you'll do anything to escape it. You'll behave recklessly and stupidly. You'll trust the wrong people, with disastrous results. Emily would still be alive if we'd stayed in New York. Matt and I would still be married—or at the very least, divorced for far less tragic reasons. I wouldn't even know what the dark web is, let alone Ağlayan Kaya. And I wouldn't be pulling into my driveway, grabbing my biggest spade out of the garden shed, roaring a mile up a mountain road, and parking at a trailhead on a freezing early February afternoon—all to dig up a gun I once tried to kill myself with, so I can protect myself from a group of murderers who have been stalking me for days.

And here, Matt and I moved to the country because we thought it would be safe.

I get out of my car quickly, running down the trail as fast as I can with the heavy spade in my hands, breathing hard, sweat pouring down my back, the cold air making my chest ache. Unicorn River is less than a mile in—a sweet, lazy hike for six-year-old Emily and me. But an exhausting obstacle course when I'm panicked and alone. By the time I get there, I'm feeling the cold and the strain of the run in my muscles, the stitch in my side a relentless, stabbing pain. I kneel next to the frozen stream and brace myself against the cold ground, breathing hard to ease the feeling, deep inhales and exhales, condensation billowing out of my mouth like smoke from a Belgian cigarette.

I bring the spade up, then plunge the sharp end of it into the icy earth. It barely makes a dent, and so I do it again and again, and it's as though I'm back in that dream—that same doomed, awful feeling, the ground just about to bleed.

Once I finally make a dent, I settle into the rhythm of digging, growing warmer with the effort, the exercise calming me down.

At some point, I find myself thinking of Carl Osterberg again, how insane I must have seemed to him, insisting that his wife was alive. Yet still he let me into his house and gave me a glass of water and patiently explained the facts until

I understood. He listened to the series of half-truths I told him, about this strange woman I'd met on a *Bachelor* Reddit who had stolen his wife's name and life story and used it as her own. "She was probably someone who knew Wendy," he had told me. "I think she was talking to some strange people online."

If you only knew, I'd wanted to say. But I kept my mouth shut because I didn't want him to become another Edward Duval. I did tell him, though, that I lost a child five years ago, and that, for a long time, I thought about ending my life every day.

"What stopped you?" Carl had said.

I think it was the first time anyone had ever asked me that question, and I tried to answer him as honestly as I could. *Therapy,* I had said. *Pills.* And then I'd thought of Luke— how, after my arrest, he'd not only picked me up at the police station no questions asked but had the couch all made up for me and how, from the moment I called him from the station—as late as I did—I'd never doubted for a second he'd do either of those things. Because I would have done the same for him. Early on in his relationship with Nora, they got into a big fight over something stupid and she ran off to a friend's place in rural Pennsylvania. Luke didn't know how to drive at the time, and so I hopped in my car, picked him up in Brooklyn, then chauffeured him another three and a half hours to the friend's house—all so that this sweet, theatrical soul could beg his girlfriend to take him back by re-creating the boom box scene from *Say Anything*. It worked. Plus, it was one of the best road trips I've ever taken. A year later I taught him how to drive, and believe it or not, that had been fun too.

"The love of a good friend," I had told Carl. "That's what's helped me most."

The tip of the shovel clinks into something metal. I put it aside and crouch down to lift it out of the hole, the dirty garbage bag, and inside, the shotgun, all the memories it comes with . . . I check the chamber to see if it's still loaded, and it is. *Protect me.*

I didn't really know how to shoot a gun when I bought this one, but I watched a YouTube tutorial and it seemed easy enough. It was. I pump the action, release the safety, aim it at a tree, and pull the trigger, the force nearly knocking me off my feet.

It is.

If those bitches come after me—and I know they will, soon—I'm going to defend myself.

Hopefully. I shoot again. I feel steadier now, but strange, as though I've lived this moment before and it isn't good . . .

I'm so deep into these thoughts that I don't hear footsteps. I don't feel her gaze on me. I feel alone. Until I'm not.

"Psst."

I look up and see the black coat, the glint of silver hair. Her hands in her coat pockets.

My stomach drops. "Penelope." I don't bother asking where she came from or why she's here. I aim the gun at her.

"I wouldn't do that," she says.

My throat clenches. I think of Wendy Osterberg, the real one, sailing off the Kingston-Rhinebeck Bridge. I pump the action again.

But then "Barracuda" erupts out of the phone in my back pocket.

I ignore it. "The collective isn't what I thought it was," I tell her slowly, the song playing under me, like something out of a cheap movie. "I want out."

Penelope's shoulders are relaxed. There's a half smile on her face. She looks remarkably unfrightened. My finger tightens against the trigger. "I said I want out."

"I'd really answer that phone if I were you."

My breath catches.

"Really."

With my free hand, I slip my phone out of my back pocket. I hold it to my ear. "Luke?" Penelope's smile widens.

"Cam. Thank God. Are you okay?"

The gun weighs against my shaking arm, my stare glued to Penelope. "Sure I am. Why?"

"You told me to come up." He sounds tense, his voice shaky like I've never heard before, and I'm worried about him. About his heart. It makes it hard to focus on what's happening right now, and I don't know what's happening, I don't. . . . "You . . . you said it was an emergency."

"Take a breath, Luke. Please."

Penelope starts to laugh, and I want to pull the trigger.

"Your email. You told me to come right up. Were you high? You said it was life-and-death."

My own heart is racing now. *They hacked my email.* "Where are you?"

"In your house. I drove up as soon as I could."

"How did you—"

"Your friend from *The Bachelor* Reddit let me in."

"*What?*"

"Wendy. You want to talk to her? She's right here. She's been trying to calm me down, but she was scared too."

I open my mouth, but my voice is gone.

Luke says, "Are you there?"

I force myself to speak, to sound calm. "Sure, I'll talk to Wendy."

Penelope nods at me. "Good move," she says quietly.

A voice pours into my ear, full of saccharine concern, that sick fuck. That fake Wendy Osterberg. "Are you okay, honey? I was so worried when I got your email. Thank God, you're all right."

"Don't hurt him. Please don't—"

"Yeah, Camille. Don't worry. We're right here waiting for you, and we care about you. Luke, honey. You okay? Hope you don't mind, Camille. I gave him some of the orange juice in your refrigerator. His sugar drops when he gets panicky, but you already knew that about him, right?"

I can't speak. I stare at Penelope. The pistol now clutched in her hand. I don't drink orange juice. I don't ever buy it.

"Hurry back, okay?" says the voice in my ear. "See you soon. Drive safely, please."

She ends the call.

"Drop the gun," Penelope says. "Or we will kill your friend."

I do. She follows me out of Unicorn River and we hike back out together, her gun at my back.

THEY PUT MULTIPLE *chips on my car.* That's the one, pointless thought that runs through my mind throughout the short drive home, and again as Penelope opens the door to my car and marches me into my house, the barrel of the gun now pressed between my shoulder blades. I suppose it's because it's easier than thinking of anything else. *I wonder how many chips. And how much each of them cost.*

Once we're in the kitchen, Penelope shuts the door and locks it. "She's here!" she calls out.

And then I hear another voice, Wendy's voice, in the living room. "About time," she says. She is on the couch next to Luke, who sits motionless, his head lolling against his chest.

"No . . ." I whisper.

She rolls her eyes. "He's alive," she says. "I only gave him enough orange juice to knock him out for a bit."

Penelope laughs.

I stare at Wendy. She's wearing baggy jeans. A sweater with candy canes all over it. Her eyes are granite behind her clear-framed glasses. "You're Triple-Oh-One."

"Yes," she says. "But Penelope's a close second. When we

were on the Kimball thing, for instance, she was the one texting the burner."

"I thought you were my friend."

"I'm not."

"Then why . . ."

"I wanted to see what you are capable of, Camille," she says quietly. "I certainly found out."

My eyes go to Luke, his breathing hard. Raspy. "He . . . he has a heart condition. The drug you gave him."

"He's fine. I'm a doctor."

She stands up, and I see it glimmering in her hand. A long hunting knife.

"Don't hurt him," I tell her. "Please. I don't want—"

"You don't want your daughter's heart to stop again? Is that what you were going to say?"

"No, I—"

"What do you think it meant, Camille, when you swore on Emily's memory?"

"I don't understand."

"Did you think it was some pinkie swear? A sorority oath? Well, it wasn't. I hate that shit. I like things that are tangible. Real. And Luke's heart—which you told me all about during the night we weren't supposed to be talking—well, that's about as close to Emily's memory as you're going to get."

"I'm . . . I'm sorry. Please don't hurt him. I won't ever go against the collective again. I swear."

"I don't believe you. But you know what? If I did, it wouldn't matter."

Penelope laughs again. "She doesn't get it," she says. "It's so strange. She has no idea."

Wendy looks at her. "I told you."

Sweat pours down the back of my neck. It's hard to breathe. "What are you talking about?"

Wendy sighs. "You murdered my daughter, Camille," she says. "You've been a target from day one."

My mouth goes dry. "What? I don't know what you're talking about."

"Joan Lowell. Your therapist. She was my only living child."

I'm frozen, unable to speak, my thoughts racing back to that night at Camp Acacia. Wendy's face in the moonlight. The first and only time I noticed the resemblance.

"I saw that tape of you at the Brayburn Club," she says, "that grief and rage, so similar to my own. The original plan had been to kill you, but in spite of all that, I had lost a daughter too. I knew your pain. I thought, *Maybe, at the very least, I can help her first.*"

My legs feel wobbly, my head light. I understand. I don't want to, but I do.

"But you didn't even appreciate my help. You didn't get to feel the joy of Harris Blanchard's death because, in spite of everything, you are still too self-absorbed to feel."

"I . . . I didn't mean to . . ."

"All that time with me when you thought I was Wendy. All those hours of spilling your guts out about Matt and Emily and Luke and your boring job. You told me about your fucking *Playboy* spread and yet not once, in that entire evening, did you ever mention my daughter."

"I . . . I loved her."

"Bullshit. You *needed* her. You called her at two in the morning and made her fall down the stairs and you were never punished," says the woman, whose real name, I recall now, is Dianne. *Friendless, joyless Dianne*, Joan said. *Ruined forever by the death of her child.* . . . "You weren't even questioned by the police," Dianne says.

I stare at her, those wide-set eyes. Same as her daughter. "I'm so, so sorry."

"They're always sorry," Penelope says. "When they know they're about to go and they're begging you to let them live, they say they're sorry and they expect you to believe it.

"It's insulting, really." Penelope looks at me. "I mean, did you ever even attempt to apologize to Dianne?"

"No." I've spent years feeling sorry for myself, drowning in guilt and self-pity and using it as a weapon against the one person who truly helped me. I caused her death—I've always known I did—and I never sought out her grieving mother. Never sent a note or flowers. Never owned up to destroying her life. I hid from her because it was easier to focus on the part of myself I have no control over—the victim part.

"I just wanted to talk to her," I try. But that isn't true. I wanted to rip her from sleep. I wanted to hurt her, the way she hurt me. . . .

You've got to stop calling me, Camille. It's not good for you. It's not good for me. You've gotten into my head, and I'm living with your hate, and your guilt and your rage and your bitterness, and it's making me drink too much and lose sleep and you're not getting any better. I can't help you. No one will ever be able to help you, Camille. . . .

Her last words to me. Her last words to anyone.

Dianne says, "I'm going to give you one more chance to do something right."

Gently, she lifts Luke's head from his chest and rests it on the couch, his face pointed toward the ceiling. "This was actually Penelope's idea, so I'll let her explain."

"It's pretty simple," she says. "You get to make a choice. Either we kill this young man, stopping your daughter's heart. Or we kill you. If he dies, we'll dispose of the body and wipe the emails from his server. You can go on with your life, free of the collective—as long as you never speak of it."

"And if I die?"

"He lives."

As Penelope speaks, Dianne stands above Luke and raises the knife over her head, the blade a few feet above his heart, my daughter's heart. My best friend's heart. "Basically," Dianne says, "you can either live or save your daughter." And then she lowers the knife.

It happens in a series of frames, the knife traveling through space, the glimmering blade nearing its target as I stand watching, unable to move. I'm aware of Penelope taking the gun from my back, of memories churning in my mind. Laughing with Luke at Applebee's, watching the Academy Awards with him and Nora, getting drunk with him one night when he lost a part, telling him, *You're too good for them.*

You're too good.

"Stop!"

Dianne puts down the knife, and I feel the barrel of the gun at my back again. There's nothing I can do. But maybe that's what's supposed to happen. Maybe there's nothing I *should* do.

No one will ever be able to help you, Camille.

"Give her the juice," Dianne says.

Penelope hands me a small bottle of orange juice, just a few sips taken out of it. The gun never leaves my back. "Drink all of it," she says.

I watch Luke, sound asleep on the couch, the rise and fall of his chest. And I raise the bottle to my lips. There's a chalkiness to the taste, but at least it's cold. I drink it all, my thoughts slowing and fogging over before I've reached the end. The room starts to blur at the corners, and then that blur bleeds into the center and everything turns syrupy. Dianne moves closer to me, that blazing candy cane sweater of hers, the torture of it, all that red in my eyes. I feel nauseous. She puts an arm around me and I can't fight, I can't move. . . .

My tongue is thick, my feet useless as she drags me up the stairs. *To bed? Is that where I'm going?*

We reach the top, and I search her blurring face. Is there something there? A hint of mercy?

"Die like Joan," Dianne says.

She shoves me hard, and there's no time for anything, even surprise. I sail in space for a moment, and then my head smacks the floor. Something explodes within me. I'm in pieces. I'm dissolving. Nothing working together anymore.

I want to say Emily's name, but I don't have enough breath for that. I'm seeing her now, though, as a baby blinking up at me, her tiny hands grasping the light. I'm seeing my own mother when I was little, her soft fingers on my cheek. I'm kissing Matt for the first time, then dancing with my dad at my wedding, then weeping at Emily's funeral, my heart ripped in two. I'm screaming at Joan over the phone. *You never loved me. You never cared.* And then, at last, this past month. From that subway ride on, every second plays out again in this one final gasp of time. It's all too much—too loud, too pointless— when all I want is to be with Luke. Watch him breathe. Listen to his heart.

EPILOGUE

One month later

A hospital isn't the place you want to be these days, what with all this talk of the virus. They're floating the idea of shutting down production on *Protect and Serve* as soon as a week from now, and if a TV set isn't safe, a New York City hospital certainly isn't. Luke still feels he should be here, though. He was requested, after all.

As he walks through the lobby at New York–Presbyterian, Luke is wearing latex gloves and one of those N95 masks Nora has been hoarding. It still feels extreme to him, all this protective gear just to take the subway. But the whole germaphobe thing is getting to be more and more normal—just this morning he saw a couple of guys on the street, hocking hand sanitizer of all things.

Maybe *normal* isn't the word.

"Do it for the baby," Nora had said this morning as she pressed the mask into his hand. And of course, he'd relented.

A father-to-be can't just think of his own vanity. Luke smiles whenever he thinks of that phrase—*father-to-be*. He never believed it would refer to *him*, but that's the way life is— unpredictable, unplannable, for better or for worse. You have to smile on those rare times when it's for better.

A month ago he and Nora had planned to go up to Camille's and tell her about the baby. Luke had pictured the three of them toasting with champagne and sparkling cider, the previous episode of *The Bachelor* playing on Camille's DVR. He'd envisioned them getting together in the future, Camille helping them choose a name, eating cake at Nora's baby shower. . . . Once the baby was born, Luke had thought, it might pull Camille out of the dark cloud she'd wrapped herself in. It might bring back some of her old self, the Camille who Luke had never fully known.

But that's not what had happened. Camille had killed herself. Luke had been in the same house with her when it happened, passed out from accidentally drinking some of the fentanyl cocktail she prepared. That's what destroyed him most. He hadn't left, like her friend Wendy. He could have saved her had he been awake when she came home. But he wasn't. From what police put together, Camille went upstairs, drank the rest of the suicide mixture, and then, as she was starting to slip out of consciousness, she lost her footing, tumbled downstairs, and died almost instantly. The fall killed her before the drugs could. And he'd been powerless to save her, either way. . . .

"I hope you're happier now, Cam." As Luke takes the eleva-
tor up to the wing where Tamara Dorsey is recovering, he says
it out loud. He often speaks out loud to Camille these days.
Nora's caught him doing it a few times, though she's been kind
enough not to say anything.

There's a crowded waiting room down the hall from where
Tamara is staying, and Luke heads over there, sits down on a
vinyl couch, and picks up a two-day-old newspaper, a headline
about the still-missing Gary Kimball. "I think he escaped,"
says the woman next to him. "They were totally going to arrest
him, you know."

When Luke looks up at the woman, she peers around his
mask. "Oh my gosh, you're Luke Charlebois." She gives him a
shy smile. "I'm Billie Dorsey. Tamara's mother."

Tamara Dorsey is a lung transplant recipient. Luke often
visits patients like her as an Organ Donor Awareness (ODA)
spokesperson. But Tamara specifically requested him, which
makes this visit more important. Luke takes Billie's hand in
both of his. Screw elbow-bumping.

"Your organization saved my daughter's life," Billie says.

Tears spring into Luke's eyes—something that never happened to him in the past, but has been close to constant since
Camille's death, his emotions churning so close to the surface. He swats the tears away and hopes Billie doesn't notice.
He's always prided himself on being the calm in the storm, the
strong shoulder to cry on. As insipid as his lines often are on
the show, he was cast as stoic Sarge for a reason. But now he's a

mess half the time, his "chill" gone to hell. Billie doesn't seem to mind, though. Her eyes aren't exactly dry either.

"Both of her lungs were punctured in the accident." Her jaw tenses. "Drunk driver. I'm so grateful Tamara made it, but my son . . . He was in the car with her. They couldn't save him."

"Oh . . ."

She takes a breath. "It's really awful to feel this powerless."

Luke watches her face, how it changes and darkens, that crumbling behind her eyes. It's as though he's looking at Camille, and he wants to pull her to him, to hug the pain away.

A nurse steps into the waiting room. "Ms. Dorsey?" she says.

Billie pats Luke's shoulder. "Are you ready to come with me and meet Tamara?"

"Absolutely."

Luke follows the nurse out of the waiting room. He turns to thank Billie, but she's still back there, talking to someone—a silver-haired woman with a telegenic look. The woman presses something into Billie's hand—a business card, he thinks, and Luke feels the most powerful sense of déjà vu. He's seen that woman before, somewhere. Maybe on TV.

ACKNOWLEDGMENTS

My enduring gratitude goes out to my agent of fifteen years (How can that be true?!), Deborah Schneider, and of course to everyone at William Morrow, particularly Liate Stehlik, Maureen Cole, Kaitlin Harri, Mireya Chiriboga, and my absolutely wonderful editor, Lyssa Keusch. Big thanks from across the pond to the great Francesca Pathak at Orion and to my fabulous UK agent, Alice Lutyens.

Much gratitude as well to digital forensics expert Josh Moulin, who gave me insight into the dark web.

On a personal note, this book was written during times that were tough for pretty much everyone on the planet, and as I tackled this challenge, I felt especially thankful for the much-needed love and laughs provided by James Conrad (shop Golden Notebook!), Chas Cerulli, and Dan, Paul Leone, Wendy Corsi Staub, Jamie and Doug Barthel, and my own personal collective, the FLs.

Thanks to my wonderful family, including my mom, Beverly, and all the Gaylins, especially Sheldon and Marilyn, who have made me a very lucky daughter-in-law. I married into a truly superb clan. (Chris, you're in for a treat!)

Thanks to Marissa, a brilliant, kind, and strong young woman who becomes more of those things every day. And to Mike, who is pretty much the best guy ever.

About the Author

ALISON GAYLIN is the author of the Edgar Award–winning suspense novel *If I Die Tonight*, and the Edgar Award–nominated novels *Hide Your Eyes, What Remains of Me*, and *Stay with Me*. Her first novel in the highly acclaimed Brenna Spector series, *And She Was*, won the Shamus Award. A graduate of Northwestern University and Columbia University's Graduate School of Journalism, she lives with her husband and daughter in Woodstock, New York.